DEADLY CARD TRICK

Mick spread the tarot cards before her. The King of Coins had to be Harry Baker. She picked up the rest of the deck and pulled the card she wanted.

"All right you bullying son-of-a-bitch," she whispered. "Let's see how you like this."

Mick placed the Death card directly on top of the King of Coins. . . .

Elaine screamed, pulled the door open, and ran out into the street, with Harry in close pursuit.

She risked one glance back over her shoulder and saw that he wasn't far behind. Alcohol had slowed his reflexes, but his legs were still longer than hers and he was gaining.

When Elaine reached the curb across the street from her house, she heard the sound of squealing tires. Behind her she heard a thud, and when Elaine turned to look, she saw only a large silver station wagon passing by. Harry had been caught by the front tires and pulled almost three quarters of a block before the car finally stopped. . . .

A CAVALCADE OF TERROR
FROM RUBY JEAN JENSEN!

SMOKE (2255, $3.95)

Seven-year-old Ellen was sure it was Aladdin's lamp that she had found at the local garage sale. And no power on earth would be able to stop the hideous terror unleashed when she rubbed the magic lamp to make the genie appear!

CHAIN LETTER (2162, $3.95)

Abby and Brian knew that the chain letter they had found was evil. They would send the letter to all their special friends. And they would know who had broken the chain—by who had died!

ANNABELLE (2011, $3.95)

The dolls had lived so long by themselves up in the attic. But now Annabelle had returned to them, and everything would be just like it was before. Only this time they'd never let anyone hurt Annabelle. And anyone who tried would be very, very sorry!

HOME SWEET HOME (1571, $3.50)

Two weeks in the mountains should have been the perfect vacation for a little boy. But Timmy didn't think so. Not when he saw the terror in the other children's eyes. Not when he heard them screaming in the night. Not when Timmy realized there was no escaping the deadly welcome of HOME SWEET HOME!

MAMA (2950, $3.95)

Once upon a time there lived a sweet little dolly—but her one beaded glass eye gleamed with mischief and evil. If Dorrie could have read her dolly's thoughts, she would have run for her life. For Dorrie's dear little dolly only had murder on her mind!

Available wherever paperbacks are sold, or order direct from the Publisher. Send cover price plus 50¢ per copy for mailing and handling to Zebra Books, Dept. 3270, 475 Park Avenue South, New York, N.Y. 10016. Residents of New York, New Jersey and Pennsylvania must include sales tax. DO NOT SEND CASH.

WILD CARD

JEAN SIMON

ZEBRA BOOKS
KENSINGTON PUBLISHING CORP.

ZEBRA BOOKS

are published by

Kensington Publishing Corp.
475 Park Avenue South
New York, NY 10016

First printing: January, 1991

Printed in the United States of America

Prologue

"There she is."

"That's her? She's not what I expected."

"What did you think — that she'd have fangs and a bat sitting on her shoulder?"

"No. But she's younger than I thought she'd be."

"Keep it down, you two. She'll hear us."

Three girls stood at a window, the scene inside the house not much brighter than the night that pressed behind. Their faces reflected the sense of excitement generated by this glimpse into forbidden, adult territory.

The house that rose high above them was two and a half stories of century-old wood, showing signs of neglect but still impressive despite an overgrown yard and the occasional cracked window. It was the Montagna house, and had always belonged to the same family, passing down from generation to generation, its reputation so much a part of it that it was generally avoided by the people in town.

The blonde-haired girl pressed closer to the window, her curiosity making her careless.

"What are you doing?" the brunette hissed, pulling her back.

"We have to get inside, don't we? Something from inside Rosalie Montagna's house. That was item number twelve on the scavenger hunt list."

The third girl, a redhead with delicate features and wide, apprehensive eyes, backed away from her friends. "Do you know how much trouble we'll be in if our parents ever find out we were out here after dark? Mine will have a lock put on my bedroom door, and I'll be thirty before I ever see the light of day again."

The other two looked at her.

"You were all for this a little while ago," the blonde reminded her.

"Yeah, I know, but I didn't expect it to be so creepy here." Doubt had crept into the girl's voice, and she looked around as though expecting the night to reach out and claim her. She wouldn't have minded leaving—even without the twenty-five points they'd get for bringing back something from the Montagna house—but she couldn't bring herself to insist. She had to admit there was a thrill in all this. It was the first time she'd ever done anything so completely disobedient, and the fact that the earth hadn't opened up to swallow her as punishment gave her the boost of courage she needed.

Besides, she wanted to see more of the inside of that house. They all knew who Rosalie Montagna was. Everyone in town knew about crazy Rosalie.

Through the window was Rosalie's large living room, a stone fireplace against one wall. Mirrors adorned the walls, reflecting dozens of Rosalies, her rich dark hair falling to a multitude of slender backs.

The blonde crept closer to the window again. She'd never seen anything like this before in all her sixteen years, and it fascinated her. She'd once believed herself to be rather sophisticated for her age, but now realized there was a great deal she had yet to learn, that her own experiences barely scratched the surface of life's secrets.

Rosalie had a man in there, but that wasn't surprising. Isolated from the townspeople who mocked her almost as much as she scorned them, Rosalie held a fascination for the men in town, stealing them briefly from their wives and girlfriends, offering them a glimpse into a dangerous place.

The light from a single lamp caught Rosalie's hair as she sat on the velvet covered sofa. Her head was thrown back, her neck white and vulnerable, the front of her dress opened to reveal the gentle swell of her breasts. Laughter tumbled from her lips as, eyes closed, she held the man's head between her breasts.

Then Rosalie lifted her hand and brought a bottle to her lips. She took a long swallow, a little of the amber liquid spilling to the base of her throat, pooling there.

The man lifted his head and put his lips to the spot, his tongue darting out to lick up the liquid.

The girl gasped and backed away from the window. Her feet caught in the weeds and she fell, landing hard on her butt, her hands going to her mouth to stifle the little cry that wanted to escape.

"Are you okay?" the brunette whispered, kneeling beside her.

She nodded and got to her feet. A quick look in the window revealed that the living room was now empty. "Where'd they go?"

"Probably to the bedroom. Did you see what they were doing? Everyone is right — Rosalie *is* a whore. I couldn't see who the man was, could you?"

The girl shook her head. "No. Maybe we should just leave. I don't care about this scavenger hunt anymore."

"This is our best chance. If they've gone into the bedroom, we can get inside now and take something. It doesn't have to be much, just some little thing she won't even miss." The brunette walked to a door several feet to the right of the window and tried the handle. The door opened with a faint squeak of rusty hinge. "Come on, it'll only take a minute, and we already know that everyone else is too chicken to try for this. If we get something, we'll win."

All three girls went inside the house, sneakers silent on the carpet, staying close together.

"Grab something, quick, and let's get out of here," the redhead whispered, her cheeks showing two bright spots of color.

They looked around the room, their curiosity temporarily overcoming caution. This was a place only speculated about, and they wanted to remember as much of it as possible.

The brunette stepped away from her friends and went to the fireplace. On the mantle rested a small wooden box, about the size of her hand, its lid painted with the faded silhouette of a tree. It looked old.

The redhead picked up the half-empty bottle of whiskey from the couch. "Here, I have something."

The blonde shook her head. "No, they'll never believe we got that here. They'll think one of us took it out of our own house."

"Well, we'll *tell* them we got it here. Why shouldn't they believe us?"

"Because Scotty Trebek is going to be furious that his team didn't have the guts to come here and we did, and he'll say anything to make us lose. We have to get something that everyone will *know* came from here."

The girl at the fireplace wasn't listening as her friends argued. The little box held her attention, and she reached out to lift the lid. The smooth surface warmed her fingertips as though it held a life of its own, or some power that, though she wanted to pull back, grabbed at her and demanded that she gaze upon the mysteries inside.

She opened it and saw the name of the owner carved crudely on the inside of the lid, the letters looking strangely childish and uneven. The box contained a deck of cards, but slightly larger and much thicker than

8

the usual deck of playing cards. The top card showed a plain blue surface with a small black crown in the center.

The girl lifted the top card and turned it over, and there saw the figure of a woman sitting on a throne, a golden cup held in one hand. The queen of something—but what? None of the usual suits, certainly, but something stronger, the queen ruling but also secondary, for there was surely a king somewhere in that deck.

Unable to resist the pull of the cards, the girl closed the lid of the box and held it possessively to her chest. This had nothing to do with the childish game she and her friends were playing tonight. She wanted these cards without knowing why, but feeling that if she left without them she would soon forget this fleeting visit to the unknown, that it would fade like a half-remembered dream. The cards would be a reminder, tangible evidence of this place and her entrance into Rosalie's world.

An overhead light came on so suddenly that it blinded them all, and an angry voice filled the room. "What are you doing here?"

Rosalie stood in the doorway, her hand still on the light switch, a flowing blue robe thrown carelessly over her shoulders. Beneath the robe she was nude, and she made no attempt to pull the garment together or to cover herself. She was as regal as the queen on the top card of the deck, but so outraged that her dark eyes flashed, and her breath came in little puffs of indignation.

The girls stood as three frozen statues, caught under the lights like bugs under a microscope.

The redhead moved first, backing toward the door through which they'd entered, ready to run for it.

"What's that you have, little girl?" Rosalie demanded. When she saw the hinged box her eyes narrowed. "Put that down," she ordered. "That won't do you any good. It's mine."

Two of the girls fled. Closer to the open door, they were out almost before Rosalie had completed her sentence.

Only the brunette remained, in the center of the room, her prize clutched tightly in both hands.

Rosalie took a step forward, red lips parted over her teeth. She looked capable of taking a bite out of anyone who crossed her. "I *said* that's mine. And I want it." Her dark eyes were slits. "What are you doing here, anyway? Is it a dare? That's usually what brings your type. Come to see Rosalie the witch? Rosalie the seducer of men, the stealer of babies? Only a small part of what you hear about me is true, little girl. But the part that is true—that's what you have to watch out for."

The space between Rosalie and the girl narrowed by the moment.

She couldn't look away from Rosalie's eyes, that beautiful face that loomed so close now that she could have reached out and touched it.

The girl turned and ran.

Rosalie sprang, but too late, and the girl actually felt Rosalie's fingers brush the back of her blouse before she was out of the house, following her terrified friends by the sound of their noisy flight as they crashed through the bushes and low branches of the trees around the house.

She ducked her head, knocking aside the twigs that tangled themselves in her hair, expecting Rosalie to catch her and drag her back into the house to meet some horrible fate.

But when Rosalie called, her voice was far behind, stopped at the doorway by some unseen barrier.

"The cards won't do you any good," Rosalie shouted. "Only a true Montagna woman can use those cards to

10

their full advantage. To anyone else they're useless. Blood is the strongest bond, child. The only bond." Her voice changed to a plea. "Bring them back to me."

The girl lost her sense of direction in the dark, and could no longer hear her friends. She stopped running only when her breath was gone, when she burned with a pain that constricted her lungs in her chest. Tears streamed from her eyes, and she wiped a sleeve across her face, smearing dirt along one cheek.

"There you are!"

She squealed and spun around, and saw the pale, slightly freckled face of the redhead.

"We've been looking all over for you," the redhead said. "We were just about ready to go back to town to get help. How would we ever have explained losing you out here?"

Together they headed for the road, where the blonde waited. When she saw them approach she laughed with relief. "Did you *see* her? She was naked and she didn't even care. She must be crazy. I'll bet if she'd have gotten her hands on us, no one would've ever seen us again."

"Do you think she'll call our mothers and tell them we were here?"

"No way. She doesn't talk to any of the women in town. Besides, she doesn't even know our names."

"I was so scared."

"Me, too. I'm *never* coming back here."

"Where's the car? My sense of direction is all messed up."

"Its over this way. Let's get out of here."

The dark-haired girl looked at the box she had some-how hung onto throughout her flight, and now she wondered why she had been so determined to keep it. If she'd given it back, as Rosalie had wanted, she wouldn't now be filled with this sense of doom, as though she'd reached her hands into Hell and pulled out a piece of

11

brimstone.

The blonde saw it. "Geez, is that what she was hollering about? I guess we have our item for the scavenger hunt, but I'll never know how you had the nerve to take it. Do you think it's true what people say about Rosalie being a witch?"

"It's true," the girl said, wiping one hand on her jeans, trying to remove the imprint of the box from her palm.

They began to walk toward the car.

"I'm glad it's over with, but wait till the others hear that we really went inside," the blonde said. "Scotty Trebek will pee his pants with envy."

Part One

Chapter One

The largest package slipped from Fran McGee's arms just as she was closing the car door, but by quick maneuvering she was able to catch it before it hit the ground. Pulling it back up she almost lost another package, and for a minute was caught up in a comical game of catch-the-bag, no sooner getting a grip on one before another threatened to slither loose.

When she finally had them all together in her arms she wondered why she hadn't thought to make two trips into the house. It wouldn't have taken any longer than this little exhibition had. Too late now. She headed for the house and realized, once she reached the front door, that she would have to put all her packages down anyway to unlock it.

Cursing and laughing at her lack of foresight, she entered the house a minute later with her packages and dumped them on the nearest chair.

From outside, the house didn't look much different from many others in Xavier, California, population less than ten thousand. It was done in the popular Spanish style: white stucco with red tile roof, black wrought iron trim, softly rounded edges rather than squared corners. The house was attractive without being ostentatious, a little nicer than most in the neighborhood, but not enough so as to cause resentment.

The McGees believed that too showy a display of wealth didn't make for good business relations in a small town.

Once inside, though, the furnishings were expensive and plush, leaving no doubt as to the quality of everything from the thick beige carpet to the original artwork on the walls.

This was Fran's private domain, and once inside that front door she enjoyed the benefits of her husband's law practice. And why not? They'd worked hard to get where they were.

Fran slipped out of her shoes and padded through the living room, following the sound of laughter that drifted in from the back of the house, from the direction of the pool. Pulling open the sliding glass door, she saw her daughter and a friend splashing in the chlorinated water, their voices louder now without the barrier of glass between them and Fran.

"Hi, girls," Fran called.

One of the teenagers, her dark hair slicked back on her head, peeked over the edge of the pool. "Oh, hi, Mom," Mick McGee said. "When did you get home?"

"Just now. I bought you some new jeans."

"Are they acid-washed?"

Fran smiled at her. "Would I dare buy you anything else?" She liked shopping for her daughter and had been forced, over the years, to keep up with the current styles lest she be faced with returning merchandise Mick refused to wear. It kept her on her toes, but she refused to do as so many of her friends had and give up entirely, letting Mick do her own shopping. She was at least reasonably certain Mick would like everything she'd bought for her today.

The other girl in the pool, Quinn Baker, pulled herself out of the water and walked dripping to the diving board. She stood poised on the end of the board, her

16

blonde hair plastered to her head, her figure slim in a modest one-piece suit that had been Mick's the year before. She jumped, hitting the water feet first, and surfaced a moment later beside Mick. Quinn smiled at Fran, water running down the end of her nose and catching in her thick eyelashes. They were both uncommonly pretty girls, tanned already even though it was only mid-summer.

A movement to her left caught Fran's attention, and she stepped out of the way just as another girl hurried past, also wearing a swimsuit, but without the tan of the other two girls.

"Hi, Mrs. McGee," Lee Sternhagen said as she dashed past, then ran to the pool and jumped in, long legs flying over the heads of her friends. Lee was a redhead, and her pale skin refused to tan no matter how much time she spent in the sun, so that she looked like the "before" picture in a tanning lotion advertisement. She hit the water with a loud splash, and Mick and Quinn shouted their protests.

"Are you girls hungry?" Fran asked after Lee had surfaced. "I could fix some sandwiches if you want."

"We had some Fruit Loops a little while ago," Mick told her mother.

Fran wrinkled her nose and said, "Not a very nutritious lunch."

The girls held a brief, whispered conference at the edge of the pool, then Mick said, "Yeah, I guess we could use some sandwiches."

"Ham okay?"

"Sure."

Fran went to the kitchen to prepare a decent lunch for the three teenagers, marveling at their ability to eat without gaining weight. She wouldn't dare top a lunch of cold cereal and milk with a sandwich — or anything else — but these girls didn't yet have to worry about

17

watching their figures. They were all beautifully slender, no doubt the result of a high metabolism that went with their age, and she felt a moment of envy for them. Mick especially seemed able to eat anything she wanted, from fried foods to an endless supply of buttered popcorn, and didn't have a spare inch of flesh to show for it. The day would probably come when she would have to change her eating habits, but for now Mick was enjoying the luxury of being able to indulge in anything that struck her fancy.

Fran fixed four sandwiches, including one for herself, remembering to make one with butter, because Lee didn't like mayonnaise, and to put a leaf of lettuce on another, as Mick preferred.

When she was finished she cut all the sandwiches in half and arranged them on one big plate. She then cabled the girls in to eat, and sat at the table to wait.

"Lunch is ready, let's chow down," Mick said, pulling herself up and out of the water near the deep end of the pool.

Lee reached for a towel on a nearby lawn chair and dried herself off as best she could. "I hope she remembered not to put mayonnaise on mine," she said.

"I'm sure she remembered," Mick said. "I wonder why Mom is buying clothes for me already. School doesn't start for another month and a half."

"She's probably wishing it was sooner."

"Maybe she's going to send you off to camp."

"No way. I stopped going to summer camp when I was twelve."

"She probably misses those days."

Mick rolled up a towel and snapped it at Quinn, the one who'd made this comment, but Quinn easily jumped out of the way.

"I wish my mother would still buy my clothes," Lee said. She rubbed the towel over her head, making her hair stand up in little red points. "Once I started baby-sitting she decided it was time I did my own shopping. That's not so bad, I guess. Her taste was really horrible. Remember that blouse with the puffy sleeves she bought me when I was fourteen? God, it was ugly."

"Yeah, and she even made you wear it."

"Until I accidentally spilled ink down the front of it."

"Some accident."

As soon as they were dry, they went inside the house and sat at the kitchen table with Fran.

Mick took diet colas from the refrigerator for everyone, then remembered the new clothes and ran into the living room to inspect her mother's choices. "Oh, I love them," she said, coming back to the kitchen with the new jeans held in front of her. "I'm going to wear them tonight."

"I thought you'd save them for school," Fran said, knowing already that this was a lost cause.

"Do I have to? Lee and Quinn and I are going to a movie tonight, and I don't have anything new to wear."

"You have a closet full of perfectly good clothes," Fran reminded her.

"That stuff is all *old*."

"Some of it as much as a month," Fran said, then smiled. "Oh, I don't care if you wear them right away. I knew when I bought them that they'd never get through the summer without being broken in."

Mick happily draped the jeans over her lap as she sat at the table, and Fran could only sigh. Probably Mick would immediately slash the knees of the jeans with a razor blade, then wash them so the cut edges would fray, as was the current style. Fran had even seen jeans in the stores already cut in such a way, but had been unable to bring herself to spend eighty dollars on a pair

19

of pants she herself wouldn't keep for the rag bag. That was a little too much, even for her.

The girls chattered happily as they ate, and Fran sat quietly, enjoying their company. They didn't exclude her, and once in a while even made an effort to make her a part of their conversation, but Fran knew the teenagers didn't feel free to talk openly in her presence. She was an adult, after all, and the talk centered mostly around how boring summer was, and other safe subjects until she'd finished her sandwich and told them she had things to do. She knew that as soon as she left the room they would heave a collective sigh of relief, but she didn't begrudge them their little secrets. She'd been the same way at their age.

"Have you heard about Blaire Campbell and that boy she's been going out with — Charlie?" Lee whispered as soon as Fran was safely out of range.

"No, what?" Mick asked, pulling the crust from her sandwich.

"They were parking out by Harris Lake the other night, and Blaire's *father* drove up and dragged her home."

"He didn't!"

"Yeah, he did. And Blaire was so embarrassed that she doesn't know if she'll be able to look Charlie in the face again."

"I'd be embarrassed, too. Her parents are so strict, it's a wonder they even let Blaire out of the house."

"Her father is really awful," Mick said. "Wasn't he in the Marines, or something?"

"Yeah, and he treats his whole family like they were in boot camp. He didn't like Charlie before because Charlie is in college, and Mr. Campbell thinks he's too old for Blaire. This is going to make it even worse. He might tell Blaire that she can't see Charlie anymore."

"Is that what Blaire says?" Quinn asked.

"It's what she's afraid is going to happen. So far, though, she's only grounded for two weeks."

"Two weeks in that house — yuk."

When they were finished eating Mick carried the plate to the sink and rinsed it. She knew she was lucky that her parents trusted her, and didn't keep tabs on her every move or embarrass her in front of her friends. Maybe it had something to do with her being an only child. But Quinn was an only child, too, and her father kept a pretty close eye on her. Apparently, Mick had just lucked out in the parent department.

She picked up her new jeans from where they'd fallen to the floor and saw that Quinn and Lee were heading toward the front door. "Don't you want to stay and swim a little longer?" she asked, following them.

"I'd better go. I've got to wash my hair if I'm going to look halfway decent tonight," Lee said.

"Me, too," Quinn agreed. "And I told my mother I'd have the car back early 'cause she has to work four to nine tonight at the store."

Mick walked them to the door and promised she would pick them both up in time for the movie later, then watched as Quinn backed her mother's rattletrap out of the driveway. When they were gone she carried her jeans to her bedroom and tossed them on the bed, along with the two sweaters her mother had also bought that day.

She liked the sweaters, but it would be months before the weather would grow cool enough to wear them, so she promptly forgot all about them. The jeans were another matter. Going to the jewelry box on her chest of drawers, Mick opened it and found the single-edged razor blade she kept there.

Then she did what her mother had known she would do: she slit open the knees of the jeans, added a couple of nicks on one thigh for good measure, and proudly

21

examined her work.

She was putting the razor blade back when she saw that her top drawer was slightly open. She'd left it that way herself earlier, but such carelessness seemed an invitation she didn't wish to extend.

Mick reached inside the drawer, and her hand immediately found the squared corners of the little box she'd hidden there, beneath her scarves and underwear. She took the box out and opened the lid. There was the thick deck of tarot cards. She would have to find a better hiding place for them. If her mother ever ran across these cards in her room, Mick knew she would have a heck of a time explaining how they'd come to be in her possession.

"Mick," her mother's voice called from down the hall. "Did you leave these towels all over the bathroom floor?"

Mick had jumped guiltily at the sound of her mother's voice. "Yeah, sorry," she hollered. She shoved the box back in the drawer, farther back this time. She closed the drawer carefully. She would hide them somewhere else later, but for now she couldn't be bothered. There were other, more important things for her to think about now. Like which blouse she was going to wear with her new jeans tonight.

The town of Xavier sat nestled in a little valley about sixty miles east of the Pacific Ocean, still somewhat isolated despite the gradually approaching cities to the north and south. It had one movie theater — albeit a theater with three screens — several restaurants, and the usual assortment of alcoholics, cheating spouses and, once or twice a year, minor drug bust.

It had only one high school, and most of the students there dreamed of leaving someday for more exciting territory.

Through the month of June, Mick and her friends enjoyed every moment of summer vacation. They spent it either swimming in Mick's pool or cruising the streets in her car, looking for adventure they rarely found. If they were feeling especially restless, they would drive down to Tijuana for the day to giggle at their broken Spanish and drag home bargains that would be in the garbage within the week.

By July they were growing bored with these activities. School started to look more attractive, if only as a social gathering place.

August brought stifling heat and short tempers. The air conditioning was turned on. They looked forward to the beginning of classes.

Mick went with her parents to Colorado for the third week of the month, where her mother had a married sister. For seven days Mick explored the beauty of the mountains and became reacquainted with cousins she saw at the most once a year. She sent three postcards to Lee and four to Quinn.

Only Fran was reluctant to return home when the week was up. She didn't see enough of her sister, and since her parents had died a few years before — together, in a car accident — her small hometown held less and less appeal for her. Every year she and Brady discussed relocating to nearby San Diego, but so far nothing had come of it.

"Did Donna look tired to you?" she asked Brady as she pulled wrinkled clothing from their suitcases. She'd done some shopping while visiting her sister, and the suitcases had been brought home filled to the bursting point.

Brady, on the other side of the room, opened his closet door. "She has five kids; of course she looked tired," he said.

23

"The kids have never bothered her before," Fran said. "She was always the original Earth Mother, ready to nurture the world. She wouldn't have stopped at five if Del hadn't finally put his foot down."

Brady pushed aside some of the clothes in his closet, trying without much luck to make some room for the shirts Fran had bought for him in Denver. "But three of her children are now teenagers," he added. "That's enough to turn my hair gray just thinking about it. If you think she needs a break, invite her here for Christmas — without the kids."

"Maybe I will."

"She'd probably enjoy it. Has she ever gone anywhere without that menagerie?"

"Not in seventeen years."

"There — what's that tell you?" Brady gave up on his closet, even though he'd promised himself that this time he would help Fran unpack, and went to her and pushed her down on the bed. It was a tight squeeze among the suitcases, but he found room.

"Hey," she protested, laughing. "I have work to do."

"It'll keep. Let's fool around."

"In the middle of the day?"

"We used to all the time."

Fran struggled, not too hard, to get away. "Mick —"

"Left fifteen minutes ago," Brady gloated. "I heard her car leave."

"You've figured out all the angles, haven't you? Is that what makes you such a good attorney?"

"Without a doubt."

Brady had managed to make Fran abandon all thoughts of unpacking. They cuddled on the crowded bed, bits of their clothing finding its way from their bodies onto the floor. At one point Brady kicked a suitcase off the bed, and they were able to stretch out.

Their tranquility was broken by a series of shouts

24

from next door.

Sitting up, Brady looked disoriented for a moment, then looked toward their open bedroom window. "Christ, it sounds like someone is being murdered next door."

"It's the Thomsen kids," Fran said. She got up from the bed and went to the window to peek through the curtains. Because they'd been gone the central air wasn't turned on, so they'd opened some windows to air out the house. The result was that all the sounds they didn't usually hear were now magnified and very distracting.

The Thomsens next door had seven foul-mouthed children who ran around unsupervised in the neighborhood. Once Fran had looked out the front door of her own house to see little Debbie Thomsen, two years old at the time, dressed only in her panties and standing in the middle of the street. She'd gone outside and retrieved the toddler, but when she knocked on the door of the house next door, Debbie's mother had only looked at her with a blank expression, said, "Oh," when Fran explained that Debbie had been in the street, then pulled the little girl inside and slammed the door.

That had been only one incident in a long chain of unpleasant events. When the McGees began to find small things around their property missing, they'd added another two feet to the top of the fence that surrounded their yard, and a new, stronger lock to the gate. The thefts had stopped then, but the older Thomsen children still liked to fight at the tops of their lungs, and sometimes Brady and Fran couldn't help but overhear.

Brady was behind Fran at the window but, because of the fence, they couldn't see anything of what was going on. However, they could hear plenty.

"Someone should wash those kids' mouths out,"

25

Brady said after a particularly choice string of four-letter words drifted their way.

"Who?" Fran asked. "Their mother? She's who they learned it from." Her blouse was open halfway down the front, and Brady suddenly remembered that they had unfinished business.

"Forget about them," he said, pulling her away from the window. "School will start again soon, and then all the little Thomsen monsters will be directing their energies elsewhere."

"Ah, yes — school," Fran said as she let herself be eased back down on the bed. "I wonder if Mick has enough —"

Brady silenced her with a kiss, and Fran forgot all about Mick, as well as the kids next door.

Chapter Two

Mick closed the bathroom door, shutting out the sounds of the party in the other room.

Not that it was much of a party. A dozen kids, fifteen at the most, gathered in the living room listening to tapes and munching on snacks. There was some conversation, but it was mostly listless, as though the prospect of school starting in two days had already sapped them of all their vitality.

Where had the summer gone? Mick wondered. It seemed as though only yesterday she'd been hanging around the pool in her back yard, wishing for something to do, and now, all of a sudden, the summer was gone.

The bathroom Mick found herself in was small, with chipped tiles around the toilet and a single dim bulb over the mirror. She looked at her reflection under the poor lighting. The shadows that dipped beneath her eyes and cheekbones made her look like a cadaver.

Still, it was nice to have some time to herself, even if it was only a few minutes stolen in a strange bathroom.

Someone knocked on the door.

"I'll be right out," she called. So much for privacy. She sighed and ran a hand through her shoulder length, dark brown hair.

The party was supposed to be a celebration of sum-

27

mer's end. The school year would officially begin on Monday, and for most of those in the other room it would also mark the beginning of their senior year at Xavier High.

Some were looking forward to it; others were dreading it. Mick remained undecided. School wasn't that big a challenge for her. She got decent grades with very little effort, and was on good terms with most of the teachers. She had her own small circle of friends, and although she wasn't likely to be voted prom queen — that was a privilege usually reserved for the head cheerleader — she dated as much as she wanted.

There was a repeat of the knocking on the door, but this time it was accompanied by a familiar voice. "Mick, let me in, it's me."

Mick opened the door, and Lee squeezed into the small room, closing the door behind her. "What are you doing?" Lee asked.

"Hiding out." Mick sat on the lowered toilet seat and rested her elbows on her knees. "I was bored to death out there."

"Do you want to leave? There's got to be something else going on somewhere in town."

"I'd like to, but Stu will get his feelings hurt if we take off early," Mick said. "It was nice of him to volunteer his house tonight while his parents are out of town."

"Yeah, I guess you're right." Lee leaned against the sink. Her short red hair was brilliant even under the dull light. She wore a loose T-shirt over faded jeans, and on her feet were one red sneaker and one yellow.

There wasn't much room in the bathroom for the two of them, but Mick and Lee were reluctant to leave.

"Hey, you want to see something really scary?" Mick asked, a mischievous expression playing over her features.

"Sure — what?"

28

"Look in the mirror."

Lee turned and gasped. "Oh, my God." She looked even worse under the light than Mick had, because her pale skin took on an eerie quality with the elongated shadows beneath her eyes. She leaned closer to the mirror, one hand on her cheek. "I look twenty-five years old," she murmured.

"Gruesome, isn't it? I've never met Stu's mother, but she must either be so gorgeous that she doesn't need special lighting to make her look good, or so awful that it doesn't matter."

Lee was still examining her reflection. "Summer vacation is over, and I didn't get a bit of tan," she said. "My skin is as white now as it was in the middle of January. What's the good of living in California if I can't even tan?"

"It could be worse."

"How?"

"You could be one of those redheads who are covered with freckles. You don't have any freckles at all. You used to have a few when we were kids, but even those are gone now."

"And you used to tease me about them." Lee turned to look at Mick.

"Yeah, I was a rotten kid, I admit it. But you used to call me bird-legs, so we're even."

"Well, you did have the skinniest legs in town."

"And Quinn had the flattest chest." Mick laughed and rocked on the toilet seat. "Remember how the three of us used to stand in front of the full length mirrors at my house and moan about all our physical flaws?"

"Yeah. Hey—you haven't said anything about Denver. How was it? Was there anything to do, or did you spend the whole week visiting relatives?"

"It wasn't bad," Mick said. "Our second night there my cousin Britney and I told our mothers we were going to a movie, but we went to her boyfriend's house instead. Then when we got home we had to try to describe the movie we'd just seen. I told Mom it was a comedy, but at the same time Britney was in the kitchen telling *her* mother we'd been to a tear-jerker."

"Did you get caught?" Lee asked, knowing already that Mick led a charmed life and always had. If Mick talked in class, the teacher would turn around and accuse the girl behind her. Mick got exposed to chicken pox, but somehow passed it on to Quinn without getting it herself. Policemen never saw her speeding, and on the few occasions she lied to her parents she was never found out.

"No," Mick said, thus confirming what Lee already knew. "I guess they never compared notes, because they never said anything to us about it. Britney was a wreck for a couple of days afterwards. She was sure they'd figure it out."

On the other side of the bathroom door someone turned up the volume on the stereo, so that it actually sounded as though there was a party going on out there. It reminded both girls that they'd been in the bathroom too long, and it was time to go back out and join the crowd.

"Where's Quinn, anyway?" Mick asked as she got up from her seat. "She disappeared a half hour ago, and I haven't seen her since."

"She went into the kitchen to get more food and didn't come back," Lee said. "She's probably hiding out in there just like we've been doing." She opened the door and made a sweeping, after-you gesture with her arm. "But we'd better get back to the others, or they're going to think we're hot for each other."

"You only wish," Mick said, hurrying past before Lee could hit her.

* * *

Quinn had taken refuge in the kitchen, but for a different reason than Mick and Lee. While they'd been bored by everyone's lack of enthusiasm, Quinn didn't like parties much in general, and had only come to this one because her date had insisted. She liked Jack enough to do what he wanted on most of their dates, even though he rarely showed her the same consideration. Jack's idea of a good time was to drink beer until he felt sick, and on more than one occasion she'd sat alone in the car while he'd crouched outside on some deserted road, making disgusting noises. At times like that Quinn wanted to tell him that he was an idiot, and that all those years of football had damaged his brain.

Quinn didn't drink at all. Jack tried to tempt her sometimes, but she stood her ground on that one. Not even a little beer. She'd seen the damage it could cause. When she tried to talk to Jack about it, he dismissed her as being a fanatic on the subject, and it had been the basis of more than one serious argument between them.

It hadn't occurred to Quinn that she and Jack simply weren't compatible. She knew the importance of fitting in, of being part of the crowd, and she was glad that few people knew just how uncomfortable she felt with the very crowd she sought to impress.

What a coward she could be at times, she thought with disgust. If she had an ounce of guts, she would get her purse and walk the few blocks to the movie theater, where she could spend a couple of hours laughing or crying in the dark, depending on the movie.

Instead, she stayed where she was, resigned to her fate.

"Caught you."

Jumping, Quinn turned around just as a pair of arms slipped around her waist, capturing her in a loose embrace.

"Jack," she gasped. "You scared me."

She put her hands on his shoulders, letting her fingertips touch his soft, perfectly groomed brown hair, and tried not to look like a criminal caught in an illegal act.

"What are you doing in here?" he asked.

"I'm a coward," she admitted. "I'd rather be alone with you somewhere than stuck here listening to music I don't like very much. Can we go soon? It's still early enough that we could drive out to Harris Lake and look at the moon." Maybe if she appealed to his baser instincts she could lure him away.

It didn't work.

"I'm having fun," Jack protested. "Besides, I like showing you off. You're the best looking girl here, and I like having everyone know you're with me. It does great things for my ego."

Quinn smiled at him, then impulsively stood on her toes and kissed his lips. "As if your ego needs any help," she said when she pulled back.

"You're tempting me," he said.

"I hope so."

"You really want to leave?"

"As soon as possible."

"Okay. I'll help you carry the food into the living room, then we'll sneak out in a few minutes. I don't think Stu will mind too much; we've been here a couple of hours already so we've done our bit."

"Great!" Quinn felt rejuvenated, as though she'd won a small victory. She rewarded him with another quick kiss—also to remind him of what he had to look forward to if they didn't waste too much time here—and pushed her thick blonde hair back behind her ears.

She forgot all her earlier irritation, and began to look forward to parking at the lake with Jack. He'd been pressuring her lately to go further than she'd really wanted, but maybe she was finally ready to take the next step. She was almost eighteen, almost a senior in high school. She and Jack had been dating for five months, longer than she'd ever gone out with any one guy. If she continued to put him off, she might end up losing him, and at the moment that wasn't what she wanted. She craved security, the sense of belonging with someone.

With this thought in mind, Quinn picked up a couple of containers of dip and turned to Jack, only to find that, holding a big bag of chips in one arm, he was already halfway through the kitchen door.

She almost laughed out loud as he disappeared into the living room without even realizing how close she'd come to telling him she was ready to do what he'd spent the past few months trying to talk her into. The mood was broken, but she'd almost let a moment of gratitude bring her to a decision she wanted a little more time to think about, and she was glad now that the feeling had passed.

She followed him, knowing that as soon as he was with people he would forget all about his promise to leave soon. She wasn't going to remind him. There was safety in numbers, and at least she had Mick and Lee to talk to.

"What were you and Jack doing in the kitchen all alone?" Mick asked as Quinn put the dip down on the coffee table. Jack was standing by the stereo, talking to a thin boy with glasses.

"Nothing," Quinn told her. "Just talking."

"Too bad."

Quinn sat on the couch beside her. She knew she could make the most of this party if she would just loosen up and enjoy herself. She would make the effort, and hope that no one noticed how uncomfortable she was.

"Do you think Stu is cute?" Mick asked, keeping her voice low enough that only Quinn could hear.

"Sure," Quinn said. "Has he asked you out?"

"No, but I'm thinking of asking him. He's kind of shy. If I wait for him to make the first move, I'll be old and gray before our first date."

A tall girl laughed shrilly behind them, and stumbled so that the beer in her hand slopped onto the carpet. "Oops," she giggled, putting a hand over her mouth.

"Way to go, Maggie," Mick said. Then she looked again at Quinn. "This is ridiculous. I am not going to sit here all night and consider watching Maggie Colin spill beer as the highlight of the evening."

She left Quinn and went to where her purse was hanging on a hook by the front door.

Reaching inside the oversized denim bag, Mick pushed aside wallet, cosmetics, a paperback book and her sunglasses until she found what she was looking for.

"Let's play a game," she said loudly to the room in general.

"What do you have in mind?" Lee asked, looking up from the handful of cassette tapes she'd been examining.

Mick lifted the hinged box in her hand, the tree painted on its lid faded but still plainly visible, the box itself about the size of her hand. She lifted the lid and took out a thick deck of cards.

"Why did you bring those?" Quinn asked. She got up from the couch and frowned as she looked over Lee's shoulder at Mick, but already she could see it was too late to stop whatever was going to happen. Still, she felt compelled to try, and she added, "You don't even know how to use them, Mick, so why don't you put them away, and we'll find something else to do."

"Hey, is that a deck of tarot cards?" Stu asked.

"It sure is," Mick said proudly.

"Where'd you get them?"

"We stole them," Mick told him, her eyes dancing with a sense of adventure.

"Not *we—you*," Lee spoke up, and Quinn nodded in agreement.

"You were both there, too," Mick said. She frowned at this unexpected lack of loyalty from her friends. Then, determined not to let them spoil what she had decided was going to be a great time, she knelt at the coffee table, swept everything to one side with a movement of her arm, and put the cards down so that everyone could get a good look at them.

Mick was finally the center of attention, and she glowed when she saw that everyone's eyes were on her, waiting to see what she would do next. With a sense of the theatrical, she spread the cards out as deftly as a Vegas blackjack dealer.

"You don't know how to use them, Mick," Quinn repeated.

"I do too. I went to the city library and looked up everything they had on tarot cards about a week ago, and I've been studying them ever since." She gathered the cards together in her hands, working slowly because the deck was so thick. "There are dozens of books at the library about tarot cards, but I picked out a couple of the best. They even had pictures of each card. The pictures were a little different from the ones on this deck, but they were close enough so that I was able to figure out exactly what each card means. Who's first?"

"Me," Jack said, moving to the front of the group.

"Okay," Mick said. "Sit there on the floor across from me, and I'll pick out a significator for you."

Jack obeyed, crossing his long legs uncomfortably in the small space provided. "A what?" he asked.

"A significator. That's the card out of the deck that

represents you." Mick turned the deck so that she could see the pictures, and began to thumb through them. "Let's see, for you I think I'll use the Knight of Staves. That's a young person, not yet an adult, with brown hair and a light complexion."

"What do you mean, not yet an adult?"

Mick smiled at him. "Don't take it personally, Jack. All it really means is someone under about twenty-five years of age. Ah, here it is." She removed the card from the deck and placed it face up on the table. Adjusting her own legs until she found a comfortable position, she took the remaining seventy-seven cards and began to shuffle them. After a minute she stopped and handed the cards to Jack. "Now you shuffle them for a minute, keeping in mind something you've been thinking a lot about lately."

"What are you going to do, read my fortune?" Jack asked, his hands struggling to accommodate the deck.

"Sort of," Mick said. She took the deck from Jack and looked around to make sure everyone was still watching. Lee and Quinn looked disapproving, but she ignored them. She was having too much fun now to listen to even her own faint inner misgivings, that nagging little voice that tried to tell her she might be getting in over her head with this.

"What I'm going to do here is called the Celtic Cross," she continued. "It's a complicated spread so I'll go slowly, but it should show us your past, present and future, Jack."

"Tell me if I'm going to be rich," Jack said. He looked up at Quinn for her approval, and saw that she was frowning, and staring at the cards Mick was now spreading out in a very specific order.

Mick was leaning forward, concentrating on what she was doing, no longer aware of the people in the room. She tried to remember everything she'd read

36

about the cards. "This one here," she said, pointing to the card she'd placed directly on top of the significator, "indicates your present circumstances. Its the Eight of Cups, which means a miserable situation in your life right now. The next card, placed crosswise over that one, shows the cause of this situation. It's the King of Coins, and he's a strong man, possibly a father figure, who can be loving but is also tough and uncompromising."

"So what does that mean?" a boy asked.

"The position of the cards in the spread tells as much as the cards themselves," Mick said. "So in this case, I would say it means that Jack's father is causing some unhappiness at this time."

Jack's smile had faded, and he shifted around as though wishing he could get up and stretch. "Go on, tell the rest," he said.

"The next card is the distant past. The Sun card indicates a very happy past. The next one, though, is your recent past, and here the Five of Swords shows quarrels, possibly even violence, and a bad time all around." She reached out and almost let her fingertips touch the cards, but held back just enough so that she didn't disturb the spread. "At the top of the Celtic Cross is the card that reveals your near future, and here the Two of Coins indicates the breakup of a home, and property being divided up, either by agreement or by law."

Mick wanted to read more. There were four cards yet to interpret, placed vertically to the right of the other cards, and they would tell more about Jack's situation, about the people around him, his inner fears and dreams, and the final outcome of the spread—but before she could continue Jack jumped up and bumped the table with his knees, sending the cards spilling onto Mick's lap.

His expression was thunderous, his usually mild face

twisted with anger.

He turned to Quinn. "You told Mick about my parents," he said.

"I didn't." Quinn backed up until she bumped into Lee. "Jack, I didn't tell her anything."

"You must have," Jack insisted, his voice rising. "How else would Mick have known about it? When I told you that, Quinn, you knew it was something I didn't want spread around. You promised you wouldn't tell anyone."

Quinn wanted to reassure him, to make him understand that she hadn't betrayed a confidence, but she could see that, no matter what she said, Jack would never believe her.

He turned on Mick then, who had retrieved her cards and was looking up at him with a puzzled expression.

"You," he said, pointing at her. "You think this is a game, to play with people's lives? This is something private, this thing about my parents. You think it's funny to spread some cards out on a table and tell everyone about what I'm going through?"

"No, Jack," Mick said. "I don't think it's a game, and I don't think it's funny. I'm sorry if I hurt you, but I was only reading the cards. I probably handled it badly, but I'm still new at this and maybe I should have downplayed the negative side of it. One important thing you have to remember, though, is that the cards don't predict the future; they only indicate the direction you're headed, and by knowing that, you can take your fate into your own hands and possibly control it." She stopped, then looked embarrassed when she saw the looks on all the faces around her, looks that were marked by awe on some, and amusement on others. "At least that's what the books say," she finished in a soft voice.

Jack, far from being reassured, looked like he longed to take Mick's throat in his hands. Instead, he slowly brought himself under control and glared at everyone in the room, daring anyone to challenge him. "I'm going home," he said. "To hell with all of you."

He'd gotten to the front door before Quinn said, "Jack, how am I supposed to get home?"

He stopped and jerked his head in Mick's direction. "Have your friend give you a ride."

Chapter Three

A half an hour later Mick's convertible pulled up in front of Quinn's house. It had been a silent ride as each girl sat lost in her own thoughts, each finding a different explanation for what had happened earlier.

Quinn had tried to be angry at Mick, had even cried a few tears on the ride home, but in the end she couldn't hold a grudge. It was a mystery to her how Mick had hit so close to the truth with everything she'd told Jack, but, since she knew she hadn't told anyone of the problems Jack was having at home, she could only assume it had been an unfortunate coincidence.

The worst part was that Jack had been genuinely hurt this evening, sincere in his belief that she had betrayed him. He would probably hate her for it, and she found that thought unbearable.

The night he'd told her that his parents were on the verge of breaking up had been one of the few times they'd ever discussed anything more serious than what was going on in town, or which movie was playing at the local theater.

It had been a rare moment of closeness between them, and Quinn had taken her vow of silence seriously, even to the point of keeping it from Mick and Lee, the two people she was accustomed to telling everything.

Jack's refusal to believe her tonight wounded her deeply, just as Jack himself had been wounded. He should have known she wouldn't break a promise. The very fact that he believed she had told revealed a lot about the true lack of depth of their relationship.

"Are you going to be all right?" Lee asked from the back seat of Mick's car.

Quinn nodded, dug around in her purse until she found a tissue that looked relatively new, and blew her nose noisily. "Yeah," she sighed. "But how am I going to face Jack after this?"

Mick, her hands on the steering wheel of her car, said, "You're better off without him."

Quinn turned on her. "Don't say that. It might be true, but that's not for you to decide. And why did you even bring those cards to the party tonight, anyway? You promised you'd get rid of them." She was angry all over again, mostly at Mick's attitude.

"I changed my mind," Mick said. "Once I dug them out again and started studying about them I decided I wanted to keep them. Okay, maybe tonight was a mistake. I really am sorry about what happened, but you have to admit it was pretty uncanny how accurate they turned out to be."

"That was a lucky guess."

"A lucky guess?" Mick hooted. "How could I ever have guessed something like that? No. Jack was thinking about it, and it came right out in the cards, just like the books said it would."

"That's bullshit," Quinn snapped.

Lee leaned forward over the seat so that she was between them. "Stop fighting, you guys. We've never fought like this before. Mick, maybe those cards really are trouble, if they're going to do this to us. And you *did* say you'd get rid of them."

Mick, outnumbered, slouched down behind the

41

steering wheel and sulked. "I'm not making any promises, but I'll think about it," she said.

Quinn opened the car door and got out. She looked toward her darkened house, but knew that appearances could be deceiving and, with her curfew almost upon her, couldn't take much more time to talk.

Even in the dark, the house that Quinn Baker lived in looked shabby and small, the yard more weeds than grass, the siding at least ten years past its last paint job. Inside wasn't much better. Only two bedrooms, with a postage-stamp bathroom and a living room that was furnished mostly from garage sales; Quinn's mother had tried to add some pleasant touches by putting in plants and covering the walls with framed photographs, but her efforts had been mostly unsuccessful.

Quinn sighed, not wanting to go inside, but knowing she couldn't put off the inevitable any longer. Maybe her father was asleep already, and wouldn't be waiting up with his usual questions. It happened sometimes, especially when he was drinking heavily—he would pass out on the couch while watching TV, and her mother would pull, push and half carry him to his bed.

But it was a chance she couldn't take, so Quinn said goodnight to her friends and headed slowly up the sidewalk.

Mick McGee's house was less than two miles away from Quinn's, on the other side of town, but the difference between the two places was so great that they might have been on different planets.

After she'd dropped Lee off, Mick drove home and slipped quietly in the back door and went straight to her room. Her bedroom was almost as large as the inside of Quinn's house. As she turned on the overhead light she kicked a pile of clothes out of the way, adding them to the clutter already gathered in the corner.

Except for the mess, her bedroom could have been featured in a magazine. It was perfectly designed to fill every teenage girl's dream. The canopied bed was so big that Mick could lie in the middle of it and extend her arms and legs out as far as she could without touching any edge. It was unmade; the comforter that rested in a heap at the foot of the bed was thick and expensive, the sheets tangled and in need of changing.

Fran, in an overdue attempt to teach Mick a sense of responsibility, had told their housekeeper not to step foot in this room, that if anything was to get done it would be done by Mick herself. The only result of this experiment so far was that the room was quickly becoming uninhabitable. Fran no longer dared to come inside, for she couldn't stand the sight of this lovely bedroom in such a state.

After throwing her purse onto the middle of the bed, Mick unbuttoned her shirt, stepped out of her shoes, and arranged herself comfortably on the sheets. She cleared a place with her hands, smoothing the folds in the sheets down, and, when she was satisfied, reached into her purse for the cards.

The box felt comfortable in her hands, fitting there perfectly as though coming home. She turned it over, looking at it, and wondered why this box, and these cards, seemed to have become so much a part of her life in such a short time.

At first they had only been a curiosity, but once she'd started reading up on the subject, she'd found her interest growing at an amazing speed.

Strange, also, was the fact that it had taken very little studying for her to come to an understanding of the tarot. The books from the library had been informative, but it had only been surface information, and couldn't explain this feeling she had that she'd at last found

43

something she was meant to have.

She shuffled the cards quickly, her hands moving with an increasing expertise. She'd picked out the Knight of Swords for herself and placed it on the bed. Although the knight himself was male, he represented a young person of either sex, and the suit of swords meant someone with dark hair and a medium complexion.

She'd used the Celtic Cross spread for Jack, but now she decided that the simpler pyramid spread would fill her needs at this time. The books had told her that this was to be used when a specific question was being asked of the cards.

A dozen or more questions swirled around in Mick's head, but she concentrated on one as she continued to shuffle. "Why have these cards become so important to me only recently?" she whispered. She'd had them for awhile, hidden in her bedroom, but had almost forgotten their existence. When she'd discovered them again a couple of weeks ago when looking for a clean bra, she'd pulled them out and decided the time might be right to put them to use.

She leaned forward, her whole being concentrated on finding an answer.

Below the significator card she placed two cards face up, showing the circumstances leading up to her question; below that went three more cards—her future. Off to the right of these went the last card—the answer to her question.

Mick's eyes scanned the spread before her, and a smile formed on her lips as she realized the cards, though certainly subject to interpretation, were telling her exactly what she'd wanted to know. No doubt about it; it was all right there on her bed.

The two cards below the significator were the Hermit and the Ace of Staves. If she hadn't already known so much about the Hermit from her studying it might have worried her, but she understood that this card didn't mean isolation so much as a need to think things through. In this case she knew it meant change, a time of reflection which would lead to a new way of life.

The card next to it, the Ace of Staves, was more specific, and meant the birth of an idea.

The three cards showing her future were the Six of Cups—a need to reach back into her past in order to build for the future, a finding of her roots; the King of Swords—a darkhaired professional man, possibly a doctor or lawyer, who would have an important influence in her life; and the Five of Coins—a sense of loss and loneliness, but with warmth and love coming from a source where the questioner least expected it.

All she could do with these cards was keep in mind that they represented what was yet to come, so if she didn't understand them completely at this time, she might soon. The king had to be her father, but that Five of Coins was puzzling. From what unexpected source would she be receiving love?

But the card that fascinated her the most, and that seemed especially revealing, was the final card. The High Priestess was a very special card that represented ancient knowledge and hidden powers. The Priestess was a message to students of the occult that the ability was there on which to expand. It was a sign of knowledge that only a lucky few possessed.

So that was it. There was something about *her* that was special, so special that with these cards she held the key to her own and others' futures. The proof was there in her very first reading, the one she'd done for Jack with such disastrous results. If she'd had a choice she wouldn't have wanted it that way, but the fact remained that, without any prior knowledge, she had seen what appeared to be a breakup of Jack's home.

"Mick?" There was a soft knock on the bedroom door, and Mick had just enough time to throw the blanket over the cards before the door opened and her mother stepped into the room. "Hi, honey," Fran McGee said. "How long have you been home?"

"Just a few minutes," Mick said, trying to hide her nervousness. Were any of the cards showing? She didn't know, but she didn't dare look and risk attracting her mother's attention to the spot.

Fran's eyes swept over the bedroom, and she winced, but managed a smile. "How was the party?" she asked.

"Mostly boring. Stu's house isn't much, but he seems nice. I think he's trying to get up the nerve to ask me out."

"And if he does, will you be put off by the house he lives in?"

Mick looked hurt. "That's not fair. I don't judge people that way, and you should know it. Quinn's house is a mess, and Lee's is only average, but I've never cared about any of that. They're my best friends and I wouldn't care if they lived in a couple of caves."

"You're right, and I apologize," Fran said, sighing. "I've had a rough day, but that's no reason to take it out on you."

"What happened?"

"Nothing that much, really. I had a flat tire on the interstate and had to wait over an hour for a tow to come. I guess what bothered me the most was that in all that time not one person stopped to offer any help. Thank goodness I was driving your father's car and was able to use the car phone to call the garage, otherwise I might still be sitting there by the side of the road."

Mick swung her legs off the side of the bed and had to suppress a smile. "But you've always told me to never stop for a car that's broken down because with all the crazies around it might be a trap."

46

Fran opened her mouth, then clamped it shut again. Finally she burst out laughing and said, "You know, you're absolutely right. It's certainly obvious that you're the daughter of an attorney."

The smile that Mick had allowed to come to her face now faded, and she frowned and looked away. Out of the corner of her eye she saw half of one card peeking out from beneath the blanket, and she quickly got up from the bed and walked across the room to her juke-box. The jukebox was nearly new, a Christmas present from the year before, and was designed with a glass top and records visible under the dome to simulate the cafe jukeboxes of the fifties. It had cost her parents over two thousand dollars, and she rarely used it.

Now she pushed at the buttons on the front of the machine and watched as a record was selected and dropped onto the turntable. Music filled the room, the primitive beat of her favorite heavy metal band, especially chosen as the most likely to drive her mother from the room.

Fran watched helplessly for a minute, knowing that any conversation she wanted to have with her daughter wouldn't be worth shouting, but that was exactly what she would have to do to make herself heard over the blaring of that dreadful music.

It was painfully obvious that Mick wanted her to leave, but Fran waited by the door for another minute, hoping for some miracle that might deliver her from Mick's sudden hostility.

This wasn't like Mick, and Fran didn't know what to do about it. For the past week or so Mick had been touchy and on edge, so that sometimes Fran felt like she was walking on eggshells in an effort to keep from saying the wrong thing.

It was exhausting, to say the least.

Fran stood the noise as long as she was able, then she

47

went to the jukebox and pulled the plug. The buttons on it looked as complicated as the control panel in an airplane to her, so this seemed the easiest way to end the barrage of sound.

In the sudden silence that filled the room, mother and daughter looked at each other.

Mick glared for a minute, then bent down to the detached plug.

"Wait a minute," Fran said, louder than she had intended. She realized that her hearing had been temporarily impaired by the screeching music, so that her own voice sounded distant and hollow to her ears. She forced herself to speak naturally. "Mick, just give me a minute to say what I came in here to say, and then I'll leave and you can blast out the walls if you want."

With her hand still on the cord to the jukebox, Mick looked up at Fran as though ready to ignore the request, but then she nodded and straightened up. Although listening now, she folded her arms across her chest to show that, though she was willing to grant the few minutes Fran had asked for, she wasn't going to make it easy for her.

"Look," Fran said, "all I want is a little consideration. I don't know what it is your father and I have done to make you so angry, but the fact remains that we all have to live in the same house together, and we might as well try to get along. Your father's law partner and his wife are coming over tomorrow for Sunday dinner, and I think it would be nice if you cleaned up your room before they got here."

"Why? They won't even come to this part of the house," Mick argued. "What difference will it make what my room looks like if no one's going to see it anyway?" Mick turned away, kicked a blue and red sneaker out of her path, and walked toward the bed. She'd intended to throw herself across it dramatically and pull the covers over her head until Fran gave up and left, but at the last minute she remembered the cards there and veered off, going to her closet instead.

Fran started to go after her, then stopped a few feet into the room, remembering that she had to be careful of every movement she made, every word she spoke.

"Even if no one sees it, *I'll* still know what it looks like in here," she told Mick. "And I won't be able to relax for five minutes tomorrow if all I can think about is this disaster you call a bedroom."

"Get Iona to clean it. That's what a housekeeper is for, isn't it?"

"Iona won't be in on Sunday morning, and you know it. Besides, that would hardly be fair." Fran looked around the room, at the banana peel on the floor next to the bed, the overflowing wastepaper basket and the thin layer of dust on every piece of furniture. She couldn't ask Iona to come in here.

"What's not fair about it?" Mick asked. "It's what she gets paid for."

Fran sighed. "This is your responsibility."

"Well, it's *my* room, and I don't care what anyone else thinks about it. I like it this way."

"Iona thinks it's a sign of rebellion."

"You let her talk to you that way?"

Fran went back to the open door and put her hand on the knob. "Iona has been with us for a long time," she struggled to explain. "She's a part of this family, and I respect her opinion."

Mick's mouth turned down at the corners. "Maybe she's more a part of this family than I am," she said.

Fran recoiled as though slapped, but shook her head to deny Mick's words. "I can't stand this," she said. "Clean your bedroom, or I'll come in and do it myself."

She left the room quickly, closing the door softly behind her.

49

Mick watched the door for a minute to make sure her mother wouldn't come back, then went to her bed and pulled aside the blanket. She looked down at the cards, wishing she could find a message there for this inner turmoil she was feeling, then gathered them together with trembling hands and returned them to their box.

Just outside Mick's bedroom door, Fran leaned against the wall and closed her eyes, fighting down the anger that crashed over her like ocean waves, tossing her about in a relentless sea.

It was several minutes before she felt some control returning, and she was able to open her eyes again.

Why was Mick doing this to her? She had expected the early teen years to be the tough ones, that was what all her friends had told her to watch out for, but Mick had breezed through that time without causing a bit of trouble.

Mick had been a sweet and loving toddler, and an affectionate preteen. Even through adolescence Mick and Fran had weathered the occasional mood swings and temper tantrums with mutual respect. Fran had allowed herself to become complacent, thinking she was having it so much easier than her sister Donna was with her brood.

Now this. Just when she thought she was home free, Fran found herself faced with a stranger.

It had to be her fault. Maybe she hadn't paid enough attention to Mick over the years, and this reaction now was a delayed symptom, a belated releasing of hostility that Mick had been holding in for a long time. Mick had always had everything she wanted, but that wasn't enough. A child needed to know that her parents were there for her, to listen to all the little troubles that a teenager usually felt were the end of the world.

If Fran had neglected these needs at times, she hadn't done so out of a lack of caring, but through ignorance. She'd placed too much importance on her husband's career, perhaps, and had been filled with a sense of self-importance as she'd attended all the events that were a vital part of creating a successful businessman in this area.

Fran knew that she was going to have to talk to Brady, to remind him that Mick's needs were more important than their ambitions.

The music was playing in Mick's bedroom again, but not as loudly this time, and as Fran walked down the hallway she struggled, again, to understand the complex needs of a teenager in this day and age.

Fran tiptoed past the closed door of the study so as not to disturb Brady as he caught up on some work he'd brought home with him, and went to the kitchen. There she opened the refrigerator and peered inside. When upset she tended to want something to eat, and right now a cold chicken leg or a sandwich sounded like heaven.

"You hungry this time of night?"

Fran straightened up, and saw Brady standing a few feet away. "I thought I'd just have something before going to bed," she told him. "Did you finish looking over those papers you wanted to read?"

He stepped into the kitchen, rubbing at the thick brown hair on his head. His reading glasses had slipped down to the end of his nose, and he pushed them back up with one finger. "Not yet, but I needed a break. Something to eat sounds good to me, too." He looked inside the open refrigerator door and pulled out a plastic bowl of soup. After asking her if she wanted some, he began to warm the soup in the microwave.

Fran sat and watched as Brady puttered around the kitchen. It was comforting to her, this small injection of

51

normalcy into a day that had been full of turmoil.

Brady began to hum softly as he worked, and Fran felt like a child in her mother's kitchen. It was so soothing that she let the fantasy drift over her, a fantasy in which Mick played no part.

Alone in her bedroom, Mick was sorry for the way she'd talked to her mother, and was wondering why she did the things she did. Some perverse little corner of her soul had made her lash out, but she wasn't proud of her behavior.

She thought about going to her mother and apologizing. Fran was the most forgiving person in the world. Mick knew that if she could just get herself to go out there and make the first move, all would be right between them again.

She turned off the jukebox and opened her bedroom door, but the sound of her parents' voices stopped her from going farther. They were talking softly—it sounded like they were in the kitchen—and there was an intimacy to the sound that was like an invisible wall, separating her from them.

Mick wanted to go into the kitchen and sit on her dad's lap and listen to her mother talk about her volunteer work at the library. That was silly, since she hadn't sat on her father's lap since she was ten, but right now it sounded like the coziest place in the world.

Instead, she closed her bedroom door again and got ready for bed.

Chapter Four

"Lee, wait!"

Quinn ran to catch up with her friend, who stopped and waited in the middle of the hall. They were between classes and had five minutes to get from one room to the next. Lee, her arms filled with books, shifted her load until Quinn reached her side.

"What's up?" Lee asked. They started walking together toward their destination, second period English Composition. The hall was crowded with students hurrying to their classes, some talking and laughing as they went, others already thinking about what was to come.

"Have you heard about Blaire Campbell?" Quinn asked, her voice low.

"No, what?"

"She's pregnant."

Lee stopped walking, shock registering on her face. "What's she going to do?" she asked.

Quinn shrugged. "She doesn't know yet. She was talking to me after she first got here this morning, and she's terrified about how her parents will react when she tells them. She says she won't have an abortion, but she's afraid that's exactly what they'll want her to do."

They continued walking. "Any chance Charlie will

marry her?" Lee asked.

Quinn shook her head. "She says she doesn't want to get married. She's only seventeen and not ready for that yet. She wants to go to college, and you know Blaire's always had big plans."

"She should have thought of that before she started fooling around," Lee said.

But even as she said the words, Lee knew she wasn't being entirely fair. She understood what it was like to believe you were truly in love, and how that feeling could sweep a person away.

Last year she'd dated, for a period of several months, Brian Frazier, a boy two years older than herself. She and Bryan had slept together, after endless discussions and much agonizing over whether or not it was what they really wanted. All the talk had probably been a smoke screen to justify the healthy lust they felt, but it made them feel that they were taking a mature approach to the subject.

Once they'd actually done it, Lee had been disappointed. It didn't seem like that big a deal for all the fuss everyone made about it. A little scary, but not a world-shattering event. It hadn't seemed impulsive or frivolous at the time, but now when she looked back on it Lee realized that she and Bryan had been doomed from the start. The relationship began to disintegrate almost immediately after the first time they'd had sex. She'd still wanted to go to school functions and be with Mick and Quinn when she felt like it, but Bryan had seemed to think they should spend all their time looking for a place to be alone. He'd obviously enjoyed it more than she had, and they'd begun to argue all the time.

When they'd finally broken up it had been an ugly scene, with accusations tossed back and forth. Her main regret now was that she hadn't waited a little longer to lose her virginity. It all seemed so shabby in retrospect.

But at least she hadn't ended up in Blaire's position. Even swept away by raging hormones, she'd had the good sense to go to the free clinic for birth control.

Bryan, on the other hand, had gone from her to Kat Rossi, and there his luck ran out. Kat got pregnant, Bryan married her, and the baby was due soon.

It all might have been an episode Lee could have put behind her if it weren't for the fact that Bryan's mother lived next door to Lee's house, and Mrs. Frazier and Joan Sternhagen were good friends. Lee had to listen to an almost daily report from her mother on how well the newlyweds were doing.

She didn't want to think about that now. "Have you talked to Jack?" she asked Quinn, changing the subject.

Quinn pulled her books up so that they almost touched her chin, and hunched her shoulders against an unhappy thought. "I've called his house a few times this past couple of weeks, but his sister always tells me he's not home. I think she's been lying, and that he told her to say that. Here at school he just turns and goes the other way when he sees me coming."

"What a creep."

"No, he has every right to be mad. Mick shouldn't have said that about his family in front of everyone. I just wish he didn't still believe I told her about it."

"He can't avoid you forever," Lee said. "This isn't that big a school. Sooner or later he's going to have to talk to you."

Quinn stepped aside to let a boy pass. "I'll worry

about that when the time comes, I guess," she said. "I don't have any illusions that Jack and I will ever go out together again. I just don't want to go through the rest of the school year with him mad at me."

Lee looked around and saw that the hallway was almost empty. Only she and Quinn, and a few stragglers, had not yet gone into their classrooms. "We'd better get in; the bell's going to ring. I'm not looking forward to this. I didn't get my assignment done."

They went into the classroom and took their seats. Quinn, sitting behind Lee, spoke in a whisper. "You didn't do your Comp assignment? Why not?"

"My mother had a long list of things she wanted me to do around the house," Lee said. "By the time I was finished it was too late to start the assignment."

Their teacher, Mrs. Pidbuhl, entered the classroom seconds before the bell rang. The murmur of conversation stopped with her appearance, and the two dozen students faced the front of the class like model prisoners.

Mrs. Pidbuhl was tall and stooped, years of disappointments etched on her face and in her posture. She might once have been attractive, but was now too thin and stern. The eyes that swept over the students were without humor. She turned her back on them and began to write on the blackboard.

Quinn took two sheets of paper from the folder on her desk, and handed them to Lee. "Here," she whispered. "Sign your name at the top of the page and turn it in as yours. Our styles are similar, so she'll never know the difference."

"But what about you?" Lee asked. She looked longingly at the papers Quinn offered, but didn't take them.

Quinn pressed the papers on her friend. "I had

56

Mrs. Pidbuhl last year, and she always liked me. She'll let me make up the assignment."

This was true. Quinn was a favorite of most of the faculty, so that on the rare occasions when she did slip up she was likely to be forgiven. Lee accepted the papers gratefully.

As the assignments were passed forward, Mrs. Pidbuhl went to the head of each row to take the work. When she reached the row in which Quinn and Lee were sitting, she looked through the papers with a frown. "We seem to be short here," she said.

Quinn cleared her throat. "I didn't get mine finished," she said. "I can have it done by tomorrow, if that's okay."

The teacher, her face beginning to take on an expression of rancor, looked disappointed to learn that it was Quinn, and not one of the others. Her mouth worked for a moment as she seemed to undergo some inner struggle. "You know my policy, Quinn," she said finally. "These compositions were due today, and I can't make an exception. If I do it this once, especially so early in the school year, the next thing I know you people will be turning your work in late all the time."

Lee opened her mouth to speak up, but Quinn pinched her shoulder from behind, a warning to keep quiet.

"Could I turn my work in later today?" Quinn asked.

Mrs. Pidbuhl considered this. "All right. That will be acceptable. As long as you turn your assignment in by three o'clock this afternoon, I'll consider it on time." She looked at Quinn from under her eyebrows. "*Can* you get it to me by three o'clock?"

"Oh, yes," Quinn said eagerly. "No problem at all."

The classroom seemed to heave a collective sigh of relief. Every student there had realized that, as unlikely as it was for Mrs. Pidbuhl to give in even that much on one of her steadfast rules, Quinn Baker was one of the few who might have some influence upon her. That Quinn had proven successful seemed a victory for them all.

Fifty minutes later, as the class ended and the girls hurried out of the room, Lee expressed her gratitude. "You saved my life," she said. "The Pit Bull never would have given me a few more hours to get that work done. She already doesn't like me, and I think she would have loved to have given me a zero on the paper." She stopped walking to look at Quinn. "But what are you going to do now?"

A boy from their class passed by. "Teacher's pet," he said teasingly, grinning at Quinn.

"Eat your heart out," she shot back.

"No, really," Lee persisted. "You got me out of a tight spot, but now you only have a few hours to do an assignment that should have taken at least a whole evening. I shouldn't have taken your work. Now I feel really guilty."

Quinn was unconcerned. "I can write a whole new composition in the study hour I have right after lunch. I've always been a fast worker, and this is my easiest class. The only thing that's worrying me is that Jack also has that study hour, and that's going to make it harder for me to concentrate. Damn. I wish Mick had just stayed home that night of the party."

"Have you seen her today?" Lee asked.

"No, but I hope she's thrown those stupid cards away by now." Quinn stopped in front of her locker.

"If she hasn't, I know they're going to cause more trouble."

"When have you ever known Mick to avoid trouble?" Lee asked.

With the cards nestled in the bottom of her big purse, Mick moved through the day feeling confident and able to handle anything that came her way. There was something about having them with her that made her feel strong.

Her dark hair pulled back in a clip, she left her last class of the day and walked to the school parking lot toward her car. It was her habit to give Quinn and Lee a ride home every day, and when she reached her car she hopped up on the hood to wait for them.

She only had one class with Quinn and none with Lee, so she hadn't had a chance yet to talk to them. Usually they all ate lunch together, but today she had come out to the parking lot during lunch break to sit alone in her car and work with her cards. She was getting really good at interpreting the meaning of each card, and she took almost every opportunity to practice and sharpen her skills.

She was getting eager to try them out again on someone. Next time she would know to soften any bad news the cards might reveal. It wouldn't do to scare people off, especially if she wanted to keep doing readings.

And she did want to continue, more than anything else in the world.

The car parked next to hers in the lot was a rusted VW that Mick knew belonged to Emma Mejia. It hadn't been there when she'd parked her car this morning, and if it had been she probably would have looked for another space.

She looked up and saw Emma walking toward her and sighed in resignation. Unconsciously her hand went to her purse, feeling for the wooden box inside.

"Hi, Mick," Emma said, her smile falsely bright. "Did you hear about Blaire Campbell?"

"I heard," Mick said.

Emma snickered as she stopped in front of Mick's car. "Serves her right, I say."

Mick tried to ignore her, hoping that Emma would get in her car and drive away. She peeled at some loose polish on her left thumbnail, scraping off the burgundy coloring as if it were the most important thing in the world, her head bent low over the task.

She didn't like Emma. Besides being brash and obnoxious, Emma had probing dark eyes and a habit of always being somehow nearby, and she seemed to watch Mick with a look that was hungry to find some flaw.

Mick assumed it had to do with envy. Emma wore clothes that were a little too gaudy and appeared hastily put together, like a hooker after a rough night. Her black hair was shoulder length and thick, but frizzy from a home perm. She had a good figure, but no subtlety.

Mick was used to people like Emma, but that didn't make them any less uncomfortable to be around. From an early age she'd noticed that a certain type of person tended to dislike her not for the person she was, but simply because her parents had money. Eventually she'd come to the realization that she was different in some way, that the very act of being raised with the last name McGee made her stand out.

Now she looked at the other girl and she knew her own face reflected the dislike painted on Emma's, a mirror giving back what it received.

"Blaire's not so bad," Mick said defiantly. "She made a mistake, that's all. It happens all the time."

Emma snorted. "All the time to sluts."

"Blaire's not a slut." Mick didn't know why she felt compelled to defend a girl she barely knew, but she was sick of Emma, sick of all the people so eager to get their pleasure from someone else's misfortune.

"Gee, McGee, I didn't know Blaire was such a good friend of yours. I thought you and Lee and Quinn were a private little club of three that didn't let anyone else in." Emma feigned a yawn, her eyes sharp behind her show of indifference. "Where are they, anyway? You three are usually inseparable."

"Get lost, Emma," Mick said, her temper rising dangerously close to the surface.

"This is the school parking lot and I have just as much right here as you do," Emma snapped. "We're not on your private property, you know."

"You're an idiot."

"And you're a rich-bitch snob who thinks she can order people around any time she wants. Well, you can't order *me* around."

Quinn and Lee were halfway across the parking lot when they saw Emma lunge for Mick, her hands outstretched like claws, a look of rage distorting her features.

"Uh-oh," Lee said, and broke into a run.

Quinn was close behind, but Lee reached the battling girls first. They were tangled together, snarling and spitting, Emma's sharp-toed shoes kicking out,

61

trying to make contact with Mick's shins. Mick had her hands buried in Emma's hair, and as she pulled she danced around in an attempt to protect her legs from the lower assault.

Not quite believing what she was seeing, Lee threw herself between the combatants.

"Mick, let go!" she begged, holding her friend's wrists. Then she yelped in pain as Emma kicked her sharply in the knee.

Quinn reached the trio and grabbed Emma around the waist from behind, very much aware that the scene had attracted a small group of curious on-lookers. She was embarrassed to be a part of this, but knew she couldn't leave as long as Mick needed help. With a burst of strength, she pulled Emma out of Mick's grasp, and she and Emma fell back and hit Mick's car with tooth-rattling force.

"You bitch!" Emma screamed, her attention still focused on Mick. "I'll kill you!" She tried to shake off Quinn but found herself held too firmly for escape.

Lee held Mick a few feet away, both breathing heavily. Mick had a thick clump of Emma's dark hair entwined in her fingers, and Mick found herself laughing as she gasped for breath. Her eyes were large and bright, a look of elation on her face.

Quinn separated herself from Emma to open the car door, and Lee pushed Mick inside. Before Emma could gather herself for a second attack, the three girls were inside the car, and the doors were quickly locked.

Lee was behind the steering wheel, so she reached inside Mick's purse for the keys, shoved them into the ignition, and looked back only long enough to make sure no one was in the way before she gunned the engine and tore out of the parking lot.

Jammed against the passenger side door, Mick had her head thrown back, one hand pressed to her chest as she struggled to contain the laughter that still bubbled from her.

"What was *that* all about?" Lee demanded when they were several blocks from the school, and she felt it was safe to slow down.

Before Mick could offer an explanation, Quinn, squeezed between the two girls in the front seat, said, "Lee, pull over so I can get in the back." She had a knee on either side of the stick shift, and every time Lee shifted gears, she felt she was in danger.

"What's the matter?" Mick gasped, tears running down her cheeks. "Is my four-on-the-floor getting farther with you than Jack ever did? Enjoy it while you can, Quinn. Now that Jack is history, this might be the most excitement you get for awhile."

"Very funny. I mean it, Lee, pull over. Bucket seats are not made for three people."

"Just a minute, I have to wait for an opening in traffic."

"Where are we, anyway?"

"I don't know. I just drove. I didn't pay any attention to where we were going."

"We're on Wesley Street, about two blocks from Burger King. No, wait, we're already past Burger King. You must have been speeding, Lee."

"Of course I was speeding! I was saving your life, if you'll remember."

Now they were all laughing, a delayed reaction to the situation, and Lee finally did pull the car over to the curb because her eyes were beginning to water, and she couldn't see the road well enough to continue driving.

"Thank God," Quinn said as soon as they were

parked. With much twisting and complaining, she managed to hike her skirt up enough to climb through the space between the seats and fall into the back. She rearranged her clothing and tried to regain a bit of her lost dignity. Her laughter caused her to hiccup, bringing fresh giggles from Mick and Lee.

"All right, now you have to tell us," Lee said to Mick as soon as she was able. "What did you say to Emma to make her jump on you like that? She hasn't liked you since you got that part in the play last year that she'd wanted . . ."

"And then you had that party a couple of months ago that you didn't invite her to," Quinn spoke up from the back.

"—but I've never known her to get violent before. I've always thought she was basically a coward. You must have really got to her for her to totally lose control that way."

Her cheeks flushed, Mick pushed her hair back from her forehead. "I told her that her mother spent so much time on her back that she got a commission from the motels in town."

Quinn gasped. "Did you really say that?"

"I sure did. Everyone knows Emma's mother will sleep with anyone who has the money for a drink. Emma knows it herself."

"But to actually *say* it—"

Mick's eyes darkened dangerously. "She's always on me, following me around and trying to cause trouble. I'd finally had all I was going to take from her." She smiled as she looked at them, a small, cold movement of her lips that did nothing to soften her expression. "You know what's funny about this whole thing?"

The hysterical laughter that had gripped Lee moments earlier was now gone, and she shook her head. "There really is nothing funny about it."

"Oh, yes, there is." Mick looked at them both, and this time her smile did reach her eyes. "My cards told me about this. I did a reading for myself last night before going to bed, and the cards revealed exactly what was going to happen."

Chapter Five

Lee stepped into her bedroom and was immediately overwhelmed by the smell of Lemon Pledge, a sure indication that her mother had recently been here. She had to open a window, even though that created the danger of a speck of dust getting in.

Her bed was made with military precision. Dimes would have bounced two feet high on the bedspread. She'd made the bed herself this morning before school, as was the rule, but it had been done over because she had a hard time meeting Joan Sternhagen's tough standards.

The whole house was like this. Starched and dazzlingly white doilies rested on the backs of every chair, the carpets were vacuumed daily and no dirty dish dared sit in a sink for longer than five minutes. Surgery could have been conducted safely in the Sternhagen home.

Lee's mother, divorced since Lee was four, was obsessive-compulsive about her children and her house. As for herself, Lee wouldn't have minded a little clutter once in awhile just to take the edge off, but she knew better than to try it. She strongly suspected her mother's housekeeping habits had a lot to do with her father's sudden departure nearly fourteen years earlier.

Going to her dresser, Lee opened it and looked at

the neatly stacked T-shirts and underwear there. Even her bras were folded in half, the straps tucked into the cups. It was a depressing sight.

A door slammed in another part of the house, and by the heavy sound of the footsteps that followed Lee knew that her brother was home. She also had a sister three years older than herself, but Liz already had a husband and a one-year-old baby. Early marriage had been her way out. Liz lived in San Diego and probably hadn't done housework since Lee had seen her last April. She'd gone from one extreme to the other. Lee hoped she would be able to find some middle ground someday.

She found her brother, Dennis, in the kitchen. He was raiding the refrigerator.

"Where's Mom?" she asked. Their mother worked as a secretary in town, but was usually home by mid-afternoon.

"Next door," Dennis mumbled through a full mouth. "Bryan and Kat are over there, and I guess she wanted to see them."

Lee groaned. She hadn't seen Bryan's car parked outside his mother's house next door. If she had seen it, she probably would have left the neighborhood for a few hours, to avoid the possibility of catching a glimpse of him. The sight of him was still painful, and probably always would be. However brief it had been, her feelings for Bryan had been genuine and deep.

"I stopped in over there for a minute myself," Dennis added. He had a chicken leg in one hand and a Twinkie in the other, and when he smiled his braces glinted silver in the sun that came through the kitchen window. "Brace yourself," he added.

"For what?"

"I think Mom is trying to get Bryan and Kat to come over here."

"To *our* house?" The possibility was too horrible to contemplate.

"That's right. Bryan didn't seem too crazy about the idea, but Mom was telling him that he had to see the new wallpaper she put up in the living room."

"He doesn't care about our wallpaper." Lee backed up toward the door, ready to make a run for it.

"Probably not, but you know how hard it is to say no to our mother about anything. She was really working on him."

Lee turned and almost made it to the back door, where she planned to duck out and become invisible, when she heard her mother call out. "Lee, look who's here!"

Too late. Her mother had probably seen her come home and now escape was impossible.

And then she was in the same room with them, for all outward appearances a cozy little group except that Lee wished she could just die and get it over with.

Quinn was wishing much the same thing as she hid in the tiny bathroom beside her parents' bedroom, where she'd gone when her father's temper had flared up and he'd begun to beat her. She could hear him outside in the hallway, pacing back and forth and muttering about how she would really get it as soon as she showed her face.

She had no intention of showing her face at all if she could help it, even if it meant staying in the bathroom all night. This was the only door in the house that had a lock on it.

The trouble had started when she'd walked in the house after school and seen that her father was already drunk. Afternoon drinking wasn't unusual for Harry Baker, but he didn't usually get really mean until he'd been at it a few hours. Something must have happened to set off his temper. It didn't have to be much. A wrong word from Quinn's mother was enough to send him into a rage, or even the cancellation of one of his favorite TV shows.

Whatever it was, Quinn and Elaine Baker were usually the ones to suffer for it.

He'd hit Quinn on the arm with his fist when she tried to prevent him from going after her mother. "Quinn, don't!" Elaine had cried. "Go to your room and close the door." But Quinn had been unable to stand the sight of her mother cowering and frightened, trying to ward off the blows coming down on her.

When he'd turned to Quinn, the girl had been almost relieved. She would rather be hit herself than to see her mother being beaten. Whatever her feelings, however, she'd only been able to take it for so long before she ran into the bathroom, feeling a coward for leaving her mother out there with him.

Then, unexpectedly, everything grew quiet. After a moment she heard her mother's voice outside the bathroom door.

"Quinn, you can come out now; he's gone."

She opened the door cautiously and saw Elaine's tear-streaked face. She fell into her mother's arms, and together they went into the living room, two survivors of a war seeking comfort in each other.

"I hate him," Quinn said, sitting with her mother on the couch.

"Sh-h-h-h. Don't say that," Elaine said. "He doesn't

69

mean it. He just can't handle the alcohol."

Quinn pulled back to look at her mother. "Of course he means it. And it's not the alcohol that does it. It's him. He *likes* to hurt us. I can see it in his face every time he hits one of us. It makes him feel big and strong." She sniffed and wiped at her wet cheeks with the back of her hand. "Why do you stay with him, Mom? Why don't you kick him out of the house? Or *we* could leave. We could move to another house, or an apartment even, on the other side of town."

Elaine Baker sat beside her daughter on the couch, looking older than her years, beaten down by almost two decades of living in fear.

Once she had been a pretty blonde like her daughter, lively and full of plans. Now she was thirty pounds overweight, and her hair had dulled to a mousy brown that she wore tucked behind her ears because styling it was too much trouble.

Swallowing several times, Elaine struggled to bring herself under control. She didn't want Quinn to see that she felt weak and incapable of making any decisions.

"He's my husband," she said. "And your father. We should stand by him. He wasn't always like this. There was a time when he was kind."

"Why is he even drinking today?" Quinn asked. "I thought he had to work tonight."

"He was supposed to, but he'd better not show up in this condition or he'll lose his job."

"Again," Quinn said bitterly. "How many jobs has he gone through in the past ten years? A dozen? If it weren't for your job, we'd all starve."

"He'll get better. There's AA—"

"Which he has no intention of ever going to. Besides, you have to want to get better for that to work. Leave him," Quinn urged again.

Elaine looked away. "I wasn't raised to walk out on a husband, Quinn. When I married him, it was forever."

"Or until he kills you." Quinn's anger was growing now that her fear had faded, but the anger was directed as much toward her mother as her father. It seemed to Quinn that for the sake of a vow she'd made over eighteen years ago, her mother was willing to risk both their lives. "Divorce isn't that big a deal anymore. Lee's parents are divorced."

Elaine moved slightly, and winced at a sudden stab of pain. "And look where it's gotten Joan Sternhagen," she said. "If she'd really tried to make a go of that marriage, she might not be as unhappy a person as she is now."

"Mom, please," Quinn said. "What's going to happen to you when I'm gone? In less than a year I'll graduate, and I'm sure not going to stick around for long after that to be his punching bag. It'll be worse for you then, because you'll be the only one he'll have to beat on."

Elaine touched her swollen jaw, but she couldn't bring her eyes to meet her daughter's. "I'll think about that when the time comes."

Quinn got to her feet, too angry now to continue this conversation, the same one they'd had a hundred times already. She didn't understand her mother's willingness to let a man neither one of them loved any more use her in this way. "I'm going to go change my clothes and wash up," she said. "Mick and Quinn will be here soon to pick me up."

"You're going out tonight?"

"I told you this morning at breakfast that I was. A

little while ago I thought I probably wouldn't get out of the house, but now that Dad is gone to find trouble somewhere else I guess I might as well go."

Elaine's expression was trapped. "What if he comes back?"

"You know he won't. He'll pass out in some bar somewhere and won't come crawling back until morning." Quinn looked around at their living room, at the secondhand furniture, the worn carpeting. It wasn't much of a home, really. She wouldn't be too sorry to leave when the time came.

"I wanted to sink right into the floor and die," Lee said, looking down at the hands resting on her lap. "Bryan looked like he wished he wasn't there, but you know Kat—she's always hated it that I went out with Bryan before she did, and she was loving every minute of it."

The scene was still too fresh in Lee's mind. Her mother had sat on the edge of the sofa, apparently oblivious to Lee's discomfort. Joan had served tea to her guests, in perfect control of the situation. Lee saw her wince when Kat put her teacup down on the coffee table and missed the coasters Joan had placed out, but Joan had waited until Kat and Bryan were gone before getting out her cleaning supplies.

"Your mother and my father would make a great couple," Quinn said. "They're both sadists."

The girls sat in a back booth at a small local cafe, where they'd gone after seeing an early movie. At first their conversation had been light and having mostly to do with school news, but eventually Lee had questioned Quinn about the fresh bruise near her temple, and Quinn had confessed to them that her father was on the warpath again.

After that they'd grown serious, each sharing a bit of her own personal unhappiness.

The cafe was nearly empty because it wasn't one of the places where most of the teenagers in town hung out. They'd chosen it especially because they hadn't felt like running into friends from school.

"I've been meaning to ask you," Lee said, turning to Mick. "What is that you're wearing?"

Mick laughed. "Do you like it," She fingered the flowing skirt that fell to mid-calf. She'd seen it in a store a few days earlier and had decided she wanted it even though she rarely wore skirts. She'd combined it with a low cut, peasant-style blouse that showed the tops of her breasts.

"I'm not sure what I think about it," Lee said. "You look completely different."

"I know." Mick shook her head so that her hair tumbled about her shoulders. Her eyes shifted away from her friends, and she smiled. "Look who just walked in."

Quinn and Lee turned and saw two leather-clad boys swaggering through the front door of the cafe. Both looked too old for high school, but neither did they appear to be college material. The taller of the two had hair almost to his shoulders and a self-confident expression as he looked around. Seeing the girls, he nudged his friend and they took a booth nearby.

Lee giggled. "Yuk," she said softly, so as not to be overheard.

"Oh, they're not so bad," Mick said. "The tall one's kind of sexy. Who do you suppose they are?"

"The short one is Emma Mejia's older brother,"

73

Quinn told her. "He dropped out of school when he was a junior, and now he works at the gas station a block from my house. I don't know who the other one is."

"Let's invite them over."

"Mick, no! I've heard so much bad stuff about Emma's brother that my mom won't even let me take the car to that station for gas any more. She makes me go a half mile to the next station instead."

"Lighten up; it'll be fun. Besides, I want to find out who the other one is." Mick made a move to get up, but Quinn and Lee both looked so scandalized that she broke out into loud laughter that drew looks from the few customers in the cafe. "Chickens," she said good-naturedly. She reached for one of the last french fries on the plate and examined it, turning it slowly back and forth before her face. "I just thought maybe he was the one."

"The one what?" Lee asked.

Mick bit off the end of the fry. "The one my cards told me about. I spread the cards for myself just before leaving home to get you two tonight, and they told me that there was romance coming in my near future." She looked over at the boys only three booths away. "My future might be sitting right over there."

"That's silly," Quinn said. "You're doing something that started out as a game, and you're taking it seriously."

"It is serious."

"Oh, come on. You don't really believe in those cards, do you?"

"I sure do." Mick looked at them both, leaning forward in her desire to make them understand. "I'll admit I had some doubts at first but I've seen too much of what they say come true to *not* believe in them. You both saw it. That very first night, at the party, the cards told us all about what was going on in Jack's life."

Quinn made a choking sound, and put one hand over her mouth.

"What's wrong?" Lee asked, concerned.

Mick looked pleased with herself. "Tell her, Quinn."

"No."

"Okay, then I'll tell her." Mick turned to Lee. "I heard it after school just today. Jack's parents are getting a divorce. His father has moved out, and the house is already up for sale. Jack's mother is taking Jack and his sister to LA, so they'll be closer to her family."

"Is that true?" Lee asked, wide-eyed.

"It's a coincidence," Quinn said, looking unsure of her own words.

"No, it's not." Mick reached into her purse and pulled out the wooden box that now went everywhere with her. She set the box down dramatically on the table and tapped it with her finger. "These cards can tell us everything we want to know. Our futures are right here, just waiting for us to ask for the information."

"You're scaring me," Lee said. She sat far back in her seat, to put as much distance between herself and the cards as possible.

Mick spoke softly. "There's nothing to be scared of, Lee. I know what I'm doing. And I want to do a reading for both of you."

"No way!" Lee said immediately.

Mick looked at Quinn. "How about you?"

Quinn started to shake her head, then shrugged. "I

don't know. What if you tell me something bad?"

"Quinn, don't encourage her," Lee said.

"Let her make up her own mind. What do you say, Quinn? It'll be fun, and it'll give me the practice I need. I'm better at it now than I was at first, so I won't see just good or bad in the cards. I'll be able to read the more subtle messages there."

"I'll have to think about it," Quinn said. Then, seeing Mick's disappointment, she added, "I'm not saying a definite no; it's just that I don't want to be pushed into doing anything tonight."

"When have I ever pushed you into doing anything you didn't want to do?"

"Since we were about eight." Quinn picked up her purse, the signal that this conversation had run its course.

They left their booth and walked through the cafe, but Quinn and Lee were already at Mick's car outside before they realized Mick wasn't with them.

"Where'd she go?" Quinn asked, looking around.

Lee spotted Mick through the front window of the cafe. "She's still inside, talking to those boys."

"Why's she doing that?" Quinn asked. "She wouldn't seriously consider going out with either of them. Would she?"

"Of course not."

"But look at her flirting with them."

"She's just teasing, because she likes ✥ drive us crazy and she knows this will do it. You know Mick— even when we were kids she had to be doing the most daring things just to see our reaction." Lee smiled and looked at Quinn. "Like that time when we were in sixth grade, and she decided she was going to climb to the top of the water tower."

Quinn had to laugh at the memory. While she and Lee had watched in horrified fascination from the bottom of the water tower, Mick had climbed halfway up before getting scared. Then she had frozen and had been unable to go either up or down. Finally the fire department had come to the rescue, after which she'd sworn she hadn't really been frightened, but only wanted to see what they would do.

"Maybe you're right," Quinn conceded. "But I wish she'd hurry up and get out here. For all we know, she might be in there right now telling those guys that *we're* interested in them."

The girls looked at each other, then both sprinted for the front door of the cafe. Lee yanked it open and called, "Mick, are you coming?"

Mick came to them after waving a good-bye to the young men. "What's the big hurry?" she asked when they reached her car. "We have a couple of hours yet before we have to be home."

Opening the car door, Quinn said, "That doesn't mean we have to spend all night here, does it? I'd like to think we could find something else to do with our time than to spend it in some old cafe."

Mick gave her a knowing look. "Yeah. And maybe you just wanted to get me out of there." She lifted one shoulder in a casual shrug. "It doesn't matter anyway. I already found out what I wanted to know."

Sitting in the booth, with a half-eaten hamburger on the plate before him, Danny Santos watched as the girls got in the car and drove away.

He and his friend, Rick Mejia, had come into the cafe and noticed the three pretty girls sitting in the

77

back booth, but, despite his interest, he had considered them all to be the snooty, stuck-up type that he liked to tease but usually considered out of his reach. Rick had told him that he knew they were high schoolers, but that he didn't remember any of their names.

The big surprise had come when two of the girls had gone out to their car and the last one had stopped to introduce herself to him as Mick McGee. He recognized the name, partly because her father was a big-shot in town, but also because he'd dated Rick's sister Emma until about a month ago, and Emma had often talked of Mick and how much she hated her.

He'd been suspicious of Mick's motives at first, thinking she was just getting some sort of cheap thrill out of leading him on. But as she'd talked, laughing and smiling, her wide eyes appraising him boldly, he'd changed his opinion of her. She might just be a kid— Emma had never seemed like a kid to him because she'd been around the block a few times—but Mick had looked so wise that he suspected she'd been around a bit, too, and not just with high school boys.

Mick had openly invited him to call her, and had leaned over their table to write her phone number on a paper napkin after digging a pen out of her purse. As she'd written the number down, the loose fabric of her blouse had gaped open, and he'd caught a delicious glimpse of soft breasts in a white bra. He'd been peeking when her eyes had lifted and met his, and he knew without a doubt that she knew exactly what he was seeing and didn't mind one bit.

He'd squirmed in his seat, wondering at that time if he could possibly unload Rick so that he could talk this girl into going somewhere with him tonight. He had the feeling she wouldn't exactly turn her nose up at the idea.

But then her friends had barged back into the cafe and dragged her off like she was in danger of catching herpes or something, and he had seen his hopes for the night vanish before his eyes.

That didn't mean the future was entirely bleak, though. Danny picked up the napkin with Mick's phone number and folded it neatly in half. He smiled secretly to himself as he tucked the napkin in his shirt pocket.

"Are you going to call her?" Rick asked, looking awed by Danny's good luck.

"Of course I'm going to call her. Did you see the way she was coming on to me?"

"How could I miss it? If she'd been around a few more minutes, I wouldn't have been surprised if she started undressing you right here in front of everyone."

Danny leaned back in his seat, glad for this opportunity to show off a little. Even if Mick had taken the initiative, she'd come after him, not Rick, and he knew Rick was sure to spread the word that all Danny had to do was flash his famous killer smile and the girls came running. It was the sort of thing that helped build his reputation in the area. "Some of us have what it takes, and some don't," he boasted.

Rick shook his head in admiration. "She sure was after you, all right."

Chapter Six

Mick closed her bedroom door and kicked aside a pair of shoes on the floor to make her way to the bed.

"What happened here?" Lee asked, looking around at the mess.

"It's called the lived-in look."

"Lived in by pigs, maybe," Quinn said.

Mick wasn't offended. "I don't mind it. At least now I know where everything is."

"On the floor, it looks like." Lee sat on the edge of Mick's bed. "I'm surprised your mother is letting you get away with this."

"She doesn't have a whole lot to say about it. It's *my* room. I guess I can do whatever I want with it."

Quinn dropped her purse on Mick's desk and said, "Let's get this over with before I change my mind. Where do you want to do it?"

"On the bed. We'll be comfortable there."

"Then you'd better get rid of all the clothes piled there."

Grabbing an armful of blouses, sweaters and blue jeans, Mick tossed the garments on the floor. "There. All taken care of."

"That's not exactly what I had in mind," Quinn said.

"Oh, stop worrying about it. We're here so I can do

a reading for you with my tarot cards, remember? Now, Quinn, you sit down there and I'll shuffle the cards." Opening the box she'd taken from her purse, Mick took out the cards and held them in her hand for a minute, eyes half closed as she tried to concentrate on what she was doing. She was sitting cross-legged across from Quinn, her skirt spread-out around her, and she let her breathing grow shallow and slow.

"What are you waiting for?" Lee asked from the edge of the bed.

Mick shot her an irritated look. "I'm attempting to get in the right frame of mind. That means blocking out everything but Quinn, the cards and myself. So if you don't mind, I'd appreciate it if you'd stay quiet and just watch."

"Sorry," Lee muttered.

The room grew silent as Mick held the cards and tried to regain some of the ground she'd lost. After a minute in which it seemed no one breathed, she began to shuffle the cards.

She could feel their strength flowing into her, up her arms until they were a part of her, as much as her heart and her lungs and brain. It frightened her for a moment, and she almost stopped. She'd never felt anything this intense before, even during all the times she'd practiced with the cards by herself. If someone had reached out and taken the cards from her then she was sure she would drop over dead, a vital part removed so that her body could no longer function.

Then the power became a separate thing, and Mick felt a sense of peace come over her. The fear vanished as quickly as it had come. It was time to pass the cards to Quinn. Now they would see just what she could do.

"Quinn, you shuffle the cards now," she whispered,

handing over the deck. "Just think about your life, and any questions you may have. Don't be afraid."

But Quinn didn't like what was happening. She'd been watching Mick closely, and the change she'd seen come over her was weird. Mick had seemed a different person somehow, as her head had fallen back, and her eyes glittered from beneath her lids. Even now, as Quinn reluctantly took the cards in her own hands, she had the feeling this was a stranger sitting on the bed with her.

"W-what am I supposed to do?" she asked.

"I told you—shuffle," Mick repeated.

"There are too many of them."

"Do your best. Go slowly until you get used to the feel of them. Concentrate."

Quinn obeyed, only once looking over at Lee, who was watching the proceedings from the edge of the bed. When she felt she couldn't bear to hold the cards any longer she put them down. "There," she said. "Is that enough?"

"It'll do," Mick told her. "Now, let's see what the future holds for you."

Fran climbed back into bed and pulled the quilt up over her knees.

"Was that Mick?" Brady asked, barely looking up from the book he had resting on his lap.

"Yes, it was. She brought Lee and Quinn home with her. I heard them talking through the bedroom door."

"You didn't go in?"

"No, I didn't want to disturb them. You known how touchy girls that age are about their privacy. Especially Mick. If I'd so much as opened the door to say hello, she would have accused me of spying on her."

"Well, at least she's home at a decent hour. One thing you have to say for Mick, we've never had to go out looking for her in the middle of the night, like some parents do."

Fran moved closer to Brady and nudged him with her toes.

That got a response from him. He looked up from his book, then reached over and pulled her closer. so that her head was nestled on his shoulder. "How's it been going?" he asked. Fran sighed.

"The same. No matter what I say or do, it's always wrong."

"She'll get over it."

"Maybe. But what are we supposed to do in the meantime?"

"Live with it, I guess. What else can we do? Let her know we love her, and that we'll always be here for her."

"I don't think Mick wants our love."

Brady frowned. "Of course she does."

Letting one hand rest on his chest, Fran sought the warmth he was offering. For a moment it almost worked, but then her mind went back to the latest argument she'd had with Mick, only this morning. All she'd done was tell Mick to have some breakfast before going off to school, and it had resulted in an explosion. "Mick acts like she hates me," she said in a low voice.

Brady rubbed his face with his free hand, then tossed the book onto the floor. He embraced Fran, putting his lips to her fresh-scented hair. "Don't worry about it, hon. If it keeps up we'll sit her down and have a long talk with her. Both of us. But I don't want to push her. Give it a little more time."

This time Fran let herself be comforted. Brady always knew the right things to say. Or maybe it was just the tone of voice he used. Low and soothing, like water running over smooth stones. Maybe that was why he was such a good lawyer. He had a way of making people trust him, of inspiring the type of confidence needed in a lawyer-client relationship.

After over twenty years together she loved him now more than ever.

"Let's go away some weekend soon," she suggested. "It doesn't have to be much—just a couple of days to put our feet up and relax. The week in Denver was nice, but there were so many people around all the time."

"Just us?" Brady asked. "Or do you want to take Mick?"

Fran thought about it. "Let's take Mick, if we can talk her into it. She's going off to college next year, and we'll have plenty of time for just the two of us then. I want to spend as much time with her as we can until that happens."

Slipping her nightgown down from her shoulders, Brady said, "You're a nice lady, Fran McGee."

"There's nothing too surprising here, really," Mick said, looking at the cards she'd laid out on the mattress between herself and Quinn. She pointed to the King of Coins in the center of the spread. "That's your father, I believe, and because the card comes out upside down, it shows that he's an overbearing, even mean man who is dominating your life right now."

84

Quinn sat perfectly straight on the bed, her hands folded together on her lap. She hadn't wanted to place too much importance on what Mick was doing, but her curiosity was getting the best of her, and she had to comment. "How do you know that doesn't mean someone else? Maybe it's Mr. LeBroc, from French class. That test coming up next week has been on my mind a lot."

"No, the general feeling here is of your family life, not school. And the strength card, here in the situation position, shows a need to overcome obstacles."

"I've needed plenty of strength since Jack dumped me."

Mick ignored the reminder that she was at least partially responsible for that. In a way, she was glad that nothing spectacular had shown up in the cards for Quinn. She wouldn't have liked seeing anything bad for Quinn, and she didn't know if she would have been able to keep it to herself if she had. Quinn knew her too well—as did Lee—for her to be able to keep secrets for long.

She didn't have that worry this time, though, for the cards that had come up reflected Quinn's unhappy home life, but didn't indicate any major changes to come.

Obviously relieved, Quinn let her shoulders relax, and even managed to smile. "Is that all? It wasn't what I expected it to be."

"What were you expecting?" Mick asked.

"I don't know. A tall, dark stranger coming into my life, maybe. You know—like those gypsies used to do at the carnival. I went to one once, and she looked into a crystal ball and told me I would be rich and famous someday."

Lee, speaking for the first time since Mick had told her to be quiet, said, "Yeah, I went to that same gypsy, and she told me the exact same thing. Looks like we threw a dollar away on that one."

Mick gathered her cards together and put them back in the box. "Since the ceiling didn't cave in on us, like you both seemed to expect, maybe we can do it again soon," she suggested.

"Maybe," Quinn said, stretching her legs to ease a cramp. "Right now you'd better take me home. It's getting late."

As soon as Mick drove up in front of Quinn's house she knew there was trouble.

All the lights were on, the front door hung wide open, and the sound of shouting could be heard coming from inside.

"Oh, no, my dad has come home," Quinn said, all the years of anguish showing in her voice and on her face.

They'd dropped Lee off at her house first, and now it was just Mick and Quinn, sitting in the front seat of the car and wondering what to do.

"Come back home with me," Mick said. "You can spend the night, and tomorrow this will have blown over."

"I didn't think he'd come back tonight," Quinn said, her eyes on the house. "He showed all the signs of going on another of his benders. Sometimes he stays away for days at a time during them."

When Quinn reached for the door handle, Mick moved to stop her. "You can't go into that," she said.

A scream pierced the night air, and the lights went

on in a house across the street. A face appeared at the neighbor's window, but no one came out to help. This was an all too common occurrence on this block, and most people preferred not to get involved when Harry Baker was in a rage.

"I have to help my mother," Quinn said, pulling her arm away from Mick.

She got out of the car and ran to the house, her hair catching the reflection from the street light overhead.

Mick waited for a minute, afraid to move, but unsure of what she could do to help.

She made her decision when Quinn's voice joined those inside. She wasn't accustomed to domestic violence, though she'd heard enough about it from Quinn over the years, and she questioned her own sanity as she abandoned her car and plunged headlong into the war zone.

As she'd feared, Harry Baker had turned his drunken anger on his daughter. He had a grip on the shoulder of Quinn's blouse, and was using it to hold her as his free hand swung at her face. Her nose was already bloodied, but she fought her father valiantly, striking out at him with her own smaller, ineffectual hands. Her defensive blows might have been rain falling on a sidewalk for all the effect they had on him.

Elaine, her hair disheveled and her eyes wild, beat at Harry's back, trying to pull him away from Quinn. She was screaming, "Harry, stop, you'll kill her!"

Mick joined Elaine in tugging at the arm that held Quinn. Harry shook her off, looking at her only briefly. "Get the hell out of here," he warned.

It didn't sound like a bad idea to Mick, but she was in this too deep to walk away as though she'd seen nothing. Just as Quinn hadn't been able to abandon her mother, Mick now couldn't leave Quinn to whatever punishment Harry had in mind.

She went at him again, seeing that she'd caused enough of a distraction at least that Quinn had managed to get herself free and had backed up a few steps. This time she hit him with her full weight, staggering him, and for one brief moment Mick almost believed she had the upper hand.

This illusion was shattered when Harry, enraged at her interference, picked Mick up with strong hands and flung her across the room.

Mick landed against an end table, the sharp corner going into her ribs and causing such pain that black and purple spots danced before her eyes. The legs of the table broke, and it collapsed beneath her.

When her vision cleared Quinn was kneeling beside her, and in the middle of the room Elaine was holding Harry at bay.

"Mick, are you all right?" Quinn asked, one hand on her shoulder.

Mick got to her feet with Quinn's help, feeling as though her ribs were broken. So this was what Quinn had to live with every day of her life. It was almost too much to comprehend. How did she put up with it? And why didn't she do something about it?

"I'm going to call the police," Mick whispered.

Fear distorted Quinn's features. "No! They won't do anything, and it'll only make it worse."

"How can it get any worse than this?"

"Believe me, it can." Quinn was leading her toward the front door.

Harry seemed calmer as they walked past him. He was no longer hitting, but was only pushing at Elaine as she tried to talk to him. She threw the girls a nervous look as they passed, keeping her body carefully between them and her husband.

At the door Mick stopped. Outside was safety, and she could see her car out there, ready to take her home where her biggest problems seemed trivial compared to this. The fight had been knocked out of her. She knew she wasn't equipped to deal with this, but loyalty to Quinn made her try once more.

"Come with me," she urged.

Quinn shook her head. "No, Mick. I have to stay. You don't understand."

"You're right, I don't."

"I'll talk to you tomorrow. You'll see, it'll be all right."

Mick was on the front porch now, and she could see the scene inside framed by the doorway, looking like something from a bizarre movie. "I want to do something to help you," she told Quinn.

"You can't help."

With that, Quinn went inside and closed the door.

Mick was pulling off her skirt almost as soon as she'd slammed into her bedroom. It was flung to the floor, followed immediately by her blouse, then her pantyhose. Her clothes felt constrictive, as though they were suffocating her, and she was glad to get them off.

In her underwear she threw herself on the bed, her hands clenched into fists. Her anger needed an outlet, but she couldn't think of what to do. Nothing in her room seemed worth breaking, nor did she think that would really do it. She wanted to break Harry Baker, to end, finally, the damage he'd been doing to Quinn and her mother for almost as long as Mick could remember.

She sat bolt upright on her bed when she thought of the tarot cards. They were in her purse, as always. But why hadn't they told her earlier what was going to happen tonight? The reading she'd done for Quinn had been as bland as cold oatmeal. There had been nothing there to indicate the violence that had happened.

Where was her purse?

She found it on the floor under her skirt. All she could think to do was to put the cards out again, exactly as she had for Quinn. There had to be some explanation.

It took her a few minutes to remember all eleven cards, and then to remove them from the deck and arrange them on the floor. When that was done she looked there for a clue, some indication of what she had done wrong.

The fault had to lie in her. She was too new at this, she didn't yet know what she was doing, and that's why she had gotten the message wrong.

'Mick's frustration mounted as she realized she still couldn't see anything of tonight's violence in the arrangement. The King of Coins had to be Harry Baker—of that much Mick was sure—but everything else was vague.

This new problem, the feeling that she had somehow failed, drove all else from Mick's thoughts, until she shifted position and again felt the pain in her ribs where she had fallen against the end table at Quinn's house. The pain brought it all back again, and with the memories came the fear over what Quinn might be going through at this very moment.

Looking down at the King of Coins, Mick picked up the rest of the deck and quickly shuffled through it. When she found the card she was looking for she removed it from the deck.

"All right, you bullying son of a bitch," she whispered. "Let's see how you like this."

Mick placed the Death card directly on top of the King of Coins.

"I've told you to never bring any outsiders into this house," Harry Baker shouted at Quinn, trying to grab her.

Quinn had gotten into the kitchen, truly terrified now at the sight of her father's prolonged anger. Usually he tired quickly, his rages burning hot while they lasted, but extinguished before he could inflict serious damage.

This time, however, he seemed to go on and on, chasing her from one room to the next, ignoring Elaine's attempts to distract him.

Quinn had gotten a kitchen chair and placed it between herself and her father, like a circus lion tamer warding off the beast. It was flimsy protection, but she hoped it would slow him down enough to allow her to escape through the back door.

She had, so far, suffered the worst beating of her life, and she feared it was nothing compared to what he would do to her if he got his hands on her again. After Mick had gone, Harry had thrown Quinn around the living room until she'd felt that every part of her body was screaming out in protest. Her head ached where it had hit the edge of the television set, her arms felt as though they'd been pulled from the sockets, and she tasted blood from a cut inside her mouth.

For once Quinn wished one of the neighbors would intervene. Once or twice in the past, when the battles had gotten too loud, the police had arrived at their front door, summoned by a concerned citizen.

It hadn't done any good. Quinn and her mother had been too frightened to speak up or to ask for help, and Harry had always managed to convince the officers that the report had been exaggerated. He could appear quite reasonable when necessary, almost charming as he apologized for causing anyone worry and promising that there would be no more trouble.

The day after one of these official visits the elderly woman across the street had found her small dog slaughtered on her back porch, and the police had not been called since.

No, it didn't seem likely that any outside help would arrive to save them. Quinn knew she and her mother were all alone in this one, and the best thing to do would be to get out of the house and disappear until things cooled down.

As she dodged her father's outstretched hands, Quinn wished she had taken Mick up on her offer and gone home with her. She hadn't known then just how bad things were going to get. She'd stayed out of love for her mother, but was ready to run now out of fear for her life.

"I told Mick not to come in," she told him, knowing it wouldn't help. "She followed me anyway."

"Who does she think she is, walking uninvited into a man's home? Don't they teach their kids any manners on the rich side of town?"

Before Quinn could answer, her father lunged and

caught a handful of the front of her blouse. He threw the chair aside, his face joyful as he realized he'd caught her at last.

This was it. Quinn knew she was going to die. She would be tomorrow's headlines, and within a few months she would be all but forgotten. Mick and Lee would cry at her funeral, her class would graduate without her, and she would never get the chance to get out of this hell and find out what a real life was all about.

She closed her eyes and braced herself for the inevitable.

The expected blow never came.

Quinn opened her eyes and saw that her mother had come up behind her father. Elaine had disappeared when Quinn had run to the kitchen, and Quinn had assumed that her mother had simply had all she could take and had retreated to a safe part of the house.

But Elaine was back now, and she hit Harry across the back with the handle of the broom she held in her hands.

Surprised by this rear assault, Harry released Quinn and turned on his wife.

"All right, that's enough!" Elaine said. She lifted the broom again and waved it in front of him. "Get out, Harry. We've had all we're going to take from you."

The expression on Harry's face was almost comical. His mouth opened with astonishment, and his hands hung limp at his sides.

The advantage of surprise stayed with Elaine only for a moment, though. Her fear showed itself on her face, and at the sight of it Harry's confidence returned.

He reached out and pulled the broom from her hands, then threw it to the floor. He didn't approve of using objects to beat his wife and daughter. A real man needed only his hands to enforce discipline.

"You're going to be very sorry you did that," he laughed.

Elaine screamed and ran from the kitchen, with Harry in close pursuit. He almost caught her once, but panic made Elaine quick, and she reached the front door before he did.

Pulling the door open, Elaine ran out into the street, thinking only to get out into the open so that she could put as much distance between herself and Harry as possible.

She risked one glance back over her shoulder and saw that he wasn't far behind. Alcohol had slowed his reflexes, but his legs were still longer than hers and he was gaining.

When Elaine reached the curb across the street from her house, she heard the sound of squealing tires, and her shadow lengthened as she was caught in the glare of twin headlights.

The toe of her right shoe hit the curb and Elaine flew forward, hands stretched out instinctively to catch herself, and landed in the soft bed of someone's front lawn.

Behind her she heard a thud that sounded very much like the watermelon she and her sister had long ago thrown from the roof of their garage, and when Elaine sat up to see what had happened she saw only a large silver station wagon already half a block down the street, its taillights swaying as the driver of the car applied the brakes and tried to stop.

Harry was nowhere in sight. All Elaine saw was

Quinn across the street, silhouetted in the open door of their house.

Quinn put a hand to her mouth to stop the sound that wanted to come out.

She'd run after her parents when Harry had chased Elaine from the house, and she'd seen the car that had hit her father. Even the driver's face had been faintly visible, a woman's face, the profile showing a mouth opened in shock at the moment of impact, then gone as the car had continued a ways down the street before finally stopping.

Harry had been caught by the front tires and pulled beneath the car. He'd been dragged almost three-quarters of a block, his body finally tumbling free just before the car stopped.

The sound Quinn tried to muffle at the sight of her father's death wasn't a scream. She'd screamed enough tonight, both in fear and anger.

A shout of delight had come to her lips. She saw a sudden, unexpected end to her torment, the bloody answer to her prayers. This was what she had secretly hoped for. In her dreams she had pictured her father quietly dropping dead of a heart attack, liberating her mother and herself. Her dreams had been of a non-violent end to the violence, and although this didn't exactly fit the bill, the end result was the same.

People were coming out of the neighboring houses. Men in hastily thrown-on clothing, women still wrapped in their robes, they came to look at the broken mass in the middle of the street. Harry's right arm — the one he'd used for years to efficiently terrorize his family — had been nearly severed from his body.

His shirt had been torn from his back and was wrapped around legs that splayed outward like a broken doll's. His face, dragged along the pavement for almost a full block, no longer laughed. It was nearly unrecognizable as one eye looked up at the sky in bloody surprise.

Some of the onlookers turned away in horror, but most pushed closer, drawn by the excitement of witnessing something usually only seen on TV or in the movies.

Quinn felt her mother's arm go around her, and she fell into those comforting arms and closed her eyes tightly.

"It's all right now," Elaine murmured, holding her close. "Everything will be all right."

Chapter Seven

Mick stumbled into the kitchen, squinting her eyes against the morning sunlight that streamed through the window. She wore the nightshirt she'd slept in, and her hair fell tangled to her shoulders.

All she wanted was a big glass of orange juice to quench the thirst she'd awakened with, but her mother was there in the kitchen, talking on the telephone, and the expression on Fran's face stopped Mick cold.

"Oh, my God," Fran said, her head bowed as she listened. "How are they doing? Yes, of course I'll tell her." She lifted her eyes and saw Mick beside the refrigerator, and her lashes were wet with fresh tears.

After a few more brief words that revealed nothing, Fran hung up the phone and put her hands out as though to touch Mick.

Taking a step back, Mick moved out of her reach. She was wide awake now, her thirst forgotten as she felt an unspeakable apprehension grip her stomach. "What is it?" she asked.

"That was Mrs. Mitchell."

"Dad's secretary? Has something happened to Dad?"

"No, dear, he's all right." Fran took a deep breath. "She called to tell me that she just heard on the radio that Harry Baker was killed last night. He was hit by a car in front of his own house. Mrs. Mitchell knows how close you are to Quinn, and she thought I should be the one to tell you."

Mick's mind was darting off in a dozen different directions at once, so that she barely heard the words of consolation that her mother now uttered.

Quinn's father was dead.

The Death card.

No. Mick shook her head to clear it. That kind of thinking would do her no good. A deck of cards couldn't have anything to do with a man's death.

But these were no ordinary cards. She knew that as surely as she knew she was meant to have them, and the implications in what she had just learned were staggering.

"Mick, did you hear me?"

She blinked and looked at her mother. "What?"

"Do you want me to go with you to Quinn's house?"

"I'm not going over there. I wouldn't know what to say to her. She might hate me."

"Mick, why would she hate you? Quinn is your best friend."

Mick turned and ran from the kitchen. She didn't stop running until she'd reached her bedroom. She slammed the door shut, panting against it, then pushed the heavy trunk that contained her records and tapes against the door.

At her bed she picked up her pillow and looked down at the box that had rested beneath her head all night as she'd slept. She had a mental picture of a deadly cancer seeping through the pillow, invading her brain with its poison, filling her until she burst.

What she was thinking wasn't possible. Her rational mind told her she was stepping over into insanity if she even entertained such a notion, yet she couldn't easily dismiss it.

Her breath was coming in painful little gasps and as though from a great distance she heard her mother calling her name.

"Go away," Mick shouted. She reached out to touch the box, and realized she didn't want to. For the first time since the cards had come into her possession, she felt something dark and sly there, a power barely contained and struggling to get out. She shook her head and backed away from the bed.

Outside the bedroom door Fran was still knocking and calling to her.

Mick cleared her throat and forced a calmness to her voice. "Go away, please. I'll go see Quinn later, I promise. I just want to be alone for a little while."

She waited through several minutes of silence before she was convinced her mother had actually gone, then Mick sat on her bed and contemplated the box. She was calmer now. The initial shock had worn off; and although still badly shaken, at least she didn't feel like she was going to fall apart.

Touching the box with only the tips of her fingers, she flipped open the lid. There was the name — Rosalie Montagna — carved on the inside of the lid. Mick had looked at this name many times in the past, but now she began to really wonder about the woman. Had Rosalie known the power these cards possessed? And what about Fran? Mick needed answers that her mother might be able to give her, but she didn't know how to go about bringing up the subject.

The deck inside the box was arranged face down, but Mick knew which card was on top. She'd gathered them together last night after her little game of revenge on Quinn's father, thinking at the time that she was only satisfying her own need to strike back.

Never had she really expected anything to come of

her innocent arranging of the cards.

Wanting to see now what she already knew was there, Mick picked up the top card and quickly put it face up on her bed. It was the Death card, of course. Different from all the others in that the picture was so completely sinister. A skeleton, its grinning face seeming to look right at her, holding a long and deadly-looking sickle in its bony hands. It stood on a barren ground, barren because nothing could flourish where death walked.

But there was nothing special here. What had happened to Harry Baker had been only an odd coincidence. He'd been drunk. He was often that way, and drunks were susceptible to accident.

Mick told herself this because it was what she needed to believe.

It was the only way she could face Quinn, to convince herself she'd had nothing to do with her father's death.

Brady found Fran waiting for him at the front door, her face creased with worry.

"I'm sorry I had to bother you at work," Fran said. "But I didn't know what to—"

"It's okay. You were right to call me. Where is Mick?"

"She ran into her bedroom and hasn't come out. I tried to get her to talk to me, but she told me to go away. I even tried the door, but she had something blocking it. I'm getting so worried; she's been in there over an hour and I haven't heard a sound in such a long time. She was very upset, Brady. You don't think she'd do anything—"

"No, of course not." He released her and closed the

front door. "This whole thing is a big shock to everyone, and you know how Mick is. She feels things very intensely, but she's basically level-headed."

Fran felt calmer now that Brady was here to reassure her, and as she sat with him in the living room she began to worry that she'd overreacted in calling him at the office and begging him to come home. He hadn't complained—he never did—but she knew that he had a heavy workload he was hoping to make a dent in, and by calling him maybe she had added to his burdens while easing her own.

But, God, how she needed him! Fran put her hands in her lap and wished she was one of those wonderfully self-sufficient women who effortlessly juggled career and family while serving on endless civic committees and baking homemade bread, all with one hand tied behind their backs.

She'd never held a real job, needed a housekeeper to keep things from falling apart, and didn't feel capable of dealing with one moody teenager.

"You must get very tired of me at times," she said, not looking up from her hands.

Brady was immediately at her side. "Fran, you know better than that," he admonished. "You did the right thing in calling me. I wouldn't even have gone in to work this morning if I'd known what had happened to Mr. Baker, but I didn't hear about it until after I got to the office. Mrs. Mitchell told me she'd already called you so I thought everything was under control. I should have known Mick would take it hard. I should have been here with you when you told her."

Fran looked up at him. She was frowning. "It wasn't just that she took it hard, Brady," she said. "She seemed terrified. I've never really seen her like that. And she wasn't making sense. She said something about Quinn hating her. What did she mean by that?"

Brady thought about this for a minute before his logical mind came up with what he believed was a plausible explanation. "Everyone in town knows what Harry Baker was like. He was a bum who abused his family and never held a job for longer than a year at a time. As close as Mick is to Quinn, she's known all about it for a long time, and as outspoken as Mick can be at times I imagine she's told Quinn on more than one occasion just what she thought of Mr. Baker. Now that he's dead, Mick is probably feeling guilty for the things she's said about him, and is afraid Quinn will hold it against her."

Fran was nodding as he spoke. It made sense. "You're probably right," she said.

Brady sighed and leaned back on the couch. "I hate to speak ill of the dead," he said slowly, "but I need to get this out. I'll say it only once, to you, and hope that I'll never get the urge to repeat it. I think Harry Baker's death is probably the best thing that ever happened to Quinn and Elaine."

Fran just looked at him.

"He was a monster," Brady continued. "He always was, and from what I've heard, he was getting steadily worse. He was dragging them both down with him. Quinn is a smart girl, and she could have a bright future, but with a father like that it was only going to get harder and harder for her to pull herself out of the muck. With him out of the way, maybe now she'll have a chance."

Fran blinked back easy tears. "It sounds so cold when you say it that way."

"Am I wrong?"

"No."

"Are you sorry I said it?"

"No. Maybe I was thinking it, too, and just didn't

have the guts to admit it. I'll have to go see Elaine, but I'm not looking forward to it."

"Do you want me to go talk to Mick now?" he asked.

Before she could reply, Mick walked into the room. She was dressed in a demure outfit of navy knit slacks and a navy and white shirt. Her hair was combed and pulled back into a pony tail. She looked pale, but calm.

Fran started to get up, but Brady put a hand on her arm. "How are you feeling?" he asked Mick.

Mick remained standing. "Better," she said. She looked at her mother. "I'm going to go see Quinn now. Is it okay if I invite her to come back with me and stay here with us for awhile?"

"Yes, of course," Fran said. "Do you want us to go with you?"

"No, I'd rather go alone." She walked toward the front door. "I don't know how long I'll be gone."

"Take your time, honey," Brady told her.

As Mick drove to Quinn's house she thought about the past hour or so she'd spent in her bedroom.

The terror had passed quickly. It seemed incredible to her now that she had, for a few minutes, actually contemplated destroying her tarot cards. She'd sat in her bedroom holding that Death card, and had wanted to take the whole deck to the fireplace in her father's den and reduce it to a heap of harmless ashes.

Then something had happened. Without really thinking about what she was going to do, she'd shuffled the deck and laid eleven cards out in the Celtic Cross spread. The cards that had come up in this impromptu reading for herself had been unspectacular. The Two of Swords here, the Page of Cups somewhere else.

But the very act of using the cards again had been

soothing, like a cool washcloth placed on an aching body part. Her hands had stopped trembling, and she'd felt as though a close friend had reached out to offer comfort.

It had taken every bit of willpower she possessed to face her parents, and especially her mother, and not blurt out everything to them.

For Quinn, the previous evening and the hours since had been a nightmare from which she couldn't awaken.

After the initial shock of seeing her father die had worn off, she had been horrified at her own reaction. The elation she'd felt, however briefly, couldn't be denied, and now she was burdened with a crushing guilt. How many times had she wished her father dead? Hundreds, at least, over the years, and it was coming back to haunt her now. If hateful thoughts could kill a person, she was as guilty as if she'd plunged a knife into her father's heart.

She was alone in the house, after spending a long, sleepless night answering endless probing questions. After the ambulance had taken away the lifeless body of Harry Baker, the police had come into the house to cover the events of the accident with her and her mother.

She hadn't been treated badly. In fact, the young officer who had sat in the kitchen with her had been sympathetic and kind. There had been many witnesses to the accident. Besides the poor woman who had actually run her father down, several neighbors had been watching the fracas from behind curtained windows. Reluctant to get involved when the family violence had actually been happening, they had been more than willing to speak up afterwards.

But, though the officer had been patient, he had known about the events leading up to the accident, and she'd felt violated by his many questions. Some things were too private to discuss with a stranger. He'd wanted to know why neither she nor her mother had called the police earlier for help, and had seemed incredulous when she'd haltingly tried to explain that to involve an outsider in their problems would only have made matters worse.

Finally she and her mother had been left alone, but sleep had eluded them both. They'd sat up in the destroyed living room for the remainder of the night, unable to talk but also not wanting to be out of each other's sight.

When morning had come Elaine showered and dressed and went to handle all the unpleasant details that had to be tended to. There was a body to claim and funeral arrangements to make, and she had to let the people at work know that she would need a leave of absence.

At first Quinn had tried to watch television, but the Saturday morning cartoons were so full of animated violence that she had to turn them off. Every smashed coyote and flattened cat reminded her that in real life people didn't get up again after being run over by a steam roller.

The local news channel had been even worse, because it was already reporting on the messy death of Harry Baker, run down in the street while chasing his wife in a violent rage. No details were spared, thanks to the suddenly talkative neighbors, and Quinn felt as though she'd been dragged out into public with no clothes on.

She was beginning to regret not going with her mother, even though at the time she hadn't wanted to.

The phone kept ringing, and after the first couple of times she stopped answering.

The calls she'd taken had been from the local and the San Diego newspapers, wanting her version and her reaction to what had happened. She was unable to answer the questions and hung up, and now she just let the phone ring and ring.

At the sound of a car door slamming outside, Quinn flinched. So far no one had actually come to the house and bothered her, but she supposed it was only logical that that would be the next invasion.

But when she pulled the curtain aside and peeked outside, she saw a familiar red Mustang.

"Mick, I'm so glad you came," she said, bursting into fresh tears as she opened the front door.

Mick pushed her gently inside. "Let's not give the neighbors any more of a show than they've already had." Once the door was safely closed, she looked closely at Quinn. "He really did a job on you, didn't he?"

Quinn touched her bruised face and knew that despite her earlier attempts to make herself presentable, she was still a mess. "I thought the makeup pretty much covered it."

Mick started to tell Quinn exactly what she saw, which was a girl who had been badly beaten recently. Quinn's left eye was blackened beneath the makeup she'd applied, and her jaw looked puffy, giving her an off-balance look. She also moved stiffly, as though she were hurting somewhere deep inside.

But Mick didn't have the heart to say all this. Quinn was suffering, and she couldn't add to it by stating just how obvious it was.

"Put a little ice on your face," was all she said, "and you'll be fine in no time."

To her dismay, Quinn started crying again, and this time sank into a chair that was as battered as she.

"What are we going to do?" she sobbed. "Mom is out right now trying to make arrangements for a funeral, but she looks worse than I do. The whole town already knows what happened. How am I going to go to school? Everyone will be looking at me, and talking behind my back. I wish we could leave town. I don't want to stick around and have to face everyone."

"*You* didn't do anything wrong, Quinn," Mick reminded her.

"Why do I feel like I did?" Quinn reached for a tissue from the box on the floor and blew her nose. "I know why—because I'm *glad* he's dead!" She said this with such vehemence that the room seemed electrified with her anger. "I'm glad, even though I tried to tell myself all night that I wasn't, that I really felt bad that my father is dead. But it didn't work, and I'm not going to pretend. Not with you, anyway. You know how I feel, don't you, Mick?"

Her face grim, Mick sat on the edge of the couch. "I was there, remember? Last night, when he was knocking us all around, I got a real good picture finally of what it's been like for you. I never really knew until then."

As though the confession had exhausted her, Quinn sagged in her chair, letting the wadded-up tissue fall to the floor. Her shoulders slumped, and her hands hung limp from the ends of her knees. Her bruised face looked too mature, aged by the years of suffering.

Mick thought of the Death card again, and in her mind its skull face was that of Quinn's father, grinning at them both even now.

Chapter Eight

Three days later Mick and Lee sat behind Quinn on uncomfortable metal folding chairs and watched as an impersonal minister said a few last words at the grave.

There were few people there. Fran and Brady McGee had accompanied Mick to the funeral service, but had decided not to come to the cemetery. The general excitement in town about the death had faded quickly, and now only a handful of friends and relatives had come to see Harry Baker buried.

As she sat and tried not to fidget, Mick had to marvel at the change in Elaine Baker, seated in the front row and to the left of Quinn. In just a very few days Elaine had lost enough weight to be noticeable, and she seemed not only thinner but also somehow taller and newly self-confident.

Gone was the woman whose very spirit had been battered into submission. The new Elaine sat with a straight back and squared shoulders, her chin held high as she faced widowhood. Her eyes were remarkably clear for a woman whose husband was being buried.

Quinn looked much worse. She was pale and obviously shaken, and her mother kept putting a reassuring hand on her arm. Quinn kept turning around to look at Mick and Lee, as though searching there for the strength to get through this ordeal.

When it was time to leave the cemetery, Lee made a move as though to go talk to Quinn, but Quinn was quickly hustled away to the waiting car by her mother and an uncle who had come down from Sacramento. Lee and Mick watched helplessly as Quinn disappeared into the back seat of the car.

Lee sighed and tucked her purse under her arm. "I'm starting to think Mrs. Baker is deliberately trying to keep Quinn away from us," she said. "Every time I called the house this past couple of days, Mrs. Baker would tell me Quinn was sleeping, or busy, or something. I finally gave up because I figured I'd see Quinn today and would get to talk to her, but even that didn't work out. What's going on?"

Mick watched as the car containing Quinn and her mother drove away. "I was with Quinn for awhile Saturday, but as soon as her mother got home she rushed me out of the house. It was strange. I've never figured Mrs. Baker for the super-efficient type, but she sure has taken charge now. I tried to call Quinn, too, yesterday, but her mother wouldn't put her on. It does seem like she's trying to shut us out." She shrugged, and they began walking toward her car. "Whatever she's doing, it can't last. Quinn will be back in school soon, and we'll see her then."

"I don't think I want to wait until then," Lee said stubbornly.

"I don't see that we have much choice."

"I do. I'm going to Quinn's house tonight, and I'll just knock on the door and tell Mrs. Baker that I want to see Quinn. I won't give her the chance to hang up on me again."

"It might work."

"I want you to come with me, Mick."

They reached the car, and Mick pulled open the door

109

and got inside without answering.

"Did you hear me?" Lee persisted. "I want you to come with me to Quinn's house tonight. She needs us now, and I'm not going to let anyone stop me from seeing her."

"I can't," Mick said. "I have a date tonight."

Standing beside Mick's car, Lee looked down at her friend with an expression of disbelief. "You can't be serious."

"Why wouldn't I be?" Mick asked.

"How can you even be thinking of going out on a date tonight? Quinn's father was buried about two minutes ago, for God's sake. It's disrespectful."

Mick drummed her fingers against the steering wheel impatiently. "It would be hypocritical of me to act grief-stricken, Lee."

"Maybe. But for Quinn's sake you could at least pretend."

"I don't think she'd want me to."

"Well, what about your parents?" Lee asked. "I can't believe they'd *let* you go out on a date tonight."

Mick didn't look at Lee as she jammed the car keys into the ignition. "They have nothing to say about it one way or the other." The engine roared to life and she added, "Do you want a ride home or not?"

"No."

"Come on, Lee. I brought you here. Let me take you home." Lee shook her head. "I'll catch a ride with someone else. I don't think I care much for your company right now."

Elaine Baker came out of her bedroom wearing blue jeans and an oversized shirt. Her large blue eyes were bright as she ran a hand through her mousy hair.

"Boy, it feels good to get out of that dress and high heels," she said. She sat on the couch and put her bare feet up on the scarred coffee table, sighing as she wiggled her toes and relished the freedom of being able to do so.

Quinn, who was still wearing the dark brown dress she'd put on that morning, stood in the doorway to the kitchen, her arms crossed under her breasts. "It doesn't seem right that it should be over so quickly," she said. "Aren't we supposed to have people over to the house now or something? That's how they did it last year when Aunt Colleen died. Everyone went to the house after the funeral and took casseroles and stuff and talked about her. Why aren't we doing something like that?"

Elaine stopped wiggling her toes. "Quinn, come sit down," she said.

Slowly Quinn approached the couch and sat beside her mother.

"How *could* we have people over?" Elaine asked, putting a hand on Quinn's shoulder. "Look at this place."

Quinn looked around. The living room was nearly empty. Only the couch, coffee table and a small bookshelf remained. The rest of the furniture had been so damaged the last night of her father's life that her mother had it removed over the past couple of days. Even the television had been broken, so now all they had was the little 9-inch black and white that had been in Quinn's bedroom. The carpet, never very attractive anyway, showed lighter patches where furniture had once stood, and every stain and worn spot seemed painfully visible.

She knew her mother was right. They couldn't possibly let anyone in to see the house in this condition, yet she suspected that her mother was merely using this as a handy excuse to avoid doing something she hadn't wanted to do anyway.

Quinn still wished they could have done a little more. She couldn't mourn her father, but if she couldn't be sorry he was dead, at least she could have given him a better send-off than this.

"I should go back to school tomorrow," she said after a silence that seemed to stretch on too long.

"Why don't you wait a few more days?" Elaine suggested. "I've told them at work that I won't be back for at least a couple of weeks. We could have some real time together for a change. If you want, we could even go up the coast on a short vacation. Then by the time we get back most of the talk will have died down."

The suggestion was tempting. When Quinn thought about going to school and seeing all those curious faces and hearing the inevitable whispers, she wanted to climb into herself and hide away from the world.

"I have tests," she said.

Elaine dismissed that with a wave of her hand. "I'll call the school in the morning, but don't worry about any of that. There isn't a teacher in the world who wouldn't let you make up the work later, under the circumstances."

"I'd like to see Mick and Lee before we go."

Elaine smiled at her. "Change your clothes, and then you can take my car. While you're gone, I'll pack our bags and make a couple of calls of my own. We can leave first thing in the morning."

Quinn felt the excitement building in her, and for the first time in days she entertained the possibility that her life was headed in a positive direction.

Yes, they could go away. She and her mother could leave town and go someplace where no one would know what had just happened to them. The swelling in her

112

face had gone down, so the bruises were more easily hidden by makeup. She wouldn't have to endure the pity she had been dreading. At least not for awhile.

She stood up, feeling animated and full of new hope. "Where will we go?" she asked.

Elaine laughed. "What does it matter? Wherever it is, it'll be better than here."

Mick missed seeing Quinn before she left by less than an hour. Mick left the house much against her parents' wishes and ran out to the curb where Danny Santos was waiting in his car.

"Hey, I would have come to the door for you," he said when she settled in beside him in the front seat.

"Not a good idea," Mick said breathlessly.

He frowned at her. "You ashamed for your folks to meet me?"

Mick shook her head. "It's not that. This is a bad night for me to be going out, and they're not too happy with me right now. I just couldn't hang around, though. It's been a weird week, and I need a little fresh air." She took a mirror from her purse and checked her reflection. "Are we going or not? I don't plan to spend the entire evening sitting in a car in front of my own house."

He obliged by putting the car in gear. "Where do you want to go?"

"Oh, I don't care." She tossed the mirror back in her purse. "As far away from here as we can get."

Danny drove around for awhile, but without actually gaining much distance. They cruised the popular areas, but because it was a weeknight they saw hardly anyone. At one point Danny took a road that rose above the town so that the night lights were visible in all their splendor.

Mick saw none of it. She kept the window on her side down despite the fact that the nights were growing cool, and leaned close to the door so that the wind whipped her hair around her head. She was wearing the full skirt and peasant blouse she'd had on the night she met Danny, and now that she was away from her parents' stifling presence, she was beginning to feel free and happy again.

Even what had happened before Danny had arrived no longer seemed important.

Mick's mother had asked her to rake the leaves in the back yard. She was almost finished with the chore when a dirty face had peered over the fence.

"What are you doing?" Hilary Thomsen asked.

"What's it look like I'm doing—I'm raking," Mick snapped. There weren't many leaves, but Mick still resented having to do it.

Hilary didn't go away. Mick tried to ignore her, but she could feel the anger building in her, anger that wasn't entirely caused by Hilary.

"My mom says your mom throws your leaves over onto our yard because you're too lazy to take care of them yourselves." Hilary stuck a finger up her nose and grinned.

Mick straightened up, leaning on the rake. "She does not."

"My mom says your mom spends all her time in the beauty parlor getting her hair fixed, and you have a housekeeper because she won't do any work herself."

"Your mother screws collies, and that's why she has so many ugly kids," Mick snapped, wondering why she was letting herself be drawn into this ludicrous conversation with a nosepicking little kid.

"You can't talk to me that way," Hilary cried. "I'm going to tell." With that, Hilary had disappeared.

Mick had thrown the rake down and gone back inside the house and straight to her bedroom. To hell with the leaves. Then she'd gotten her cards, and a short while later a commotion next door had brought her out.

She'd gone to the front door just as her mother was coming in. "What happened?" she asked.

"Oh, little Hilary Thomsen next door fell off her bike," Fran said. "They think her arm might be broken. Cindy is taking her to the hospital."

"Gee, that's too bad," Mick had said.

Now, with the breeze on her face, Mick forgot all about Hilary and her accident.

"God, what a beautiful night," she said, leaning forward so that she could see the stars overhead through the windshield.

"Yeah, it's not bad," Danny said. He looked at the girl next to him, trying to figure her out. "What time do you have to be home?"

Mick sat back in her seat with a jerk. "Any time I want."

"You sure do run hot and cold," Danny observed. "I never know what to say to you. One wrong word and you're ready to bite my head off. I'm beginning to wonder if you're worth all the trouble."

Mick slid across the seat so that she was very close to him, and let her hand rest on his leg, just above the knee. When she spoke, her lips were less than three inches from his ear. "Danny, if you don't like it you can always drop me off at the next corner. I promise you I'll get along just fine without you." She squeezed his leg lightly.

Danny took his eyes off the road just long enough to look at her. "Yeah, I just bet you would." He was trying to match her tough tone of voice, but he knew he'd failed. His words came out in a breathless whisper, and to his disgust he felt his leg trembling under her hand.

"Do you have anything to drink?" she asked.

"There's a bottle under the blanket in the back seat," he said. "I think it's almost full."

"Good."

Fran McGee let Quinn in the front door and gave her a quick hug before leading her into the living room.

"You just missed her," Fran said in response to Quinn's question. Her eyes were dark with sadness, not only for what had happened to Quinn, but also because she now had to tell Quinn that Mick wasn't home. "She went out for the evening. With some boy."

Sitting on the comfortable chair Fran had indicated, Quinn couldn't hide her surprise. "She's out on a date?"

Fran nodded, wringing her hands. "I tried to talk her out of it, but these days there's no talking Mick out of doing anything once she sets her mind to it. I'm so sorry, dear. I know it seems heartless of her."

Quinn slumped and had to look away from Mrs. McGee. She couldn't face those tormented eyes, especially when she had no comfort to give. How could Mick have gone out on a date only hours after the funeral? She had expected her friends to rally around her at this time when she felt she needed them the most, but instead she was all alone.

She felt betrayed by Mick, who was out having a good time somewhere. Maybe she wasn't being completely fair, expecting Mick to put her life on hold for her, but at the very least Quinn would have expected Mick to wait a day or two.

She looked around at the living room she'd always

admired. The McGee's furniture was all lovely, and so clean that it almost hurt her eyes. The carpet was thick, always looking as though it had just been vacuumed, and no dust would dare settle on the hard surfaces here.

It was such a stark contrast to her own house, and she'd enjoyed spending time here for that very reason. She'd been to parties in this room. Mick's sixteenth birthday party had rivaled any ever seen in town. Almost fifty kids had come, and Mr. and Mrs. McGee had stayed discreetly out of sight, never once coming in to complain about the noise or the mess. Music had blared loudly from the stereo system in the wall, and Quinn had danced with a boy who had later kissed her out on the patio.

That happy memory helped dispel some of the pain Quinn was feeling. Almost two years had gone by since then, and so much had changed.

The biggest change, of course, was in Mick. At sixteen she had been happy and loving toward her parents. They'd given her the Mustang as a birthday present, the exact car she'd wanted, and she'd been appreciative. She seemed to know, then, that the car was a symbol of their love for her.

Now Mick didn't appreciate anything, even her friends. How could she, if she could go out on a date the day that Quinn's father had been buried?

"I was just thinking about Mick's birthday party," she said suddenly, wanting to share a little bit of the memory.

Fran looked confused. "Which one?"

"Her sixteenth. We really had a great time that night, and Mick couldn't talk about anything else for weeks afterwards."

Smiling only slightly, Fran nodded. "Oh, yes. That was a long time ago, wasn't it?"

"It sure seems like it. I haven't had a birthday party since I was seven, and even that was a disaster. My dad showed up drunk and mean and made everyone leave. I'd almost forgotten about that. I wonder why I'm thinking of it now."

"Well, I suppose it's only natural that your mind is on your father. Maybe you should try not to think of the bad times, though. Try to think of the nice things he did."

Quinn looked at her. "He never did any nice things for me. No, I take that back. He left us a life insurance policy. My mom told me about it this morning. It's why we can afford to go away for awhile." Her face brightened, and she could almost forgive her father. "Mom says it's enough that she wouldn't have to work at all if she didn't want to, but she likes her job and will just take a leave of absence. And I can go to college."

College had always seemed out of Quinn's reach. Even though her grades were good, the money just wasn't there. At the most she had hoped she would be able to further her education a little at a time through night courses while she worked during the day to pay expenses.

All that was now changed. Her mother had carefully explained the facts to her, and to Quinn it had seemed, as the meaning of the words had sunk in, that a whole new world was opening up for her. If they were careful and didn't spend the money foolishly, she could go to a real college. She would still have to work part time, but her tuition would be paid.

"But my mother and I are going to take a vacation first," she told Mrs. McGee. "Just the two of us."

"Where are you going?" Fran asked, relieved to see that Quinn's mood was lifting.

"We haven't decided for sure. That's what's fun about

it. We're just going to get in the car and drive north until we see something interesting. That's why I wanted to see Mick tonight. To say good-bye and tell her I'll see her in a couple of weeks. Will you give her the message?"

"Of course I will." Fran wanted to hug this poor girl, but held back. She'd known Quinn most of the girl's life, but theirs had never been a demonstrative relationship. She'd seen Quinn grow from a shy, awkward child to a lovely young woman. She'd noticed when, at thirteen, Quinn had come to the house to proudly show Mick that she was wearing her first bra; and although touched by their sweet innocence, Fran had wisely not made a big deal out of it. She'd watched Quinn swim in the pool in their back yard, her straight little body gradually growing taller and more curved.

In a way, she almost felt as though Quinn were a second daughter to her, though she knew Quinn would be surprised to learn this.

She'd also taken comfort in the fact that Quinn seemed a steadying influence on Mick. No matter how rebellious Mick became, she hadn't abandoned her old friends Quinn and Lee.

Until now.

But maybe even this was temporary, and Fran clung to that hope.

Impulsively, Fran got up from her seat and went to the desk drawer for her checkbook. She wanted to do something for Quinn, and out of a habit of too many years with too much money, she equated showing affection with the giving of money or goods.

"Quinn," she said, opening the drawer. "I don't think your mother quite realizes that insurance companies sometimes take awhile to actually settle these matters. I'd like to give you a little something so that you and she

119

can enjoy your vacation without worry."

When Quinn realized what Mrs. McGee was doing, she stood and protested. "Oh, no, you don't have to do that. We'll be all right."

Fran held her pen poised over the blank check. After giving the matter only the briefest thought, she filled in the amount for a sum that would ensure that Quinn and Elaine Baker would not have to worry about which hotels they stayed in or if the car broke down. With a rip, she tore the check loose and held it out to Quinn. "I *want* to do this," she said firmly. "I made it payable to your mother, and she can get it cashed in the morning."

Quinn kept her hands at her sides. "Mom won't accept it, Mrs. McGee."

"Tell her it's a loan, then. Until the insurance money comes in." Fran smiled. "Tell her it's for that time when she helped me sneak in the bedroom window."

Quinn laughed nervously. "What?"

Fran explained. "When your mother and I were in high school—I think I was about sixteen—I stayed out way past my curfew with a boy I was crazy about. My parents were asleep, but I didn't know how I was going to get in the house without waking them. Your mother and I only lived a few houses apart then, so I went to her house and knocked on her bedroom window and woke her up. She slipped out, came home with me and stood outside my bedroom window in the bushes so that I could climb up on her shoulders and get inside. Later, as she was trying to get back inside at her place, her parents woke up and *she* caught hell. But she didn't tell on me."

Quinn laughed again, but with delight this time at this unexpected picture of her mother as a girl. "She never told me anything about that," she said.

Fran shrugged, a little sadly. "Your mother and I

drifted apart after high school, but a long time ago we were good friends. Now, I insist you take this check, and tell her what I said. I want you two to have the best vacation you've ever had."

Taking the piece of paper from Fran's fingers, Quinn said, "We will. I just know it."

Chapter Nine

Lee stood beside Mrs. Pidbuhl's desk, her head lowered as she looked at the paper that trembled in her hands. The grade that jumped out at her, made all the worse by the fact that it had been written with a thick red marker, was a "D."

"D" for disastrous.

"D" for degrading.

"I don't deserve this," Lee said as soon as the last student had gone and she was alone with the teacher.

Mrs. Pidbuhl struck a familiar pose. Sitting perfectly straight behind her desk, she steepled her hands beneath her chin as though praying, and looked at Lee over her glasses. "Just what is the problem, Lee?" she asked.

"This grade," Lee's voice had risen in anger. She lowered it, knowing that to show her feelings was a mistake. She tried to proceed calmly. "I worked hard on this book report. Almost three evenings. There isn't a spelling or punctuation error in the entire five pages. Why did you give me a 'D?' "

Mrs. Pidbuhl lowered her hands, her eyes hard despite the smile on her lips. "Lee, your mistake is glaringly obvious. Your report states that the *man* was the focus of the book."

"He is."

"No. The woman is the central character. The book starts with her, and it ends with her."

Lee looked down at the neatly typed pages in her hands, now wrinkled and creased from the sweat on her palms. "Yes, that's true, but she still only serves as a voice for what the man goes through—"

"Her voice, as you put it, is what the book is all about."

"The man's ordeal is what the story is about."

The teacher's smile faded. "Lee, are you trying to tell me that I don't know my job?"

"No, but—" Lee stumbled to formulate an answer that wouldn't get her in deeper trouble, then thought she found the solution. "The assignment was that we read the book and give our opinion of it. That's exactly what I did."

"Your opinion is wrong," Mrs. Pidbuhl said. By way of dismissal, she began to shuffle around the papers on her desk.

Lee's hands tightened so that the papers made a sound like dry leaves being crushed. "This is the third unjustified 'D' you've given me since school started," she said. "If I get less than a 'B' in this class I won't make the honor roll for the semester."

The teacher looked up at her, her mouth turned down at the corners, and her meager breast heaving with indignation. "You think I've been grading you unfairly?" she asked in a dangerous voice.

Lee kept her gaze steady. "Yes."

"Then you think my years of college, and almost twenty-five years of teaching in this very school mean nothing? You think you know more than I do? Maybe you should be teaching this class, since you've gained so much wisdom in such a short time."

All of Lee's instincts told her to back off, that she had

stepped into perilous territory. But despite knowing that the longer she stayed the worse things would get, she was unable to just give up without a fight. The stubborn streak her mother was always telling her she possessed had taken over.

"I don't deserve a 'D' for this book report," she said. "It's well written. Probably one of the best in the whole class. I don't know what it is you have against my work, but I know Mr. Trepanier will agree with me that this is at least 'B' work."

Mrs. Pidbuhl put her hands on her desk and pushed herself to her feet. She leaned over the desk and pointed her face at Lee. "Mr. Trepanier was your English teacher *last* year. He has nothing to do with this class."

"But this year he's been promoted to vice-principal," Lee reminded her.

"Are you threatening to go over my head with this matter?"

"Yes."

"It won't do you any good. Mr. Trepanier respects my position here. I've been with this school for almost—"

"Almost twenty-five years," Lee interrupted.

Mrs. Pidbuhl's color darkened alarmingly. She looked in danger of having a stroke. "Have you ever thought, Lee, that it's your very attitude that is dragging your grades down? It gets worse every year. Kids like you waltz in here like we *owe* you an education. You sit at your desks and barely listen to anything the teachers say, then act surprised when your grades reflect your inattentiveness. You're disrespectful, foulmouthed—"

"I've never—"

"—and scantily dressed." The teacher looked at Lee's short skirt with undisguised contempt. "The girls especially. You spend so much time flaunting yourselves, showing off, that it's a wonder you get any work done at all. This school never should have abolished the dress code. It's indecent, the way you expose yourselves."

Lee had backed up toward the open door. This was too much. She should have kept her mouth shut when she'd had the chance, but she'd pushed her luck, and now it seemed that Mrs. Pidbuhl had decided to blame her personally for everything that was wrong with the world.

Her face burning with embarrassment, Lee saw that a small group of students was standing in the doorway, gaping in astonishment. They had been on their way to their next class, and had stumbled upon a scene that would provide enough gossip for days.

She felt humiliated and tried to push her way through the growing crowd of students. Someone snickered, and she looked up and saw Emma Mejia's eyes on her. Emma looked especially delighted to be a witness to Lee's downfall.

Finally she broke through and stumbled out into the hallway, almost falling as she pitched forward. Strong arms caught her, and kept her from being further embarrassed.

"Come on, let's get out of here," Jack said, keeping an arm around her waist.

Grateful to have someone else take charge, Lee let him lead her down the hall and out the side door of the building. The sunlight assaulted her, and she shielded her eyes with one hand until they reached Jack's car in the school parking lot.

Salvation had come in the form of Quinn's ex-boyfriend, and as Jack opened the car door for her, she felt the tension break and she began to giggle. It was a nervous reaction, and Jack sat beside her and waited patiently for her laughter to subside.

When she was finished, she wiped her eyes on the back of her hand and looked at him gratefully. "God, that was awful," she said.

"What happened in there?" he asked.

Leaning back against the seat in exhaustion, she explained it all to him, from the bad grade on her book report to Mrs. Pidbuhl's attack on her very character. When she was finished they were both laughing.

It all seemed so ridiculous now. She should have known better than to argue with the Pit Bull. The teacher had always disliked her, but instead of going through the proper channels Lee had foolishly confronted her and had paid the price.

She was missing a class, but she didn't care. To hell with it. If she had to, she would go to the school nurse tomorrow and claim that she'd had a sudden attack of cramps. That excuse always worked, and she hadn't overused it in the past, so she wouldn't be questioned. Maybe she would even stay out of school for a couple of days, just to give things a little time to settle down.

She ran a hand through her hair and wondered if she dared ask Jack to give her a ride home. He'd been great so far, but she was keeping him out of school, too, and she didn't want him to get in trouble because of her. He couldn't very well use menstrual cramps as an excuse for leaving.

"You'd better get back inside," she said, deciding that she could walk home. "You hang around out here, and they're likely to send out a posse."

"Not for me," Jack told her. "I'm out of that school. I'm moving to LA, remember? We're leaving tomorrow. I just came by the school today hoping that Quinn would be back. I wanted to say good-bye to her."

"Oh." Lee looked at Jack, really looked at him this

126

time, and saw a sadness in his expression she hadn't noticed before. Of course she knew he was moving to Los Angeles with his mother and younger sister, but she'd forgotten all about it in the two weeks since Mr. Baker's funeral. Now she realized that Jack had problems of his own, and didn't need to have her dumping hers on his shoulders.

"Have you heard anything from her?" he asked. "I thought she'd be back by now."

"So did I," Lee admitted. "I got a postcard about a week ago. She and her mother were in San Francisco. She didn't say anything about when they'd be coming back."

Jack rested his hands on his knees, his long legs squeezed in the small space under the steering wheel. "I didn't want to go until I had a chance to talk to her," he said. "I've always felt bad about the way Quinn and I broke up. I mean, we got along pretty good for awhile there, it was just too bad that a little thing like Mick and those crazy cards of hers had to come between us."

"When Quinn gets back, I'll tell her what you said," Lee offered.

"Okay. I guess that's better than nothing. I just want her to know that I really thought she was special, and that I'll miss her."

"I'll tell her," Lee promised.

The bell rang inside the school building. It didn't seem possible that fifty minutes had passed already, but they must have because that was the signal that the period had ended, and it was time for all students to rush from one classroom to the next.

A half dozen boys burst from the side door and immediately lit cigarettes, laughing softly as they exhaled white plumes of smoke.

Lee hunkered down in the seat, not wanting to be

seen.

"Do you want me to drive you home?" Jack asked, making the offer she hadn't been able to ask for.

"Yes," she said, relieved. "Are you sure you don't mind?"

"No trouble at all."

As the car left the schoolgrounds, neither Lee nor Jack saw the lonely figure watching them from an open doorway of the building.

Mick had been in study hall when word had gotten to her about Lee's run-in with Mrs. Pidbuhl. It never took long for gossip to spread in school, especially when it was juicy or amusing. Too many people had heard what Mrs. Pidbuhl had said to Lee, and by the time it'd reached Mick's ears, it had been blown all out of proportion.

"The Pit Bull was yelling at Lee about coming to class practically naked," Karen Bishop had whispered to Mick over the study hall table they shared. The tables seated four, but as that particular study hall was only half full, Mick and Karen had the table to themselves.

Mick had asked her for an explanation, and Karen had provided all the distorted details. She'd heard about it from Todd Belzer, who'd heard it from Emma Mejia, but Karen swore every word of it was true.

As soon as study hall had ended Mick had gone looking for Lee, only to learn that Lee hadn't gone to her next class and hadn't been seen since the incident. That could only mean that Lee had decided to go home, and Mick sneaked out the side door herself, planning to go to her friend. Lee probably needed her.

But almost immediately she'd spotted Lee, sitting

with Jack in his car, and before she could recover from her surprise, they'd driven off.

Mick went to her own car, a little hurt that Lee had found comfort so quickly, and from such an unlikely source.

She flopped down in her front seat and sulked for a few minutes. First Quinn had run off, sending only one brief postcard in two weeks, and now Lee was out joyriding with Quinn's old boyfriend. So much for the loyalty of friendship.

Reaching into her purse, Mick pulled out the box. The cards were her friends now. They spoke to her in an ancient tongue that she was getting increasingly adept at understanding. They asked nothing of her, but they gave so much.

She flipped open the lid and held the cards lovingly in her hands, feeling the strength there. The strength was hers now. It flowed into her, making her forget the pain of abandonment, taking away the hurt.

She didn't need anything or anyone else.

Jack stopped the car in front of Lee's house.

"Thanks," she said, reaching for the handle.

"Lee?"

She turned to look at him.

"You won't forget to tell Quinn what I said, will you?" he asked.

"No, of course I won't," she said. Then, because he seemed to be waiting for something, she added, "Good luck in LA, Jack. I hope everything works out great for you there."

"It probably will." He grinned, looking more like his old self. "It's gotta be more interesting than around here, right? Xavier has never been exactly the excitement center of California."

"Oh, I don't know about that," Lee said. "Only about an hour ago I had all the excitement *I'm* going to need for a few days."

Jack laughed and impulsively leaned over to kiss Lee's cheek. "You take care. Would you mind a whole lot if I wrote to you once in awhile? I'd kind of like to keep in touch with the old gang. Just because I'm moving doesn't mean I want to forget everyone."

"Sure. I'd like that." Lee spoke haltingly, still in a slight state of shock over the kiss he'd planted so lightly on her skin. She wanted to reach up and touch her cheek to see if he'd left some mark there, but she didn't want him to see the gesture.

She did open the car door this time, and ran toward her house. Jack had awakened something in Lee, an old feeling that she'd thought she'd buried so deeply that it could never surface again.

She wasn't pinning any false hopes on Jack. He was moving away, and she would probably hear from him a couple of times before he lost interest in his old friends and stopped writing. But it was nice to know the old spark was still there in her, and that one bad experience with a boy hadn't ruined her forever.

She'd forgotten all about Mrs. Pidbuhl, and even Quinn, as she opened the front door of her house and went inside.

Quinn dropped her suitcase inside, feeling happier to be home than she would have imagined possible.

True, the home wasn't much to look at, but for two weeks she and her mother had talked about what they were going to do with it as soon as the insurance money came in. Furniture was the first thing it would need, and they'd spent endless enjoyable hours looking in furniture stores and getting an idea of what they wanted.

It had been fun because for once they'd known their window shopping wasn't an exercise in futility. The heavy ceramic lamps, sofas of thick, plush fabrics, and comfortable recliners were suddenly a possibility, and they'd had an orgy of speculation, imagining how they would arrange their new furniture, and changing their minds every other day.

"Carpet!" Elaine proclaimed, moving past Quinn and carrying her own suitcase to the old sofa. "The very first thing we'll need is new carpet. There's absolutely no point in putting new furniture on top of this old rag."

Hands on hips, Elaine stood and looked around the room critically. She'd lost at least fifteen pounds in the past two weeks, and when they were in Anaheim she'd had her hair trimmed, styled, and highlighted so that it now more closely resembled the soft attractive blonde of her youth. The puffiness from years of worry was almost gone from her face, and she'd begun, with Quinn's help, to experiment with makeup. Her eyelashes fluttered attractively, enhanced by mascara, and her skin was lightly tanned from all the walking outdoors they'd done.

"It feels good to be back," Quinn said. "I actually missed school."

"Beige, I think," Elaine said, running the toe of her right shoe along the bald surface of the old carpet. "Beige carpet would look nice with that blue and beige sofa we saw in Pamona. Or was it Pasadena? Well, it doesn't matter. I'm not going all the way back anyway, but it gives me an idea of what I want."

Quinn went into the kitchen, her rumbling stomach reminding her that she hadn't eaten since breakfast. "Are you hungry?" she called out to her mother, opening a cupboard.

"Not at all." Elaine came into the kitchen and looked at the scratched and dented refrigerator. *"That* is going to the dump, too. When was the last time we had anything new around here?"

"It's been longer than I can remember." Quinn found a package of macaroni and cheese in a cupboard, and set a pan of water on the stove to boil. "Are you sure you're not hungry? There'll be enough here for both of us, and you haven't been eating much lately." She looked sternly at her mother. "You aren't getting anorexic, are you?"

Elaine ran her hands along her hips, definitely narrower than they had been, but still well rounded. "I'm a long way from that. I don't know what it is, Quinn, but I don't think of food now the way I once did. It used to be I ate when I was lonely because it made me forget, or when I was sad because it would cheer me up. Let's face it, I ate all the time. But all the time we were on vacation, I felt like I'd thrown away a crutch. The need to stuff my face is gone. I feel lighter, and not just in body."

Quinn stood at the stove, watching as the water began to show the first few bubbles rising to the surface. She didn't begrudge her mother her new happiness. It would be foolish to deny that they'd both enjoyed the past couple of weeks more than any other time in recent years.

But she wouldn't dwell on the fact that a man's death had everything to do with the fact that they both felt as though they'd been reborn. They were being given a second chance, and Quinn intended to take that chance and not look back. All the painful memories had been given a decent burial, and they were going to stay buried if she had anything to say about it.

"It'll be nice to have the house fixed up enough to have people over once in awhile," Quinn said, turning the topic of conversation over to a subject that she knew her mother would be delighted to discuss. She dumped the macaroni into the pot of water and turned down the heat. It wasn't going to be a gourmet meal, but then she wasn't exactly a gourmet cook. "Can I get a new bedspread and curtains for my room?" she asked.

Elaine threw her arms out in enthusiasm. "Of course you can. In fact, why don't we get you a new bed? You're too big for that old twin bed you've had since you were three. It's about time you had something you can roll over in without falling out onto the floor."

Quinn laughed. "I haven't fallen out of bed in years, Mom. And I appreciate the thought, but there's no point in buying me a new bed now. If I really am going to college next year I can't be hauling a bunch of furniture along with me. No, a bedspread and some pretty matching curtains will make me very happy."

"Well, all right, but if you change your mind, let me know." The phone rang in the other room, and Elaine went to answer it. A minute later she came back into the kitchen to tell Quinn that it was for her.

"Mick!" Quinn shouted with delight when she heard her friend's voice. "How did you know we were back?"

"I didn't." Mick's voice came through the wires sounding small and distant. "I've been calling your house every day, figuring that sooner or later you'd show up."

"Where are you now?" Quinn asked.

"Home, but I'd love an excuse to leave. Can you get out?"

"I don't know. I should probably stick around and help Mom unpack. We bought a few things on our trip." Quinn looked up when, out of the corner of her eye, she caught her mother waving at her.

"Go ahead and go," Elaine said. "I'm not touching a thing until tomorrow. Take the car if you want."

Quinn started to protest, thinking how much her father hated it when she drove the car, then she remembered that he was no longer a factor. "Where should we meet?" she asked Mick.

"How about the little cafe on Crimson Street? It'll be quiet there tonight, and it's not too far from either of us."

"I'll meet you there in fifteen minutes," Quinn said and hung up the phone.

Chapter Ten

Mick leaned against her car, both glad the parking lot of the restaurant was nearly empty, and lonely for company.

It was a conflict of emotions that was familiar to her lately. When alone she felt restless and in need of adventure, this need causing her to behave recklessly at times, staying out late and not always choosing her companions wisely.

But, if too many people were around, she began to feel hemmed in. More than once she'd had to leave a party abruptly because she hadn't been able to breathe, and panic had threatened to press in.

Danny became angry with her at these times. His friends were beginning to think she considered herself too good for them.

And that was another problem. She'd been seeing a lot of Danny Santos, but he was becoming too possessive. On her first date with Danny, she'd lost her virginity. The act itself hadn't meant much to her. She'd simply decided that the time had come and she preferred to begin with someone like Danny, who wouldn't fumble or make her feel like a fool. In that, she'd made a good choice. Danny's hands on her were smooth with experience, and she made it through the uncomfortable first half hour with a minimum of embarrassment.

After that first time she'd even come to enjoy it, her heat matching his as her body responded with a hunger that surprised and pleased Danny. He called her a wildcat, and when they were alone together he whispered her name over and over in her ear.

But she was tiring of Danny. He was crude and emotionally immature. He'd decided that he owned her, and that was something Mick was not going to tolerate.

Tonight he'd called, right after she'd talked to Quinn, and demanded that she see him. When she refused, telling him she had other plans, he flew into a rage. She cut off the flow of angry words by hanging up on him, and left the house quickly. She didn't know if he called back, and she didn't care.

Through the window of the restaurant she could see the few diners who were inside, but she had no desire to join them. She felt separated from them by more than just glass and brick. She was different from them in a way that she didn't entirely understand.

She felt like an exotic jungle cat, forced to live with ordinary domestic animals, but with a wildness deep within her that struggled to be free. Those people inside could no more understand her than a parakeet could understand the mind of a leopard or ocelot.

A dog barked off to her left, and Mick jumped, banging her elbow on the hood of her car. She swore softly under her breath, her heart hammering in her chest as she searched the darkness for some sign of movement.

There was someone out there. She was sure of it now, even though the dog had fallen silent after that single, startled yelp.

If only Quinn would hurry up and arrive. Mick rubbed her arms nervously and looked again toward the cafe. The lights inside there were beginning to look

136

appealing. Usually she liked the night, but now the shadows felt unfriendly.

She'd made enemies lately. Emma Mejia had taken to following her, always showing up where Mick was, presumably by accident. The first couple of times it happened Mick shrugged it off, telling herself that Emma, though a pest, could do her no actual harm. But the incidents were growing more frequent, reaching the point finally where Mick half expected to look over her shoulder and see Emma on every street corner.

The situation wasn't helped by the fact that Emma had dated Danny for awhile before he'd started seeing Mick. If Emma had disliked her before, that dislike had now become full-fledged hatred, and Mick thought with exasperation that if she'd known Emma was interested in Danny, she never would have gone out with him in the first place. Who needed the aggravation? There were plenty of available men around.

The heavy throb of an unmuffled engine penetrated Mick's thoughts, and she looked up just as Quinn's car reached the corner of Crimson Street. Without the aid of either blinker or hand signal, the car turned into the parking lot and came to a halt less than a yard from Mick's toes.

"Who taught you to drive, lady?" Mick called out as both doors opened and first Quinn, then Lee, climbed out of the car.

"You did!" Quinn shouted happily. "Don't you remember? It took a week, and I put the first dent in your new car. Did you ever tell your father the truth about what happened?"

"No way. If I'd told him you'd sideswiped a parked police car he'd have confiscated my keys so fast your head would spin. Better to let him believe that I was innocently parked at the mall when some unknown driver scraped the side of my car, then left without so much as leaving a note on the windshield."

Then the girls were all talking at once, their voices rising as each tried to drown out the others.

"I called Lee right after I talked to you, then picked her up on my way here."

"How was your vacation? You were gone such a long time I was starting to wonder if you were going to come back."

"I could have stayed away another week at least, but Mom started getting restless to come back."

"Did you meet any guys while you were gone?"

"No, we just drove up the coast and saw the sights and did some shopping. One weekend we stayed in a hotel that had a jacuzzi in our room. I'd never been in a jacuzzi before. If felt great, all bubbly and soothing."

"Did you get in it naked?"

"No, I wore my swimsuit."

"Jack has left for LA," Lee said. "He told me to tell you good-bye. He said he's going to miss you."

"Really? This is the first time I've even thought about Jack in ages. I guess I've been too busy. Did he really say he was going to miss me?"

"Forget Jack. I got my cards out and did a reading for you right after I talked to you on the phone, and they said that a new romance will be coming to your life soon."

Lee and Quinn fell silent at Mick's words. The atmosphere, so joyful a moment earlier, had become, quite suddenly, uncomfortable.

Thirty feet away Danny Santos stood in the protective shadow of a Winnebago camper with a FOR SALE sign in the window, watching the three girls.

138

It was blind luck that had brought him to this spot. After Mick had hung up on him, he'd slammed his own phone down hard enough to crack the receiver, infuriated at the way she treated him, but powerless to do anything about it. If she had been in front of him at that moment, he thought, he'd have given it to her good.

No, that wasn't true. He wouldn't have hit her. He was unable to lift a hand against Mick, simply because she had some hold on him. He loved her, for her arrogance and her strength. She laughed at him, and though he hated it when she did, he admired her ability to do it.

Only a week ago they'd gone to his apartment, and she'd looked around with her nose in the air. "What a dump!" she'd said in a funny voice that hadn't sounded like her own.

When he'd gotten mad, she'd just smirked.

"Oh, come on, Danny," she'd said. "That was my Bette Davis impression; don't take it so personally. Haven't you ever seen a Bette Davis movie?"

"Sure, I have," he told her, getting on the defensive. "But that doesn't mean you have to say that about my apartment." He wouldn't have admitted it to her — or to anyone — but he'd spent over an hour cleaning the place up when he'd known she was coming over. He'd wanted her to like his place because it was, after all, his, and he was hoping they would be spending a lot of time there together. If things worked out between them, he'd even thought about inviting her to move in as soon as she finished school.

Seeing his hurt look, Mick had gone to him and put her arms around him. "Forget what I said. Let's start over again at the beginning. Are you going to offer me something to drink?"

Since then Mick had been to his apartment four times. It was hard for him to believe so much had happened in such a short time. Since their first date, he'd been thinking about her constantly. He thought they had a pretty good thing going, most of the time.

They'd been to a couple of parties together, even though both times she'd wanted to leave early, and one Sunday they'd spent the day in Tijuana, just looking around and acting like tourists. He'd bought her a silver and turquoise necklace there, for more money than he'd ever spent on a girl.

That she obviously cared for him less than he did for her ate at Danny like a worm in an apple. She drove him crazy with her soft, willing body, and when he was at his most needy, alone with her and begging her to love him back, she gave him her flesh but withheld what he desired most — her heart.

Tonight had been the last straw. He'd jumped into his car immediately after throwing the telephone across the room, and had headed in the direction of her house, determined to catch her there and force her to see him.

He'd traveled only a few blocks when he'd seen her little convertible ahead of him, and he'd followed it from a safe distance to the parking lot of the restaurant.

It was a dark night, but the parking lot was well lit and he'd been forced to park a block away to avoid being seen. He'd walked slowly along a fence, cursing once when a dog on the other side of the fence had barked at him, all the while keeping his eyes on Mick. She'd gotten out of her car and seemed to be waiting.

He'd waited with her, keeping out of sight as an impotent rage filled him. She had to be waiting for some man. Why else would she be out here?

So convinced was he that Mick had cooled toward him because she'd found someone else, Danny had been ready to step out from the shadow of the Winnebago and confront her when Lee and Quinn had arrived. The relief he'd felt at the sight of them had left his legs feeling weak, and he'd been forced to lean against the camper.

It was humiliating, feeling this way about any girl. He should have stuck with Emma, who'd at least known enough to be grateful for the time he'd spent with her. Emma wasn't as pretty as Mick, and not half as exciting, but she was always eager to be with him and didn't try to boss him around. Emma knew her place, and the more time he spent with Mick, the more he appreciated the Emmas of the world.

But he couldn't walk away from Mick. She was like a fever that had gotten into his blood.

"Why are you still messing around with those cards?" Lee asked, angry with Mick for bringing the subject up in the first place.

Mick was surprised at the hostility in Lee's question, but smiled quickly to cover it. She wasn't going to do anything to spoil this reunion. She still wanted to believe that the distance that had grown between her and her oldest friends was a temporary thing, and that eventually they would come around to understanding how she felt about the cards.

She was puzzled by their continued lack of acceptance. Why couldn't the three of them share this wonderful new adventure together, as they'd shared everything else for the past dozen years?

Mick's first impulse was to defend herself. But she saw, in Lee's face, a stubbornness that she recognized all too well. It was a look she'd seen often, and she knew the best thing to do was to just let it go. With a little time Lee might change her opinion of the cards, but if Mick tried to force her, Lee would only dig in her heels all that much harder.

"I only play around with them a little," Mick said lightly. "It's like a game."

"Some game," Lee said, still frowning. "I think they're dangerous. And I think you do a lot more than just play around with them."

"What, exactly, does that mean?"

"It means it's not a game when you really believe in them. *I* don't believe in them. But you do, and it's changing you. Remember Stu? There was a time not so long ago when he was hot to go out with you, but he's not interested any more — have you noticed that? People are talking about you." Lee's eyes swept over Mick's flowing skirt and hooped earrings. "And you dress like a gypsy. That's something that only started recently. Even your face looks different, but I'm not really sure how. It's something I can't put my finger on, but I don't like it."

Mick threw up her hands. "Well, by all means I should dress and look exactly the way *you* think I should, Lee Sternhagen. By the way, as long as we're on the subject, I've always hated that ugly sweater you're wearing. Are you going to throw it away because I don't like it?"

Before Lee could respond, Quinn stepped in. "Come on, you two! This is the first time we've been together in weeks. Let's not spoil it by fighting." Her voice quivered, and immediately both Lee and Mick looked contrite.

"You're right, Quinn," Lee said. To Mick she added, "I'm sorry about what I said. You're absolutely right — it's none of my business what you wear, and if I ever bring it up again you have my permission to remind me of what I just said."

Mick just nodded. More than anything else she wanted to enjoy this time with her friends, and she was already sorry she'd brought up the subject of her tarot cards. Knowing as she did how Lee felt about them, she should have kept her mouth shut.

"Hey, we can't hang around here all night," she said. "Let's go somewhere."

"Where? There's not much going on in the middle of the week." This came from Quinn.

"Harris Lake," Mick said. "It's not far. We'll take my car, and I'll bring you back here later." She opened her car door for them. "Remember last summer, when Maggie Colin and Snooze Shonoway were caught skinny-dipping in the lake?"

"I heard Maggie's mom got so mad when she heard about it that she just about burst a blood vessel."

"Can you imagine what Snooze must look like naked? He looks goofy enough with clothes on. Bareassed he must really be a hoot."

"Do you really hate this sweater? I've always kind of liked it."

The dog on the other side of the five-foot chain-link fence growled threateningly, and Danny Santos picked up a jagged rock that fit neatly in the palm of his hand. His lips pulled back in a snarl that resembled the dog's, he approached the fence and threw the rock, aiming at the animal's head.

With a satisfying yelp, the dog retreated to the safety of its yard, its eyes now fearful.

Danny turned and saw that Mick's car, its headlights on high beam, was leaving the parking lot. He hadn't seen the girls get in the car — that must have happened when he'd had his attention on the dog—but Quinn's car was empty and still parked in the lot, so he figured all three were now in Mick's car.

Probably going out cruising, he thought angrily. He didn't waste time dwelling on it. Mick was already almost out of sight, and without thinking it through he hurried to his own car and, without turning on the headlights, followed.

Mick dug the toe of her shoe into the sand, and watched as the dark green water of Harris Lake lapped close. There was just enough of a breeze to cause a few small waves to form at the edge of the water, and as she played with the waves she wished desperately for a drink.

She had a bottle under the back seat, but she didn't dare get it out. Lee and Quinn were so touchy about every little thing lately. If she produced her half-full bottle of Jack Daniels and suggested they all share it, they would surely find fault with that, too.

"Blaire Campbell left school a week ago," Lee told Quinn. "She's gone to stay with her sister in San Diego. She's going to give the baby up for adoption."

"That's probably best," Quinn said. "She's too young to—"

"I heard about what Mrs. Pidbuhl did to you the other day, Lee," Mick broke in. She sat on the dock, which had been pulled up out of the water for the winter and now rested on the beach. "Was it really as bad as I heard?"

"Worse," Lee said. "I don't know what's going to happen now. She hasn't said anything more to me about it, but I can tell she's still angry. She shoots daggers at me in class every day."

144

"What happened?" Quinn asked. She hadn't heard about it, so they quickly filled her in on the details.

"Why is the Pit Bull so hard on you all the time?" Mick asked, scooting over so they could join her on the dock.

"I don't know. She hasn't liked me since school started, and it's getting worse."

"It's not fair that she's singled you out for her post-menopausal fantasies."

"I don't know what I can do about it. I don't mind her picking on me all that much, but if she keeps giving me these low marks it's going to throw my whole grade average off."

"Can you talk to someone about it? How about your guidance counselor?"

"Mr. Lyttle? He thinks Mrs. Pidbuhl is the next thing to God. He's not going to take my side in this." Lee sighed and looked down at the sand on her shoes. It was caked there, and she wiped it off by rubbing the tip of first one shoe, then the other, on the leg of her jeans. "My mother is going to have a fit when she sees my report card."

"If you ask me, Mrs. Pidbuhl should be forced into early retirement. She's obviously not fit to be a teacher any more—if she ever *was* fit. I don't know why they even keep her on. Nobody likes her, and—" Mick stopped talking as the headlights of a car topped the hill on the road leading to the lake, and slowly approached.

The lake was a popular make out-spot on weekends, being far enough away from town to afford a little privacy, but on week nights it was usually deserted. At first Mick thought that some couple, too passionate to wait for Friday night, had come to the lake to be alone together. But as the car drew nearer she recognized it, and she felt her anger, so close to the surface, well up

145

inside her.

"Who's that?" Lee asked, frowning in the direction of the car.

"I think I know." Mick hopped down from the dock and walked toward the car, which was now right behind hers.

She reached it just as Danny turned off the ignition and opened his door.

"What are you doing here?" she demanded, hands on hips.

Danny looked past her at Lee and Quinn a few yards away, then his eyes swept over the otherwise deserted beach. Not satisfied, he yanked open Mick's car door and peered inside. "Where are they?" he asked.

"Where are *who?*"

"You know who." He pushed her aside and walked around to the other side of her car, glaring at the row of trees there.

"Danny, whatever you're doing here, I suggest you leave right now, before I—"

He whirled and faced her. "Before you what?"

"Before I get so mad that I decide to never speak to you again. I'm here with my friends, and we don't need you showing up and making trouble."

"Who else is here?"

Mick's laughter was a harsh sound that broke through the silence of the lake. She finally understood what Danny was thinking. "The entire male population of Xavier is hiding in the bushes, Danny, just waiting for you to leave so we can continue with our orgy. We have to hurry, though, because Lee has to be home by ten."

Danny's face colored, and he hooked his thumbs in the front pockets of his jeans, trying to strike a pose of nonchalance he didn't feel. "Maybe I was wrong," he mumbled.

"It's a miracle!" Mick cried. "Danny Santos finally admits he's an idiot."

"What did you expect me to think, after the way you've been sneaking around."

"I don't expect you to think, Danny. That's not one of your strong points."

"You bitch." He reached for her, but Mick stepped quickly back out of his reach.

"Go home, Danny. I don't want you here."

He ran both hands through his long hair, and looked over to where Lee and Quinn were still sitting. They were trying to act like they weren't listening, but he knew that every word Mick had said to him must have carried clearly to her friends, and he could almost hate Mick for what she was doing to him. Then his anger deflated like a punctured balloon, and he was suddenly worried that he'd gone too far this time. Mick wasn't one to easily forgive even his minor mistakes. Right now she looked like she could happily tear him apart.

"Okay, I'll go," he said, backing up toward his car. "Look, you know how crazy I get when I think of you with anyone else. I'm sorry I made you mad. Call me when you get home later. It doesn't matter what time it is."

He went to his car and got inside without looking at her again.

Mick waited until he had driven away before she let her breath out in one long, relieved sigh. She had no intention of calling him later. As far as she was concerned, Danny had overstepped his boundaries, and whatever happened now was not her fault. He had been fun for awhile, but he wanted more of her than she was willing to give.

The problem was, she had a feeling he wasn't going

to just walk out of her life without a struggle.

After she'd taken Lee and Quinn back to Quinn's car, Mick was too restless to go home. She'd had such high hopes for tonight, but it had been ruined not only by Danny, but by the disagreement she'd had with Lee. She shouldn't have said anything about her cards. She knew Lee and Quinn didn't understand, but she was so accustomed to telling them everything that it had slipped out before she'd had a chance to think.

She would have to be more careful in the future. Keeping secrets was getting to be a way of life with her. Lee and Quinn knew she was dating Danny, but they had no idea that she'd slept with him, and there was no doubt in her mind that they would strongly disapprove if they did know.

Reaching into her purse for her car keys, Mick's hand brushed against the box. She pulled it out and opened the lid, looking at the name there.

Maybe she didn't have to go home yet, after all.

"I've only been gone two weeks—what on earth has been going on in that time?" Quinn asked. She looked at Lee and waited for an answer.

"How would I know?" Lee said, holding her hands out helplessly.

"Haven't you been talking to Mick?"

"Not much. She's hardly ever at home any more, and school isn't exactly the best place for meaningful conversation. People are starting to wonder what's happening with her, though. Emma is spreading it around school that Mick's been seen at some pretty wild parties."

They were sitting in the front seat of Quinn's car, parked in Lee's driveway. Quinn had been stunned at the change in Mick since she'd seen her last. They'd both heard all too clearly the way she'd talked to Danny, and although Quinn didn't think much of him, she'd almost felt sorry for him.

"I'm afraid Mick is headed for big trouble," Quinn said softly.

When Mick got out of her car the sight of the isolated old house was almost enough to make her turn around and go home. It was creepy here, all right.

She didn't know what she'd expected. The Montagna house rose high above its overgrown yard, surrounded by a dense growth of trees that blocked the sliver of moon overhead. She'd been curious about it since she'd found the cards, but it wasn't until tonight that she'd actually thought about coming here.

Maybe this house would shed some light on the enigma of the tarot cards that had once belonged to Rosalie Montagna.

No one lived in the house any more. Rosalie was gone, but her memory was like a cloud of mystery hanging over the house and surrounding property.

Steeling herself, Mick walked closer, with only the headlights from her car to illuminate her way. What would she find when she got there? She felt as though she were expected. The house seemed familiar to her, yet she had no memory of ever having been here before.

This was the origin of the cards, of that she was certain. If she were to fully understand the cards, it was necessary that she learn something of Rosalie Montagna.

It didn't end there, of course, but at least it was a beginning. She would take this one step at a time.

And how did her mother figure in all this?

Mick couldn't picture proper Fran McGee ever having anything to do with someone like Rosalie — but she must have at one time, because it was at the back of Fran's closet that Mick had first found the cards.

Part Two

Chapter Eleven

There used to be so many of us. What happened? My sister died. Father died. Mother took her own life. We're cursed, and I find myself alone with my thoughts and the brief company of stupid men. If I were a stronger person I'd leave here and go to Tia Celestine, like she wants me to, but I'm not ready to abandon my home.

Mick sat hunched over the diary, so absorbed in the words that time ceased to have any meaning. Reading the leather-bound journal was like peeking uninvited into another person's mind. And it was slow reading because Rosalie's mind tended to wander off in several directions at once.

This was Mick's third trip to the house in the past week. The first night here she'd gotten in through a back door by jimmying a lock with her credit card. She got in only to find that the electricity didn't work, and she stumbled around like a fool. By feeling her way carefully until her eyes adjusted to the dark, she found candles, but that discovery didn't do her any good because she had no way to light them.

On her second visit she came in the afternoon when there was still enough light to see, and was prepared with a flashlight and some matches. Then she began exploring, her fascination increasing with every closet she opened and each room she wandered through.

On this, her third visit, Mick discovered the diary in a desk in one of the upstairs bedrooms. Her excitement grew as she read the words Rosalie had scrawled on the unlined pages. Rosalie's handwriting tended to run uphill, and in places almost fell off the end of the page, but with practice Mick was getting more adept at deciphering the words.

Mick felt some sympathy for the woman. Rosalie had been a pariah in her own hometown, and it hadn't been entirely her fault. It was true she'd done nothing to endear herself to the people of Xavier, and she'd seemed to dislike them intensely, but it hadn't started with her. From what Mick learned from her reading, Rosalie's parents had also kept to themselves, instilling in their daughter a sense of isolation she hadn't been able to overcome later, when she'd been alone.

I went into town today. Mr. Trebek in the hardware store took almost half an hour to wait on me, even though there was no one else in the store. When he finally did he sneered at me. Has he ever been to the house? I can't remember. There have been so many that they tend to run together in my memory. I know he has a small farm on the outskirts of town. When he wasn't looking I reached behind the counter and took a leather glove from the pocket of the jacket he had hanging there. I wonder how he'd like it if all his livestock suddenly died . . .

Mick put the diary down and stretched her arms out to ease a cramp in her shoulder. The sun was going down, so she got up and lit a few candles in the bedroom. Not too many, just enough so that she could read for a little while longer. She had to be careful. The house was far enough out of the way that she felt fairly safe, but she didn't want to risk having the light seen by someone who might come down the road accidentally.

It would be time to leave soon, but it was hard to tear herself away. So far Rosalie had mentioned the cards only once. Her Tia Celestine had come for a visit, and Rosalie had done a reading for her with the tarot deck. She hadn't gone into any more detail than that, and Mick was disappointed. She had so much to learn, and Rosalie's diary was her only source of information.

Fran folded the last pink flowered sheet into a neat square and put it on top of the pile of clean laundry. Smoothing the fabric with the palms of her hands, she found she was actually enjoying the small rituals of doing laundry and housework.

Iona's brother-in-law had died, and she'd gone to Arizona for a couple of weeks to help her sister out, so while she was gone Fran had taken over the running of the house.

It had been so long since she'd been without a housekeeper that at first she doubted she would be able to do it all herself, but after the first few days she grew more confident in her ability. It reminded her of how it had been earlier in her marriage, when she and Brady were a young couple struggling to make a life for themselves. It hadn't always been easy, but somehow that brought a closeness to their marriage. It was fun, those times of learning together, and mistakes only made later victories all that much sweeter.

Not that they'd ever suffered financially. Brady's family was already well established when she married him, and he was a new attorney making a niche for himself in the community and the family practice, so they had it easier than most newlyweds. At least they never had to worry about how they were going to pay the bills.

The adjustments they'd had to make in those early years were of a personal nature. She was blindly in love with Brady when she married him at age nineteen, and she expected their life to be like one of the romance novels she'd often read.

Of course it hadn't turned out that way. Life never did. Although she never doubted that Brady loved her, he was slow to give up his bachelor ways. About three years into their marriage, when she finally learned of his infidelities, it almost destroyed her.

She actually packed to leave him, and that had shocked Brady into realizing how important Fran — and their marriage — was to him.

Even with a firm, mutual resolve to make it work, there had still been rough times, and Fran had often thought they wouldn't make it.

They had, though, with the arrival of Mick doing much to keep them together. Although Mick hadn't come into their lives at quite the time Fran would have wished, she had, nonetheless, loved the baby from the first moment she laid eyes on her.

That was part of what made it so difficult now for Fran to understand the changes in Mick, the growing hostility.

Picking up the bundle of clean sheets, Fran carried them from the laundry room, down the hallway, through the kitchen and to Mick's bedroom.

She opened Mick's linen closet and put the sheets inside, then took a deep breath and turned to look, really look, at the room.

It wasn't as bad as she'd expected.

Mick had done some cleaning in here, had picked up most of the clothes that had been spread around on the carpeting, and had even made her bed.

It was a pleasant surprise that reinforced Fran's hope that Mick would snap out of this mood she'd been in. Maybe Brady had been right all along when he'd insisted that the best way to handle it was to just ride the wave and let Mick have some space.

She was turning to leave the room when something caught her eye. The room was different somehow — and not just cleaner. As Fran looked around she realized what it was. There was a small, brass-framed mirror hanging on the wall beside Mick's dressing table. Fran went to it, wondering at this new piece of decoration that seemed out of place in the pink and white bedroom. The mirror was only about a foot tall by eight or nine inches wide, and the glass was wavy and speckled in one corner with age. The frame was tarnished and had been carelessly dusted.

The mirror stood out on the wall like a scab, dark and unclean.

Brady stood in the doorway of Mick's room and looked inside.

"See what I mean?" Fran said. She was right behind him so she couldn't see his face.

"It's just some old mirror she found somewhere," Brady said. "Probably picked it up at a garage sale or flea market."

This didn't sound likely to Fran. Mick had always been something of a snob when it came to her clothes and possessions. She liked new, expensive things, not secondhand junk.

Brady looked puzzled when he closed Mick's bedroom door and walked to the living room. Fran followed and asked, "What is it?"

"I was just thinking—" he stopped.

"What?"

"No. Forget it."

But Fran wasn't going to forget it. She was tired of having her fears brushed off, and for once she was determined not to take the easy way out. "It's something about that mirror, isn't it?" she said, pacing the room. Brady had sat in his favorite chair and didn't look up at her.

"I think I've seen it before," he said.

"When?"

"When Mick was a baby. And even before that."

Fran had been leaning toward him, but now she straightened up. It was a pulling back, and she realized that this conversation was going to take a turn she hadn't expected. "I'm worried about what's happening to Mick *now,*" she said.

Brady looked up at her, his eyes probing. "That's all a part of it."

She wanted to argue with him, dissuade him from that way of thinking, but she couldn't. He had, after all, merely voiced her own fears.

Mick sat at the dining room table, picking at the food on her plate, too excited to eat. Every bite she took stuck in her throat, but she knew she had to get through this half hour with her parents or suffer more of their endless questions.

And she sensed a storm brewing on the horizon. They hadn't said anything to her yet, but she could tell something was up.

"This is really good," she said, using her fork to push around some of the meat on her plate. "What's it called?"

"Meat loaf," Fran said, her voice flat.

"Well, it's really good. Much better than Iona's meat loaf."

"Thank you." Fran looked at Brady, but he frowned slightly and shook his head.

Mick missed the exchange. She was pushing the meat around a little more, trying to figure out how much of it she would have to eat before she could safely ask to be excused. She had so much to think about, and she needed to be alone.

"How is Quinn doing now that she's back in school?" Brady asked.

Mick looked up at him. "She's doing okay," she said. "Better than okay, actually. She's dating a little bit, and she and her mother are fixing up the house. Her mom even bought her a little second hand car, and they're looking into some colleges. I think her father's dying is the best thing that ever happened to Quinn."

Fran's fork hit her plate with a clatter. "Michelle! That's a horrible thing to say." She didn't look at Brady. They had said the same thing themselves, but it seemed so much worse coming from Mick.

"It's true," Mick said.

"The man's dead. If you can't speak well of him, then don't say anything at all."

Despite her earlier resolve to avoid another confrontation, Mick didn't back down. "Did *you* like him?" she asked.

Fran's eyes shifted away from Mick's. "I didn't know him."

"But you knew of him."

"Mick," Brady said softly. "We all know what kind of man Quinn's father was. But we don't know what made him that way. Maybe he was more to be pitied than hated."

Mick removed the napkin from her lap and put it on

the table beside her plate. "May I be excused? I have homework to do, and when I'm done with that, I'll need help hemming my costume."

Fran's expression was blank.

"My costume for the Halloween dance at school," Mick reminded her. "Remember? I told you it needed to be shortened and you said you'd help me with it."

"Oh, yes, that's right."

"Do you have a date for the dance?" Brady asked.

"I'm taking Danny," she told him. She knew they didn't approve of Danny, but that wasn't going to be a problem much longer. She was taking him to the Halloween dance only because the plans had already been made before he'd embarrassed her so badly at the lake, but this was going to be their last date, of that she was determined.

"You've been seeing a lot of him," Brady said. "I'm surprised he'd want to go to a high school dance. He's a little older than most of your friends, isn't he?"

"He's twenty-two."

Fran looked a little upset at this revelation, but before she could say anything Mick hurried to put her mind at ease.

"And you're right," she said, "he *is* too old for me. To tell you the truth, if it wasn't too late to get another date, I wouldn't take Danny at all. We haven't been getting along all that great, but he's still better than no date at all. I don't think I'll be seeing much of him after this weekend."

Their relief was pathetically obvious, and for a moment Mick was sorry that she'd been so difficult lately. They weren't used to it. But before her pity could take hold, she remembered Rosalie's tarot cards her mother had kept so carefully hidden in her closet. If Fran could keep her little secrets, Mick felt she had every right to

160

do the same thing. Obviously, trust wasn't a big thing in this family.

"Don't forget about my costume," she said to her mother, and left the table.

Quinn's hair kept falling in her eyes as she leaned over the brown turtleneck on the table, and she impatiently pushed it back with her wrist. She couldn't use her fingers because they had glue on them, as well as sticky bits of cotton.

She was cutting the cotton balls into quarters, and sticking them onto the front of the turtleneck and a pair of brown tights. When the glue dried she would turn the outfit over and repeat the process on the back.

The front door opened, then closed again, and Elaine came into the kitchen. "How's the costume coming?" she asked, putting a package down on the floor. The paper rustled.

"Okay." Quinn looked at the package. "What's that?"

"Some clothes. A couple of skirts and a sweater. Everything I have is too big. I needed some new things for work." Elaine went to a basket on the counter and examined some apples there, chose one and bit into it.

Quinn looked up from her work, a cotton ball stuck to her fingers. She tried to pull it off, but it merely stuck to her other hand.

Elaine laughed at her predicament, then put her apple down and went to help. When Quinn was free of the cotton she went to the sink to wash her hands.

"I think you're thin enough now that you could probably wear my clothes," she said as she dried her hands on a paper towel.

It was true. Elaine Baker could now pass as Quinn's older sister, if she were so inclined. She seemed to be shedding years along with the pounds, and when she walked it was with the bounce of a much younger woman.

It was precisely because of this that Quinn could no longer share her innermost feelings with her mother. Where once she had felt free to discuss any problem with Elaine, now Quinn couldn't even bring up the subject that was eating at her.

Only a couple of days ago Mick had told her the most incredible thing. Here, in this very house, Mick had, with an air of confession, told her that she might have had something to do with the death of Quinn's father.

"I didn't really mean to hurt him," Mick had said, her eyes searching Quinn's for understanding. "And I don't *really* know if the cards had anything to do with it, but I can't get it out of my head that they might have."

Quinn had tried to refuse to listen. She'd even, at one point, put her hands over her ears, but Mick had been adamant.

"Please, Quinn, I need to know that you don't blame me."

"Of course I don't blame you. You weren't even here."

"But I told you—"

"Yes, I know. You told me that you put the Death card over the card that was supposed to be my father, and then he died. But that's crazy, Mick. That's something from a bad movie. It's not real." Quinn had felt her hands trembling, and she'd wanted to reach out and shake Mick. "Why are you telling me this?"

Mick, her face pale, had looked momentarily doubtful. "Because I've never kept anything from you before. Sometimes I feel like—like I've found something dangerous. It scares me."

It scared Quinn, too, but not in the same way. Mick

had left eventually, but before going she'd given Quinn a terrible burden to shoulder. Quinn genuinely feared for Mick's sanity, and this unhealthy obsession she had with those cards.

Not knowing what else to do, Quinn had called Lee and shared the story with her. Lee had been properly shocked, but could offer no real advice.

Mick was drifting away from them, farther every day, and Quinn felt helpless to prevent some tragedy she knew was about to befall them.

She watched her mother finish the apple, then dutifully expressed her approval of the new clothes Elaine had bought. Something must have shown on her face, though, because Elaine put the pink and beige sweater down and asked, "What's wrong, honey?"

Everything, Quinn thought. Her best friend was getting weirder by the day, but she had to go to school and to dances and act like all was right with the world.

"Quinn?" Elaine moved toward her.

"I'm okay," Quinn said quickly, backing up. She didn't want her mother to touch her. If she did, Quinn might be tempted to tell her all about it, and that wouldn't help anything.

"Oh, I've been selfish," Elaine said. "Maybe I shouldn't have gone back to work full time. I could have my hours cut to part time. That way I could be with you more."

Quinn turned and ran from the room. She ignored her mother's hurt expression, and didn't stop until she'd gotten to her bedroom and shut the door.

The new flowered curtains and bedspread did nothing to cheer her. As the tears seeped from her eyes, Quinn felt more alone than she ever had in her life.

Chapter Twelve

Lee, balanced precariously near the top of the ladder, used the staple gun in her right hand to attach the orange streamer to the ceiling of the gym.

"Who talked me into this job?" she asked, her eyes on her work. She didn't want to look down and be reminded of just how high up she was.

"You volunteered," Quinn called up to her.

They, along with about a dozen other students, were decorating the gym for the dance, blowing up orange and black balloons, hanging streamers, and cleaning.

Quinn was at the bottom of the ladder, holding it steady for Lee, secretly glad that she wasn't the one up there. "Have you finished your costume?" she asked.

Lee looked down at her briefly, then quickly looked up again. "I'm going to use the same one I wore last year. The Spanish lady outfit, with the full skirt and sombrero. I haven't had time to figure out anything new. Mrs. Pidbuhl's running me ragged. I work twice as long on her assignments as for any other class, and she's still never satisfied. I heard she's going to be a chaperon at the dance. Do you suppose she'll come as a witch?" She stapled the streamer again, to make sure it was secure. "What about you? Have a costume yet?"

"It's a surprise. You'll see it when everyone else does."

Climbing down carefully, the staple gun still in her hand, Lee descended. When her tennis shoes touched down on firm ground she sighed in relief and handed the staple gun to Quinn.

"What's this for?" Quinn asked.

"Next time you go up, and *I'll* hold the ladder."

"We need more balloons," a boy called from the other side of the gym. "More orange balloons."

"If I blow up one more balloon I'll pass out," a girl answered, and there was a general murmur of agreement.

A piece of black crepe paper clung to Lee's hair, the color contrasting with her bright red hair and making her look somewhat like a Halloween decoration herself. Quinn plucked off the paper, and they walked over to the bleachers to take a deserved break.

They both had dates for the dance, but they were dates of convenience more than anything else. Quinn was going with Todd Belzer. She liked him, but she knew they were just two friends going to a dance together so they didn't have to go stag.

That was okay, because she didn't feel much like getting heavily involved. Too much was happening right now. Besides Mick's odd behavior, Quinn was finding that her senior year in school wasn't going to be quite the breeze she'd expected. She was taking a heavy load of classes, the hardest of which were Advanced Algebra and Biology. She was also trying to catch up with what she'd missed while she'd been gone with her mother, and she couldn't let herself fall behind.

The dance was going to be a welcome relief. For one whole night she planned to do nothing but have fun. All too soon it would again be time to hit the books, and to worry about other matters.

Lee, on the other hand, wasn't looking forward to the dance at all. Her school work seemed to be on a downward slide that she couldn't control, and it was affecting her ability to find pleasure in outside activities. No matter how hard she worked, she couldn't pull her grades up in Mrs. Pidbuhl's class. The result was that she was neglecting her other classes, and the strain was starting to take its toll.

Even her date was something that she'd had no control over herself. Todd Belzer had a cousin visiting him for the weekend, and Todd and Quinn had set Lee up with the cousin. She was sure the whole thing was going to turn out to be a waste of time.

With her legs stretched out in front of her, Lee slumped down on the bottom row of the bleachers and looked at her shoes. They were just about shot. She needed new ones, but was having trouble talking her mother into getting her a pair. Her mother expected her to buy her own clothing, but her savings was nearly depleted, and her studies kept her too busy to take on any of the babysitting jobs she usually counted on for extra money.

"I wish I knew what to do," she said to Quinn.

"What do you mean?"

"I don't know what I want, or don't want, or even if I'm coming or going most of the time. Is all this confusion just part of being a senior, or is there something wrong with me?"

"It's not you," Quinn said. "I feel the same way sometimes."

"Hey, you two. There's a lot more work to do here."

Addie Briscoe, her hands on her hips, stood on the other side of the gym and glared at Lee and Quinn.

166

When neither girl jumped up, Addie walked over to where they were sitting and began to list what needed to be done to get the gym ready for the dance.

"This isn't the army, Addie," Lee said. "We've been working all morning, and we just sat down for a minute. It'll be time for lunch in little while anyway."

"Lunch!" Addie looked as though Lee had suggested they set fire to the school.

"Yes, lunch," Quinn spoke up. Her own stomach growled noisily as though on cue. "It's a meal most people eat about this time every day."

Addie began to stammer. "But we still have to set up the stereo equipment, and sweep the floors, and make punch, and—"

"It'll all get done, Addie," Quinn assured her. She never doubted her own words. Over a dozen students were working to get the gym ready, and they'd been going hard at it all morning, but somehow Addie's sense of impending doom was contagious, and Quinn found herself getting to her feet. "Oh, all right. We'll work for another half hour before we go to lunch. But we're going to have to eat, Addie."

Slightly mollified, Addie left them and crossed the gym to make sure no one else had decided to sit down on the job.

"I'm not going back up on that ladder," Lee said. "Maybe I'll set up the refreshment table instead. That sounds safe."

"Everything we need is in the Home Ec room," Quinn told her. "Do you need help?"

"No, I don't think so. Is the punch there, too?"

"The teachers will bring the punch later, right before the dance." Quinn gave her a lopsided grin. "I think they're trying to prevent a repeat of what happened at the spring dance last year."

"What happened?"

"Don't you remember? Bo Sutherland made the punch and he spiked it. Emma got drunk and threw up in the girls' bathroom,"

"Oh, yeah. I'd forgotten. Bo got suspended for that, didn't he?"

"Three days, but he said it was worth it."

Lee left the gym and headed for the Home Ec room. Hauling boxes of paper cups and napkins wouldn't be exciting, but at least her feet would be safely planted on the ground.

Edwina Pidbuhl pulled the glass punch bowl from the cupboard and inspected it inside and out. It was less than spotless, so she took the bowl to the sink in the Home Ec room and rinsed it out, then wiped it down with a towel.

She was going to be a chaperon at the dance not because she wanted to, but because the teachers were on a rotating schedule for these events, and it was her turn. She would have gotten out of it if she could have, and had even tried to switch with the new art teacher, Miss Hamilton, hoping that the other teacher's youth and relative inexperience would make her eager to ingratiate herself with a senior member of the teaching staff. It hadn't worked. Miss Hamilton had failed to respond to pleading, bribery and even a thinly veiled threat. Edwina was stuck with this dance, like it or not.

She took longer to wipe down the punch bowl than was necessary, but she was using the time to enjoy this rare bit of solitude. The longer she'd been teaching, the more she had come to dislike teenagers. It was ironic that, as a young, idealistic woman, she had gotten into the teaching profession with the hope of guiding young minds. Her hopes had gradually, over the years, been crushed until now she only put in her time and looked forward to her retirement. She felt so completely out of touch with her students now. She didn't understand them, and she had given up trying.

This last couple of years had been the worst. She was only fifty, but knew that she looked ten years older. Menopause had been especially hard on her, and even the medication she took didn't always help her mood swings. Sometimes she overreacted, and regretting it afterwards still did nothing to repair the damage that had been done.

Her latest scene with Lee Sternhagen was a perfect example. The girl rubbed her the wrong way, that was all there was to it, but she was disappointed in herself for her inability to keep her feelings in check. Every day she told herself that she would teach her classes and try to instill some knowledge in those stubborn children, but the sight of their uninterested faces always destroyed her resolve.

She wasn't even sure what it was about Lee to make her dislike the girl with such intensity. Maybe it was the very fact of her youth, that unlined skin and perfect figure, that inspired jealousy.

Whatever it was, Edwina Pidbuhl knew she wasn't always entirely fair with Lee, and once again she promised herself that she would set her personal feelings aside. She was reaching her final years as a teacher, and she didn't want to go out with the memory of unprofessional behavior forever burned into her mind.

She still had her dignity, and with that thought felt sure she could get through this Halloween dance. It might even be fun, if she would only allow herself to join in the spirit of the occasion.

The punch bowl was dry now, and sparkled brightly as she carried it toward the door. She almost felt good as she thought about the costumes she would see, and would take part in judging. She might even do something herself, see if she couldn't improvise a quick, simple costume.

The heels of her flat shoes clattered on the tile floor, and she held the big bowl high, balancing it carefully in the crook of her left arm as she reached for the doorknob with her right hand.

The tips of her fingers had just touched the doorknob when it suddenly jumped toward her. The door hit her and sent the punch bowl flying up and out of her grasp.

For a moment it caught the light coming through the window, and she had the disjointed, confused thought that it looked almost beautiful as it flew through the air.

Then the bowl hit the tile floor and shattered into a thousand small pieces.

Edwina Pidbuhl let her breath out in a gush of sound, only then realizing she had been holding it in.

She raised her eyes and looked directly into the horrified face of Lee Sternhagen.

Chapter Thirteen

Somehow the mess in the Home Ec room was cleaned and a new punch bowl borrowed from one of the teachers, but for Lee the incident only confirmed her feelings that no matter what she did, no matter how good her intentions, something would always happen to screw things up for her.

Word got out quickly about what had happened. No one openly blamed her, but Lee still felt that all eyes were on her at the dance not because of her costume, but because she had once again been thrust into the middle of trouble with a capital 'T'.

"The gym looks great," her date said, looking into a cauldron that bubbled with dry ice. "You and Quinn must have worked all day."

"We didn't do it alone, we had plenty of help," she told him. The black wig she was wearing itched, and she felt fat in the dress with its full skirt and petticoats, but at least her date had turned out to be okay. Todd Belzer's cousin was dressed as a caveman, complete with shoulder-draping pelt and club, and even though he was a sophomore in college, he didn't seem to mind being at a high school dance.

The gym did look good, she had to admit. Besides the balloons and streamers she and Quinn had put up, black netting hid the basketball hoops and eerie lighting completed the picture.

And the costumes were outstanding. Half the fun was trying to figure out who was behind the masks, and Lee had already decided that Quinn's costume should win an award for originality.

Quinn swept through the room on the arm of her date, dressed in the brown turtleneck and tights dotted with bits of white cotton. She was a pretzel, and at the slightest encouragement she would twist herself into difficult shapes, laughing with delight at the applause it always brought.

"Want some punch?" her date asked.

Lee winced. "Not yet, thanks. You go ahead if you want."

She stood alone only for a moment after he'd gone, then she made her way through the crowd to Quinn. Progress was slow because she kept having to stop to admire costumes.

"How did you know it was me?" Addie Briscoe cried after Lee told her she liked her hula-girl outfit. Addie was wearing a mask over her eyes and had thought she was unrecognizable in her grass skirt and flowered halter top.

"Your braces," Lee told her. "They're a dead giveaway."

"Oh, yeah." For a minute Addie looked crestfallen. Then she shrugged and smiled, removing her mask. "Oh, well. This thing was making my mascara run anyway. Hey, have you seen Mick? She came in just a minute ago with her date. Is she really going *out* with him? I've heard he's been in jail."

"That wouldn't surprise me a bit," Lee said.

"Her costume is beautiful, though. Must have cost a fortune, but I guess her parents can afford it."

"Where is she?"

"Over there by the door. See her?"

Lee looked in the direction Addie was indicating, and saw Mick, who did, indeed, look beautiful. Mick was dressed as a fairy princess in a diaphanous blue gown that looked as light as a feather, complete with transparent wings and gold, star-tipped wand.

Danny was standing close to Mick, his face set in a frown as he jealously guarded what he considered his territory. In contrast to Mick's elaborate costume, Danny had barely bothered to dress up. He had a bandanna on his head and a gold hoop earring in one ear, and looked like he hadn't shaved in a day or two. Even this half-hearted stab at making himself up as a pirate seemed to bother Danny, and as Lee watched she saw him lean toward Mick and whisper something in her ear.

"Talk to you later, Addie," Lee said, and walked toward Mick and Danny. They were an odd couple, all right, and Lee could see that even now, only a few minutes into the festivities, there was friction between them. Where Mick had been smiling happily only moments before, she now mirrored Danny's frown, and when Lee got closer she heard Mick say, "You can leave right now, Danny, if this is so far beneath you."

"You'd like me to leave, wouldn't you?" he snapped.

"I don't really care, if you want the truth."

Danny looked ready to drag Mick away, and Lee, heart thumping heavily in her chest, approached them with an artificial smile. "Hi'" she said. "Mick, you just had to outdo us all, didn't you? That cos-

173

tume is incredible. Where'd you get it? Hi, Danny. How are you tonight?"

They looked startled to see her, but Lee's chatter had the desired effect. Danny stepped back and mumbled a reluctant greeting.

"Mick, can you come with me for a minute? I need to talk to you. You don't mind, do you, Danny? We'll be right back. Have some punch while you wait."

"What did you need to talk to me about?" Mick asked when they were in the clear.

"Nothing," Lee said. "But you looked like you needed help."

Mick's dark hair sparkled with gold glitter as she shook her head. "I appreciate your concern, but I can handle Danny."

"It didn't look like it. Why did you bring him? He doesn't fit in with this crowd, and he sure doesn't look like he's having any fun."

Mick waved her wand. "Oh, he's just a little uncomfortable because he's older than anyone else here. He'll settle down. He always does."

"I think he's spooky."

Mick laughed, then put one hand over her mouth when several people turned to look at her. "He's not, really, so stop looking so worried. Lee, you have to have a little faith in me. I know what I'm doing."

"Addie says he's been in jail."

"A couple of times, yeah."

"You mean you *knew* that, and you still go out with him?" Lee couldn't hide her shock.

Mick touched Lee's arm with the tip of her wand. "It's part of what I like about him. The boys at this

174

school, they're so—predictable. I could tell you exactly what any one of them will be doing one year from now. At least Danny is different."

Before Lee could think of anything to say to that, someone turned on the stereo system on the far side of the room, and the gym was filled with music.

"Now tell me," Mick said, raising her voice to be heard over the music. "What's this I hear about you breaking the punch bowl?"

Mick had cleverly brought up the one subject that could distract Lee from what they'd been talking about. "Oh, God, it was awful," Lee told her. "Mrs. Pidbuhl turned so red I thought she was going to have a stroke, and the worst part was she didn't say anything. She just looked at me, and if I could have dropped dead right there I would have gladly done it. I cleaned up the mess, and someone found another punch bowl, but I know I haven't heard the last of this."

"What can she do to you?" Mick asked.

"Make my life miserable."

"Only if you let her." Mick lifted her wand and touched it lightly to the bangs of Lee's wig. "I grant you one wish. What do you wish for?"

"Peace," Lee sighed. "That's all I ever really wanted. And it's the one thing I can't seem to find."

"Never fear, fair lady. Your wish has been granted."

Prizes were given at midnight for the best costumes. Quinn received honorable mention for her pretzel costume, and Danny, though he'd been bored and angry all night, resented the fact that Mick didn't win anything. She tried to explain to him that the winners had all made their own costumes, while she'd only bought hers, so they'd deserved the recognition. But Danny wasn't listening to her.

Mick had been looking forward to this night, as a chance to again be with the people she considered her friends. Once she'd been big on these school activities, never missing a game or dance. She'd been avoiding these events lately and had thought this might be a chance to recapture something that seemed to be slipping away from her.

It hadn't turned out that way, as she might have expected. She realized she was no longer one of them as she stood alone and waited for Danny to return from the bathroom.

She was no longer sure she ever had been one of them.

Danny seemed to be taking a long time, so she wandered toward the refreshment table. A boy she had dated a couple of times asked her to dance when she reached the table, but she smiled and shook her head no. She wouldn't have minded dancing, especially since it was a fast number and so far Danny had only agreed to dance to a few slow songs with her, but with her luck Danny would get back when she was out on the floor and would raise a stink. Better to avoid trouble, especially since most of her friends had a low opinion of Danny already.

Mrs. Pidbuhl was standing behind the punch bowl, dressed in a plain navy dress with a white collar. "Hello, Michelle," she said as she ladled some punch into a plastic cup. "That's a very nice costume."

"Thanks." Mick took the cup the teacher held out

to her, thought about attempting small talk, then decided against it. She'd just brought the cup to her lips when, out of the corner of her eye, she saw Danny. A splash of bright red had caught her attention, that color being in the form of Emma Mejia, dressed in a tight devil costume that was pressed against Danny as he tried to get through the doorway.

Mick watched with a mixture of amusement and irritation, because Emma kept glancing in her direction, obviously hoping that Mick was watching. When Danny finally extracted himself from Emma's groping arms, he made his way to Mick's side and shook his head when she asked him if he wanted some punch.

"Nah. Let's get out of here. This is a bore."

"You didn't look bored a minute ago," she said. She knew he hadn't encouraged Emma, but couldn't help teasing him a little. He was so easy to tease, because he never really knew she was doing it.

"That's just Emma," he said. Then he broke into a grin. "It's not my fault she's hot for me. The Santos charm is hard to resist."

Mick became aware that Mrs. Pidbuhl was hanging on their every word, and she put her cup down and took Danny's arm. "You're right, this is a bore. Let's go. I have someplace special I want to take you."

"Where?"

Mick smiled up at him. "It's a surprise," she said.

Chapter Fourteen

"This is it? Some surprise. Everyone knows about this house, Mick. Big deal."

Mick ignored him as she took a cigarette lighter from her purse and lit two candles. They'd stumbled through the living room until she'd found the candles, and now the feeble light showed only a dusty room full of crumbling furniture and abandoned hopes.

Putting the candles back carefully on the mantle, Mick stepped back from the big fireplace and breathed deeply of the stale air. She felt better now than she had all night, and attributed it to the fact that she now had her purse with her. It would have clashed horribly with her costume, so while she and Danny had been at the dance she'd left her purse locked in his car, carefully hidden under the front seat. Her cards were in the purse, and she'd fretted about their safety even though she'd known that in Xavier car break-ins were almost unheard of. Having them with her again gave her strength, and even Danny's lack of enthusiasm couldn't dampen her spirits.

"Sure, everybody knows about it, but who ever comes here?" she asked.

"Why would they want to?" Danny touched the back of the couch, then wiped the grime on his fingers onto his jeans. He watched Mick warily, wondering what she was up to. She looked beautiful in her costume, but there was something in her expression he didn't like. Her eyes took in everything in the room, but never came to rest for long on any one object. He felt like he was trapped in this old house with a stranger. "I'm not sure it's even safe here," he said, hoping to persuade her to leave. He would have taken her arm and pulled her out if he could, but something kept him from touching her. "The floors are probably rotten. And those candles aren't a good idea. How did you even know they were here?"

"Because I've been here before. There are candles in every room. Rosalie Montagna must have liked candlelight."

"Either that or she didn't pay her electric bill."

"Maybe. I prefer to think she liked the way candlelight looked in these rooms." Mick turned, her arms wide, the skirt of her costume billowing around her slender legs. When she faced him, the shadows beneath her eyes made her look less like a fairy princess than anything Danny had ever seen. "This is my secret place. I've been exploring."

"Find any ghosts?"

"Not yet. But I'm still looking." She brushed past him and headed for the stairway.

"Hey, don't go up there," Danny said, catching up with her. His voice was tight with alarm. "Come on, Mick, this place isn't safe. You shouldn't be coming here alone. Anything could happen."

She'd let him stop her from climbing the stairs, but Mick couldn't hide her disappointment. She'd hoped Danny would find the house as intriguing as she did, and had wanted to share it with him. Maybe if he'd shown some interest it might have breathed new life into this dying relationship. Instead, she found his reaction cowardly, and not at all worthy of him. Danny's love of adventure was one of the few things that attracted her to him. To learn now that he was as ordinary as everyone else in town made her realize how alone she really was.

"I thought you'd like this place," was all she could say.

"Why? It's not the only deserted old house around town."

"But it's the only one with all the furniture still left in it. There are even clothes in the closets, and dishes in the cupboards."

"Yeah, so what?"

Mick was standing on the bottom step, looking down at Danny. She suspected that if she tried again to climb the stairs he would pull her back. She made one last stab at making him understand the mystery of this house. "Don't you ever wonder about it?" she asked. "Rosalie is gone, but I heard that she was crazy. And why hasn't the house been sold, or at least cleaned out? Everything is a mess now, but this furniture must have been worth something. There are silver ornaments in a couple of the bedrooms upstairs. Why haven't vandals broken in and stolen them?"

Danny's eyebrows rose an inch. "Real sliver?" he asked.

"Yes, and don't you go getting any big ideas."

"Why not? If no one seems to want them, I'm sure I could find a buyer." He looked past her, up the stairs, as though tempted by the thought of easy riches. But as quickly as it had come, his greed disappeared and he was again wary. "Ah, hell. I don't care if the door knobs are giant diamonds, I don't want anything out of this house. Let the spooks have it all."

Mick reached out and took his hand eagerly. "That's exactly the attitude everyone seems to have, and I want to know why. I come here, usually during the day so I don't have to light candles, and I feel like I belong here. Almost like *it* belongs to me. I'm not afraid. Why is everyone else so scared?"

Danny straightened his shoulders at this insult. "I'm not scared," he insisted, though his mouth felt dry, and he had the urge to look back over his shoulder. "It's just that—"

"What?"

"I don't know. People say she was a witch."

Realizing that she was digging her fingernails into Danny's hand, Mick loosened her grip, though she didn't release him. She was afraid that if she did he would leave. "Do you believe it?" she asked.

"Hell, no," he said too quickly.

"Why not?" She moved closer to him, really wanting an answer. She had none of her own, only more questions that haunted her sleeping as well as waking hours, but maybe Danny could help her unravel the mystery. "We've both heard the stories. They're probably exaggerated, yet they never really die completely down. Maybe she really was a witch.

181

Maybe this house is haunted, or possessed, or—I don't know what."

Her face was very close to his, and Danny saw a need in her eyes that he didn't understand. He loved Mick, would have done anything for her, but he knew he wasn't even close to possessing her. She was miles away from him, her wide eyes almost black with desperation.

He put his hands on her waist and pulled her to him. Physically they were good together, and he hoped to remind her of that. *"You're* the only witch I've ever known," he said, right before he kissed her.

Lee opened the front door, surprised to find lights still on in her house. Usually her mother went to bed by eleven or so; it was strange that she'd still be up.

But there was Joan Sternhagen, sitting on the edge of the couch, a mug of coffee in her hands. "How was the dance?" she asked when she saw Lee.

"It was okay."

"And your date?"

"He was okay. What's going on? I thought you didn't like to drink coffee after six p.m."

Joan looked down at the mug in her hands. "Oh, yes. I didn't even think. I'll be up all night now, won't I? Gloria just left. She brought some good news."

Lee didn't want to hear it. She knew what the news was going to be, and she didn't want to face that just yet.

"Bryan and Kat had their baby tonight," Joan

said. "A little girl. Isn't that exciting?"

Lee closed her eyes and prayed for the comfort of her own bed. "I'm tired. Goodnight."

Joan wasn't ready to let her go. "I thought I'd send flowers to the hospital, from all of us. A little pink arrangement would be nice, don't you think?"

"I'll talk to you in the morning." Lee took two steps toward her bedroom.

"Do you want to go to the hospital with me tomorrow afternoon to see Kat?" Joan asked.

"No!"

"It would be the polite thing to do."

Lee lifted one hand. "No, Mom, I don't want to go to the hospital. I don't want to send flowers. You go ahead and do what you want, but leave me out of it."

Joan put her mug down on the coffee table, so distracted that she didn't even reach for a coaster. "Really, Lee, I would have expected you to be over your petty jealousy by now."

"Goodnight."

"Don't walk away from me when I'm talking to you."

Lee turned around and faced her mother. Lee kept her face blank, giving away nothing, but she couldn't help wondering why her mother had such a thing about Bryan and Kat. Most of the time her mother was okay—Lee didn't even mind all the house cleaning that much. It was better than living in a dirty home. But when it came to Bryan, Joan was completely insensitive to Lee's feelings.

"Gloria has been a friend of mine for years," Joan said. "She's known you since you were a little girl, and she'll be hurt if you don't go to that hospital with me tomorrow."

"Mrs. Frazier isn't the one who's in the hospital; Kat is," Lee pointed out. "If it was Mrs. Frazier you wanted to go see, I'd go with you."

"Kat is her daughter-in-law, and this is Gloria's first grandchild. It means a lot to her."

"I really don't think she'll mind if I don't go to the hospital."

"*I* mind. You're going with me."

"No, I'm not." Lee knew it was foolish to argue, but for once she wasn't going to back down. She stood with her feet planted firmly apart, feeling silly in her costume, but unwilling to compromise. "I'm not going."

Mick dropped her key, almost couldn't find it in the dark, then located it and tried again. The light over the back door had been left on, as it always was when she was out at night, but the shadows around her feet were deep, and an item as small as a key could easily be lost.

She managed to get it in the lock on the second try.

She couldn't stop her hands from shaking, that was the problem. They shook so badly that her arms vibrated, and her breath came in little gasps that sounded almost like sobs.

The door rattled on its hinges when she opened it, and she slipped in quickly and pulled it shut before the noise could wake her parents.

The trembling had climbed from her arms now

and was invading the rest of her body. She had to get to her own bedroom before someone came to ask her what was going on. She couldn't face questions right now.

She felt slightly better once safely in her bedroom. At least here, with the door closed, she could think. Her brain had been working on auto-pilot for the past hour—it had gotten her home but had been shut down to any real thought or analysis.

Sitting on the edge of her bed, she stripped off her ruined shoes and soggy tights. Even the bottom half of her costume was soaked through and muddy, and when she removed it she knew it was beyond saving.

That didn't matter. She never wanted to look at this outfit again. It would be only a reminder of the horrors she'd been through tonight. Horrors of her own making, without a doubt, but no less frightening for that fact.

When she was stripped down to her underwear, Mick rolled the costume into as tight a ball as she could, then went to her closet and found a plastic bag with a drawstring and shoved the whole mess of fabric and shoes inside. She then pulled the drawstring closed and put the bag as far back in her closet as she could reach.

With that task out of the way, Mick was forced, finally, to think.

"Oh, God," she moaned, bending over and pressing her fists into her stomach, fighting the nausea that gripped her body. For a moment she thought she was going to lose the battle. Only by closing her eyes tightly and concentrating with every ounce of her will was she able to drive the sick feeling down.

It was several minutes before she was able to straighten up again.

Hugging herself and pacing, Mick saw Danny's face again, his anger matching her own, that anger finally giving way to fear.

Why couldn't he have left her alone?

After they'd left the Montagna house she'd tried to talk to him, tried to make him understand why he could no longer be a part of her life. She'd hoped to share something special with him, and when he'd shown absolutely no understanding of her feelings for the house, she'd realized it was finally, irrevocably time to cut him loose.

Despite his outer veneer of toughness, Danny had crumbled when she'd tried to tell him she wouldn't be seeing him any more. His pleading had been an act of desperation, and when he'd realized that it wasn't going to work he'd turned on her, telling her he would kill her before he would let her go.

She'd managed to calm him down, but Mick had known then that he meant what he said. She would have to resort to desperate measures if she were to ever be free of him. She'd seen the future stretching ahead of her, had seen how it would be. Wherever she went, Danny would be there. If she tried to date other men, he would show up and might even use the knife he'd reminded her he always carried.

He would cut her, he'd promised, starting with her face.

Still, she couldn't quite believe that excused what she'd done. At the time there'd seemed only one solution, and she'd talked Danny into, for the first and last time, letting her read her tarot cards for him.

Now, in the safety of her own bedroom, Mick contemplated the enormity of her actions.

When she finally fell asleep, still in her underwear and with a blanket pulled up over her shoulders, the first sign of a cheerless dawn was peeking through her bedroom window.

Chapter Fifteen

"Mr. McGee, you've let this refrigerator get almost empty," Iona complained, looking for something to prepare for that night's supper.

Brady had come into the kitchen for a cup of coffee, and he stopped to look over the housekeeper's shoulder into the nearly bare refrigerator. All it contained now was a half gallon of milk, a large cardboard bucket holding only one piece of dry chicken, a six-pack of diet pop and a cellophane-wrapped piece of pizza.

Brady gave Iona an apologetic look. "Yeah, you're right, we've neglected your kitchen while you were gone. Sorry."

"What did you folks eat for the past three weeks?" Iona closed the refrigerator door.

"Fran's been cooking most of the time, she just hasn't done much grocery shopping," Brady explained. "She knows you have your own method of shopping, and she thought you'd rather stock the kitchen with the things you like to have around, rather than filling it with a bunch of stuff you don't want."

Iona sniffed. "Well, it's your kitchen, I imagine you folks can put in it whatever you wanted."

Brady smiled and shook his head as he poured

his coffee. "Oh, come on, Iona. You know this hasn't really been our kitchen since the day you came to work here. You've taken it and us over, and I'm afraid we just couldn't get along without you."

Waving her hands and blushing all the way up to the roots of her gray hair, the housekeeper tried to deny his words. "That's nonsense, Mr. McGee."

"Is it? Just look what's happened to this house since you've been gone."

"Looks to me like Mrs. McGee's done a pretty good job of keeping things in order."

"Pretty good, but still not up to your standards."

Iona looked pleased, despite her efforts to hide it. "You're just trying to butter me up," she said.

"You bet I am." Brady took his coffee cup. As he passed her, he added, "I'm hoping to get you to make your famous lasagna tonight. Nobody makes lasagna as well as you."

After he was gone, a greatly pacified Iona made up a lengthy grocery list. Her initial irritation at finding the kitchen so depleted had given way to delight at knowing she was needed. He was right, this family couldn't get along without her.

When she was finished with her list—the longest one she'd made since coming to work for the McGees—she took the filled-to-overflowing garbage bag out from under the sink and carried it to the big metal trash can outside the kitchen door.

She'd almost replaced the lid on the trash can when she noticed the bag from one of the clothing stores Mick shopped at. It was the type with a drawstring, and ordinarily Iona wouldn't have given it a second thought, but this one obviously had something in it, so she reached inside the trash can and pulled it out.

The costume was halfway out of the bag before Iona realized what it was. Halloween had been over a week ago, but just this morning she had listened to Mrs. McGee talk about how lovely Mick had looked in her fairy princess costume. Iona hadn't seen it herself, of course, because she'd still been in Arizona at the time, but she knew this had to be it.

Then she found the slippers, and saw that they were nearly black with mud, and completely ruined. The tights, too, and a good part of the skirt were filthy.

That girl had no appreciation for the fine things her parents bought her, Iona thought. That costume probably cost a fortune — certainly it had cost more than anything she'd ever worn on *her* back — yet Mick treated it like a baby treated a disposable diaper. Mess it up and throw it away.

Kids these days had everything handed to them on a silver platter. All that did for them was make them expect more, and most were too lazy to work for what they got.

Iona didn't have anything against Mick. The girl had always been polite to her even if she didn't know enough to pick up a wet towel from the bathroom floor. But Mick had no respect for money, which was obvious by the way she'd thrown out an expensive costume rather than go to the trouble to have it cleaned. Such waste was something that Iona couldn't abide, but this wasn't her house and it wasn't her place to say anything.

Iona shook her head at the ways of the world, and put the costume back in the garbage.

"What are you doing here?" Mick sat beside Lee at the library table and put her books down in front of her. "Quinn told me you were in here for detention. What gives?"

"Talking in class," Lee said. She kept her voice low to avoid further trouble, and leaned close to Mick.

"Everyone talks in class," Mick said. "Is that all you did?"

"Yeah."

"Let me guess—Mrs. Pidbuhl."

"How did you ever figure it out?"

Mick frowned and looked around the library, where about a dozen students were studying or talking softly among themselves. Most were here for the same after-school detention as Lee. "How long did you get?" she asked.

"Three days." Lee propped her chin on one fist and let her shoulders sag. "It's not so bad, really. Three days isn't much, and it gives me a little extra time to work. I'll need to really push it these next few weeks if I want to raise my grade point average by the end of the semester."

Mick knew that Lee had gotten an expected but still devastating "D-plus" in English Comp for the first quarter.

Mrs. Shipley, the librarian, approached the table before either girl saw her. "Mick, are you supposed to be here?" she asked, not unkindly.

"Not exactly," Mick admitted. "I just wanted to talk to Lee for a minute."

"Well, keep it short, all right? This is supposed to be detention. I can't let it turn into a social hour."

"Okay. Thanks," Mick said as Mrs. Shipley walked away. She turned back to Lee. "Let's do something together this weekend. Quinn, too. Do you know how long it's been since the three of us went out together?"

"I don't know," Lee said. There was a piece of paper on the table in front of her, and she began to shred it into tiny squares. "My mom said something about stripping the wax off the kitchen floor, and I know she'll want me to help. I can't get out of it because she's kind of mad at me anyway, and—"

"Okay, okay," Mick said, leaning back in her seat. "Maybe some other time—"

"Forget it. It's not that big a deal."

Lee had run out of paper to shred. She chewed on a fingernail, and tried not to feel like pond scum. The job her mother wanted her to help with this weekend would take only a couple of hours. There was no real reason for her to reject Mick's suggestion, except that she didn't *want* to go out with Mick.

That didn't, however, mean she had to be cruel about it. "What's that you're wearing?" she asked. "You look almost like your old self again."

Dressed in jeans and a plain pink sweater, Mick looked considerably less exotic than she had for the past couple of months. She'd put away the loose skirts and peasant blouses after Halloween. Since the night of the dance she'd been struggling with herself, trying to recapture some of the innocence she'd lost these past months.

She wasn't sure why she wanted to go back to the old, simpler ways. Something had happened to her, something that had frightened her enough to make her question the path her life was taking.

The problem was, she still wasn't sure what she really wanted. At first she'd enjoyed the feeling of power the cards had given her—and she believed, with all her heart, that the cards were at the center of all this—but then she'd begun to feel that she was no longer in control. She'd gotten on a roller coaster without even realizing it, and now she was on an up and down ride without a seat belt. She had to hang on tight or fall off, but the ride wouldn't stop.

Although she'd put the cards away for the time being, they were rarely out of Mick's thoughts. Fear had driven her to put them between the mattresses on her bed, far enough back so that she was sure no one would stumble across them accidentally. She'd decided she would keep them there for now, rather than carry them around with her all the time, so that she could think and decide what she wanted to do with them.

Realizing Lee was watching her and waiting for some response, Mick struck a pose. "This is my new look. What do you think?"

"It's an improvement."

"I thought you'd like it. Hey, if we can't get together this weekend, maybe some time next week will work out. Or maybe we can study together."

"Yeah, maybe," Lee said, without committing herself to anything. "I'll be doing a lot of that in the future."

"You don't have to put up with Mrs. Pidbuhl, you know," Mick said.

"Oh, no?"

"No." Again Mick found her thoughts drawn to the tarot cards hidden between her mattresses. They were like a toothache, always there no matter what she did to try to forget.

"I don't know what you think I can do about it, Mick," Lee said. "It could be worse."

"How?"

"I could be a freshman. I could have three more years of this to look forward to. I consider myself lucky that I didn't get the Pit Bull for a class until my senior year. At least this way I know it will be over within about six months."

"What about college? You were counting on a scholarship."

Lee winced at this reminder, and Mick was immediately sorry she'd brought it up.

But she couldn't stop herself from saying, "There *is* something that can be done."

Inside the Montagna house an hour later, Mick felt better, safer. She moved around from room to room, touching the dusty furniture with her fingers but being careful not to brush up against anything that would dirty her clothes.

Late afternoon light filtered weakly through windows that were filthy from years of neglect, but enough so that she didn't have to light any candles yet. She was coming here more and more, first drawn by a simple curiosity that had quickly become an obsession. Besides the feeling that this house was somehow important to her, Mick had a sense of belonging when she roamed the rooms.

And she didn't feel one bit guilty about taking things out of the house, even though she hadn't wanted Danny to. At first it had been only the small mirror she'd hung on her bedroom wall, but since then she'd added a couple of candlesticks, a small porcelain statue, and other items that she could carry easily.

She liked the way they looked in her bedroom, and was strangely comforted having them around.

She didn't have much time today. She was expected home for supper because her parents were having company, and she knew she'd better show up on time.

Fran and Brady's tolerance had been stretched almost to the breaking point, and she didn't want to attract any more unwanted attention to herself. She didn't want anyone watching her too closely now, not when she was so close to finding what she needed.

Taking the diary from the desk, Mick opened it to the pages she had marked, about a quarter of the way into the book.

There's a wall up around my house. No one can see it but me, but it's there. I can't get out. When I try, I get sick and I sweat and shake. It doesn't matter. I'm safer here anyway and I have plenty of company . . .

195

Mick turned the page slowly. Rosalie didn't bother with dates in her diary. Only an occasional reference to the weather gave Mick a hint as to the seasons, but for all she knew this entry could have been written twenty years ago or last month. There were too many gaps in her own knowledge, and Rosalie wasn't doing much to help.

> . . . *I've started having my groceries delivered to the house i can't go shopping any more. i tip big, and that helps. At first the boy was afraid of me but he's not so afraid any more. i see him watching me when he thinks i don't know. He's very young . . .*

"What were you up to, Rosalie?" Mick whispered, the sound of her own voice filling the room.

The time was going too quickly, and she wasn't making much progress in the book. Shimmering knowledge was just out of her reach, and every time she tried to grab it, she was perplexed by the limitations everyday life placed on her.

Impatience plagued Mick like a spider crawling down her spine. She flipped through the pages of the diary, sorry to miss the chapters of Rosalie's increasingly distorted views, but forced to skim if she were to cover any real territory this day. She told herself she could always go back and read more thoroughly later.

As the shadows in the house deepened, Mick felt the sharp edge of uneasiness she always felt this time of day. A floorboard somewhere creaked. A curtain rustled in a room without wind. Mick kept her unprotected back to a wall, and her eyes darted from corner to open doorway.

The feeling always passed. As she grew accustomed to the house — or as it grew accustomed to her — she was enveloped in a sense of acceptance. A soft voice whispered encouragement in her ear, and Mick continued to read further into the book.

Here she made her biggest discovery yet, the one she'd been waiting for.

> . . . *they stole my precious cards. I'd kill them if i could. Those cards have been in my family for two hundred years passed down from mother to daughter and now they're gone in one careless nite. i don't know the girls who were here and the wall outside my house kept me from going after them. When it was all over I looked for something they'd left behind. not a button or a single strand of hair remained for me to . . . if i'd found anything i would have destroyed them happily, but they weren't here long enough. i could have caused them to wither and die slowly or quickly if i'd felt merci . . . what will Tia Celestine say when i tell her, she was always jealous that the cards were mine but she has treasures of her own. i have nothing but this prison of a house . . .*

After that Rosalie's words fell into an incoherent rambling, and Mick lowered the book to her lap to rest her eyes.

Her mother had to have been one of the girls who'd stolen Rosalie's book, but Mick had no way of knowing how old Fran had been at the time, or why'd she'd come to the house in the first place.

Even with Rosalie's account of what had happened, there were still too many blank places that needed to be filled.

Obviously Fran had never known about the power in the cards, which might have been for the best. The cards might have punished her as a thief if she'd ever tried to use them. There was no longer any doubt in Mick's mind that Rosalie's tarot cards offered a dark gift, but only to the right person.

She wished she could ask Rosalie for the instruction she needed. Instead, she was forced to go along blindly, learning by hit-or-miss what could and couldn't be done.

She became aware of the time again, and reluctantly put down the diary. She would have to look through it more another time. For now she had to get home.

Something kept her from taking the diary with her, even though she knew that would be the sensible thing to do. It belonged here, in this house, much more so than the knick-knacks that Rosalie probably hadn't cared much about. She would have to come back to read the diary, but Mick knew she wouldn't wait long. She was eager to travel down this road to discovery.

Brushing the seat of her jeans as she hurried down the stairs, Mick moved through the rooms as easily as if she'd spent her life here, past the big fireplace, through the kitchen and out the back door. She hated to leave, but couldn't waste any more time. She'd stayed too long already and would have to hurry if she were to get home in time to shower and change.

The route home took her within a block of Lee's house, and as she drove past the street that the Sternhagen house was on, she glanced down that way. Parked in front of Lee's house was Quinn's new used car, the one Elaine had bought for her when they'd gotten back from vacation.

Mick was tempted to turn around and go back to Lee's house, to stop in and surprise them, but she couldn't.

It wasn't just that she had to get home. It was something more than that. Since they were kids she and Lee and Quinn had been almost like one person, doing everything together and sharing all the secrets they'd once considered so important.

Those days were gone. Things had changed too much for her to recapture the past. *She* had changed too much. It saddened her to think that way, but she knew it was true nonetheless.

The last time she'd tried to talk to either of them about anything meaningful was when she'd told Quinn about her trips to the house. Quinn hadn't even wanted to listen. After that, if Mick so much as mentioned the Montagna house, Quinn would turn around and walk away from her, her retreating back a slap in Mick's face.

Mick was almost to her own house when she reached up and wiped away a tear with the back of her hand. Another followed, then another.

She was crying not only for her own lost innocence, but for the fact that she felt her life was somehow careening out of control, and she had no idea how to check the deadly progress.

* * *

"When was the last time you were in Mick's house?" Quinn asked.

Lee shrugged. "I don't know. Before Halloween, at least."

"I haven't been there since I stopped in the day before my mom and I left on vacation, and even then I didn't see Mick. I just talked to Mrs. McGee for a few minutes, then left."

"What's your point?" Lee asked.

Quinn, sitting on the floor beside Lee's bed, and with a pillow across her lap, looked up at the ceiling. "My *point* is that we used to spend practically half our lives at Mick's house. Doing our homework, listening to the jukebox or just hanging around the pool. Now it's like we've been shut out."

Lee was sitting on the edge of her bed, with her legs hanging over the side and her bare toes worrying the carpet in front of Quinn. Quinn had been in the school parking lot waiting for her when she'd finally been sprung from detention, and it was Quinn who had suggested they come to Lee's house to talk.

She should have known the talk would revolve around Mick and The Big Change in Her Lately. It seemed like every conversation ended up on that subject, even if it didn't always start out that way.

"I don't know what you think we can do about it," Lee said when she realized Quinn was still looking at her. "So we haven't been to her house much lately. So what? We still see her in school."

"Fifteen minutes here, a half an hour there — that's nothing compared to the time we all used to spend together."

"She came into the library after school today to see me."

"She did?"

"Yeah. I was going to tell you, but I forgot. She suggested that we all do something together this weekend. It was her idea, so she's not avoiding us, if that's what you're thinking. I had to tell her I can't."

Quinn smoothed the fabric of the pillowcase with the palms of her hands, her brows drawn together in a frown. "I wonder why she doesn't have plans with Danny this weekend," she said.

"We've both known all along that wasn't the smoothest relationship in the world," Lee said. "Maybe she finally gave him the brush-off. Remember how mad she was that night he showed up at the lake?"

"Yeah." Quinn smiled and looked relieved. "Now that I think about it, I haven't heard her mention anything about Danny in at least a couple of weeks. Have you?"

"Not a word." Lee got up from her bed and went to her bedroom door, opened it and listened, then closed it again. "I thought I heard something, but I guess not. My mom will be getting home pretty soon, and she'll want me to help with supper. She tells me I can't cook anything without ruining it, but she expects me to keep trying. When I move out, I'm going to eat all my meals in restaurants; that way I won't have to worry about poisoning myself or catching the building on fire."

"You make good popcorn."

"A person can't eat popcorn three times a day."

"I could."

Lee giggled. "Yeah, you probably could. Remember that time we made that huge bag of it and ate it all in Mick's bedroom? I couldn't *look* at popcorn for a month afterwards." She frowned, realizing Mick had again been brought into the conversation, and this time it was her own doing. It was just that it was almost impossible to talk about anything from the past without including Mick.

"Has Mick said anything more to you about those cards of hers?" Quinn asked, going for the opening Lee had provided.

"Not much. Just the usual garbage."

Quinn nodded. "But there's more to it now. She called me a couple of nights ago, and after we'd talked for a few minutes she brought up the subject of the cards." Quinn's eyes darkened at the memory. "She wasn't making much sense, but she—she started to cry, I think. She was sniffling, and her voice sounded funny, but when I asked her she denied it. I think she really wanted to tell me something, Lee, but the way she sounded scared me, and I kept changing the subject. Then she gave up and hung up on me. It's been bothering me ever since."

Lee pulled her shoulders up in a familiar gesture of withdrawal. "It doesn't concern us."

"We can't just write her off. Mick is still our friend."

"I know." Lee sighed deeply and looked away. "But lately she makes me very nervous."

Chapter Sixteen

"Where is he?"

Mick turned away from her car door and saw Emma standing much too close. She could feel Emma's breath on her face, and could see the angry frustration in the other girl's eyes. Turning back to her car, Mick tried to open the door, but Emma reached out and pulled her hand roughly away.

"Where *is* he?" Emma repeated. "Where is Danny? No one's seen him in at least three weeks. You know something about it."

"He's probably gone into hiding from you," Mick said. She was backed up against her car now as Emma pressed closer, and she felt at a distinct disadvantage. Usually Emma didn't frighten her, but this time she sensed that Emma's anger had gone beyond the rational, and might result in serious violence. Last time they'd tangled it had resulted in some mutual slapping and hair pulling, but without much real force behind the blows. This time it would be different, and Mick didn't feel up to a fight. Besides, she was having trouble even looking Emma in the eye, so how could she defend herself? "He's probably tired of having you follow him around all the time and is avoiding you," she added, but there wasn't much strength behind her words.

"Nobody's seen him," Emma hissed. As though sensing her advantage, she pressed closer. "He hasn't

shown up at work. His family is worried. His parents went to his apartment, and all his things are still there. His rent is overdue, and the landlord was going to put an eviction notice on the door, but his father paid another month's rent in case he comes back. Something's happened to him." Emma's voice crackled with emotion.

"I don't know anything about it," Mick said.

"You were the last person anyone saw him with."

"That doesn't mean anything."

"His parents have gone to the police."

"The police?" Mick couldn't keep her fear from showing. With her hand behind her, she groped for the door handle and finally managed to get it pulled up and out.

"I haven't talked to them yet, but I'm going to," Emma added. "I'm going to tell them *you* did something to Danny."

"That's crazy." Mick got the car door opened and tried to squeeze in, but Emma was blocking her way.

"Everyone is talking about you. I'm not the only one who thinks you had something to do with Danny disappearing so suddenly."

"It's just talk. It doesn't mean anything."

"I'll find out. Somehow I'll find out what you did to him."

"Leave me alone," Mick said.

"You're not going to get away with this!"

Mick reached out and shoved Emma with all her force. Caught off guard, Emma stumbled backwards, and Mick used the opportunity to get inside her car and punch down the lock button before Emma could pull the door open.

She got the key in the ignition as Emma began pounding on the window with her fists.

Mick put her foot down on the gas pedal with all her strength, so that the car lurched forward, and Emma was left behind in the school parking lot, her arms raised in the air as she shouted and waved her fists.

The car had traveled less than one hundred yards when Mick spotted Lee, walking with an armful of books. She hit the brakes and leaned over to open the passenger side door. "Get in," she called out.

Lee looked up and saw Mick. She didn't want to get in the car. Mick looked wild-eyed and out of breath, but Lee could think of no good reason to refuse. Reluctantly, she approached the car and got in.

As she drove away from the school, Mick chattered nervously, holding the steering wheel tightly. She didn't tell Lee about the incident with Emma; instead she talked about school, the upcoming Christmas holidays, anything she could think of to keep her mind from going back in the direction of Emma's accusations.

She realized that Lee was eyeing her warily, pressed up against the car door, and Mick forced herself to keep silent until she felt in control again. Once her near-hysteria was in check, she tried to smile. It was shaky and less than completely convincing, but it *was* a smile, and at least Lee no longer looked like she wanted to jump out of the car.

. . . *Emma* . . .

. . . *Danny* . . .

. . . *What could the police really do?* . . .

"Sorry," Mick said as she touched the brakes and slowed down for a car ahead that was signaling to turn right. "It's been one of those days."

"Yeah," Lee agreed. "I've had a few of those myself lately. Hey, you missed my corner."

"I thought maybe you'd come to my house for a little while. I could use the company."

. . . Danny's face, his mouth open but no sound reaching her ears. His fists beating on glass . . .

"I have a ton of homework," Lee began.

"That's okay. I have some, too. We can study together. Just like old times." Mick didn't want to beg, but she was ready to stoop to that if it became necessary. She didn't want to be alone.

. . . Danny's eyes full of panic. His eyes haunting her sleep . . .

"Just for a little while," Lee said, and Mick sighed with relief.

Thank God.

They had the house to themselves when they got there. It was Iona's half-day, and Fran, who didn't like putting things off until the last minute, was Christmas shopping. The girls settled at the kitchen table with their books, and Mick poured two tall glasses of diet cola.

"The ice machine in the refrigerator went on strike a couple of day ago," Mick explained as she set a glass down in front of Lee. "But the pop's cold, so it should be okay."

"It's fine, thanks," Lee said.

"They were supposed to get it fixed this morning, but it looks like the repairman didn't show up. Or maybe they decided to just buy a whole new refrigerator."

"The pop is fine just like this."

"I swear, things are falling apart around here. Last week the washing machine overflowed all over the laundry room, and you should have heard Iona." Mick paced around the kitchen as she talked, her own glass in her hand. She was full of nervous energy, unable to relax.

"That stuff happens," Lee said, her eyes following Mick's every move.

"But why does it happen all at the same time?"

"I don't know."

"My dad is talking about moving down to San Diego, did you know that?"

It took Lee a moment to adjust to this sudden shift in conversation. When she realized what Mick had said, she asked, "Alone?"

"What? Oh, no, it's nothing like that." Mick looked down at the glass in her hand. "No, it's just that he thinks he's gone as far as he can in Xavier, and he wants to move his law practice to the city. I don't really care. By the time he got anything like that organized, I'd be out of school anyway."

The mention of school reminded Lee of something she'd heard just that day. "Have you seen Danny lately?" she asked. "I heard a couple of people talking during lunch today, and they said he's vanished right off the face of the earth and—"

The glass in Mick's hand shattered. Cola splattered the front of her blouse, and broken pieces of glass landed on the kitchen floor with a delicate tinkling sound.

Lee gasped and jumped to her feet. "Mick, are you all right?" She went quickly to Mick and saw that the palm of her right hand was cut. "Oh, my

God, you're bleeding." She pushed Mick toward the sink, turned on the cold water, and held the hand under running water.

"Why did you say that?" Mick asked, ignoring the blood that swirled with the water at the bottom of the sink.

"I don't think you're going to need stitches, but we'd better make sure there's no glass still in there."

"Why did you say that about Danny?" Mick persisted. "Have you been listening to Emma?"

"Is there a first aid kit in your bathroom? I think I can bandage this myself, and it'll be okay, but you'd better show it to your mother when she gets home. She might want a doctor to look at it."

Mick jerked her wrist out of Lee's hand so suddenly that they both stumbled, their shoes crunching on broken glass. "I thought you were my friend!" she cried.

Her mouth hanging open in surprise, Lee could only stare at Mick, who seemed to have lost her mind.

They stood beside the kitchen sink, one bleeding and angry, the other too astonished to speak, and stared at each other until they both heard the front door slam.

"That's my mother," Mick said, grabbing a handful of paper towels. "I don't want her to see this—she'll probably want to rush me to the hospital or something, and I don't need that."

"It might not be such a bad idea," Lee tried to say, but Mick was already mopping up the floor and wasn't listening.

"Get the bigger pieces of glass and throw them in the garbage," Mick ordered. "Hurry!"

Not knowing what else to do, Lee obeyed. They could hear Fran moving around in the other rooms. Mick's agitation prompted Lee to move as quickly as she could to hide the evidence of the accident. Within a matter of a few moments the mess was cleaned up, and Mick pulled a clean dishtowel from a drawer and held it into the palm of her right hand to staunch the flow of blood.

"Let's go to my room," Mick whispered.

They were halfway there when Fran called, "Mick, is that you?"

"Yes," Mick hollered. "Lee's with me; we're going to my room."

Fran's voice again drifted toward them. "Hello, Lee."

"Hi, Mrs. McGee."

"Would you girls like any—"

"We don't need anything. Thanks anyway, Mom." Mick pushed Lee ahead of her through the bedroom door.

Fran heard Mick's bedroom door close just as she reached the kitchen. It was just as well, because she'd brought Christmas presents home with her, and she wanted to do a good job of hiding them.

Even as she thought this, Fran knew how unnecessary it really was. When Mick was little, they'd practically had to put her gifts under lock and key to keep her from finding them and peeking. Mick had outgrown that youthful temptation years ago. But it was a tradition, the hiding of presents, and Fran clung to tradition. Besides, it was fun.

In the kitchen she found Lee's still full glass of

209

pop on the table, and she put it into the sink, no-
ticing as she did so that the soles of her shoes were
sticking to the floor. Bending down, Fran touched
the tiles with her fingertips to find more stickiness
and several small shards of glass.

She mopped up the floor, shaking her head all
the while at the carelessness of teenagers.

"I want you to do something for me," Mick told
Lee after she felt sure Fran wasn't going to come
snooping.

"What?" Lee asked.

"Let me read the tarot cards for you."

"Oh, Mick. I've already told you I don't like that
stuff—"

"Just this once. What can it hurt?"

"I don't know, but I'm not sure I want to find
out. Besides, how can you even do it with your
hand all cut up?"

Mick bent her head low as she pulled the dishtowel away from her palm to check out the damage.
It wasn't as bad as she'd thought at first. There
were three cuts, all less than an inch in length, but
the bleeding had stopped, and now it was possible
to see that the cuts were not terribly deep.

Mick showed the hand to Lee.

Lips pursed together and eyebrows forming a "V"
of concentration, Lee examined Mick's hand. "Okay,
it's not too bad," she admitted. "But I still think you
should bandage it up. To keep it clean."

"If I go into the bathroom right now and take
care of it, will you let me read the cards for you?"

Lee hesitated, and it was enough for Mick to

pounce.

"I'll be back in a minute. You won't regret this, Lee."

"I already regret it!" Lee called out as Mick disappeared through the bedroom door.

True to her word, Mick was back in no time with a big square bandage taped to her palm. She sat down in the middle of the floor and indicated that Lee was to do the same.

Only this morning she'd taken the deck from its hiding place and returned it to her purse. Now she took the box out of her purse and opened it.

Shuffling the cards was a slow process, but she managed it, then passed the deck to Lee.

"What do I do now?" Lee asked.

"Shuffle them, and think about something."

"Like what?"

"Anything to do with your life. What's been on your mind a lot lately?"

"You know the answer to that one—the Pit Bull. Will I even get a passing grade in her class this semester?" Lee had begun shuffling the cards slowly, handling them as though she found their very touch distasteful. "You know, I tried talking to Mr. Trepanier about her, but all he could do for me was give me this big lecture about how in the future I'll run into plenty of people in positions of authority who I might not like, and how it's important to learn to get along. Then he looked at his watch and said if there was anything else he could do to help to be sure and stop in and see him again. Some help."

Mick reached out and took the cards from Lee. "That's probably enough," she said. "Now, let's see what we can see."

"I don't like this; why did I let you talk—"

"Sh-h-h-h!"

Mick spread the cards out slowly, hindered by the bandaged hand. Soon, though, she had eleven cards placed on the carpet between them, and she leaned forward to search for a meaning there.

"What do you see?" Lee whispered. Despite herself she was getting caught up in this mysterious process.

"Not that much, really," Mick admitted. She sat back, not very disappointed. She was only putting down a foundation on which she could later build. "The Page of Cups means a time of study and passing exams. That would coincide with your concerns about school. This one here"—she pointed one finger at a card—"is the Queen of Swords. That could be a tough, uncompromising woman."

"Mrs. Pidbuhl, she's tough all right," Lee said.

"The Seven of Staves means problems that need to be sorted out, and the Temperence card indicates that you've been overdoing and need a break from pressures."

"I didn't need your cards to tell me all that," Lee said. She reached a hand up to rub the back of her neck, rotating her head to loosen the tight muscles.

She got to her feet, but Mick remained seated, her attention still on the cards.

"I've got to go now," Lee said. She stopped at the bedroom door to look back at Mick. "I'll walk home. It's not that far. Mick, are you all right?"

Mick looked up, her expression distant.

"Are you okay?" Lee repeated.

"Yeah, sure. I'm just thinking."

"Don't hurt yourself." Lee smiled, but the joke

212

was lost on Mick.

"Hm?"

"Forget it. I'll see you tomorrow."

After Lee had gone, Mick continued to contemplate the cards. She reached out to gather them up, but stopped before her hands actually reached the cards.

She knew she should put them back in the box now. That would be the smart thing to do, and a part of her wanted to do just that.

But another part, the part that was intoxicated with this feeling of barely-harnessed energy that came whenever she handled the cards, wanted to go on, to test that energy to the very limit.

Handling the remainder of the deck slowly, almost lovingly, Mick thumbed through the cards without knowing exactly what it was she was seeking.

When her eyes fell on the Hanged Man, she knew this was the one.

Edwina Pidbuhl opened the front door of her house and immediately stepped on her husband's discarded sweater. She bent over to pick it up, long ago resigned to this annoying habit he had of dropping his clothes when he took them off.

"That you, Ed?" Charlie's voice called to her from the other room.

"It's me," she answered, opening the closet door. She pulled out a hanger and draped the sweater over it.

"What are you doing?"

"Hanging up your sweater." She closed the closet

door.

"Oh — sorry."

"Sure." Wearily she climbed the stairs to her bedroom without going to see what her husband was doing. She already knew. He was parked in front of the TV in the den, with his feet up on the ottoman. It was where he would stay until she called him to supper, and where he would go when he was finished eating.

The house was too big for them. Every step she climbed reminded her of this fact. At the top of the banister was a large wooden ball the size of her fist, and she paused there for a moment and leaned on it to rest. Twenty years ago this house hadn't seemed so large, but they'd been younger then, and it hadn't seemed to matter.

In her bedroom Edwina slipped out of her high heels and eased her tired feet into a pair of comfortable old slippers. That was such a relief that she already felt slightly better.

After putting her shoes away in the closet, she turned and smacked, for the hundredth time, into the macrame plant hanger that hung from the ceiling in front of the window.

Mick took the Hanged Man and looked at it for a long time. Her hands were shaking, but she did what she'd known all along she was going to do.

She put the Hanged Man over the card that represented Mrs. Pidbuhl.

Edwina brushed the macrame hanger aside with

an air of annoyance. The plant in the clay pot was dead; it didn't get enough light from this northern window.

She looked at the dry and withered plant in the center of the knotted macrame, and thought that the plant looked like she felt inside.

Angrily, she yanked at the macrame until it came loose from the hook in the ceiling, and the heavy brown twine fell around her. She caught it loosely in her arms, determined to throw the whole works out. The plant was dead, and she wasn't going to replace it. Why bother, when the next one would only die as surely as her own expectations.

Mick had broken out in a sweat, and she rubbed the palms of her hands on her jeans. The cards before her seemed to waver and swim as her vision blurred.

It was too hot in the bedroom. She would have opened a window, but all strength had left her limbs. She felt as insubstantial as a rag doll and would have fallen over on her side if the pull of the cards hadn't held her up. It was as though everything inside her was concentrated on this moment.

Her heart rabbitted in her chest, and she sucked in ragged gulps of air. Bile burned the back of her throat. Instead of feeling detached from the cards, as she had in the past, Mick had become one with them.

The macrame hanger was like a snake in Edwina Pidbuhl's arms. She would just get one end gathered up when another end would slither out of her grasp. The clay pot dug into her skin, and the dead leaves on the plant crumbled so that dust tickled her nose.

She noticed it was too hot as she left the bedroom with her burden. She was sweating even though it wasn't really warm in the house. The walls of the hallway undulated as perspiration trickled into her eyes, and she wondered briefly if this was a hot flash more severe than any she'd ever known, or if she were coming down with something.

"What are you doing up there?" Charlie's voice drifted up to her as though from a great distance. "Ed?"

She looked down and realized the pot had escaped from the tangle of macrame, and the pieces of broken clay littered the floor at the top of the stairs. When had that happened? She didn't remember dropping it, hadn't heard it shatter.

She tossed one end of the hanger over her shoulder and reached a hand out for the banister. If she could only get downstairs to Charlie, he would know what to do.

Edwina's foot came down on one of the larger pieces of the broken pot, and she felt herself going sideways. Thrown off balance, her hip hit the banister hard, so that she was propelled over it.

Her hands groped for something solid to hold onto, but there was only open air around her. Vaguely she felt the long, knotted length of macrame burn her neck as it tightened so suddenly that she didn't even have time to gasp.

Her feet kicked out wildly, hitting nothing, one slipper falling off and sailing through the air. Her head felt as though it were going to burst. The weight of her body tried to pull her in two, and her vision purpled. Her fingers clawed at her neck, digging into the skin, drawing blood.

Then her hands fell to her sides.

The last sound she heard was Charlie's voice, so small that it seemed to be traveling through a long, long tunnel: "Edwina, would you stop fooling around up there and see about my sup—"

Mick fell back with such force that it was as though she'd been shoved, and she hit the back of her head on the base of her bed.

Stars danced before her eyes as she pulled at her throat, fighting with whatever was there cutting off her oxygen. Her fingers met only smooth skin, but still she couldn't take in air.

She was on the verge of blacking out when she rolled from the bed and landed on the floor, and suddenly she could breathe again.

For several long minutes she lay with her face pressed to the carpet, its rough texture against her cheek. Her throat hurt, and her hands and feet tingled as though she'd gone without oxygen for much longer than the few seconds the experience had actually lasted. Finally she was able to get up, but she had to move slowly, testing her body for signs of further rebellion.

The horror stayed with her for a long time, and an hour later, when Fran came to the bedroom door and told her it was time for supper, Mick was under the blankets in her bed, still pale and shaken, and she begged off, claiming a headache.

Fran went to her and hovered over Mick, looking concerned. "Is it bad?" she asked, "Do you want an aspirin?"

Mick scrunched under the covers, her hands hidden so her mother wouldn't see how they trembled. "No," she rasped. "I think it'll get better if I get some sleep." She closed her eyes again and didn't open them until she heard her mother leave the room. Then she opened them and sighed.

Her mind kept going back to what had happened to her, even though she tried to block it out.

What had she done? She knew something had happened, not just to her, but to Mrs. Pidbuhl, and suddenly she wished more than anything else in the world that she could take back the last hour or so, that she could erase it all and start over again.

Tomorrow she would have to go to school, and then she would find out what she'd done. Maybe Mrs. Pidbuhl would be sitting there behind her desk, looking sour as usual but unhurt.

Mick clung to that hope, but sleep was still a long time coming.

When it did, Danny Santos, his hair plastered to his head and his clothes dripping, pointed an accusing finger at her. When he grinned at her, his face changed to Edwina Pidbuhl's.

Mick woke screaming.

Chapter Seventeen

Quinn had barely reached the front steps of the school when Addie Briscoe greeted her with the news.

"Quinn, have you heard about Mrs. Pidbuhl?" Addie asked breathlessly. Her eyes were wide, and she looked as though she didn't know whether to look excited or saddened by what she had to tell.

Holding her school books under one arm, Quinn stopped on the bottom step and knew that she didn't want to hear whatever Addie was going to tell her. So much had happened that was bad lately that she didn't know how much more she could take. All she wanted was to get through this school year with a minimum of difficulty, so she could go off to some nice, safe college where her biggest problem would be getting to her classes.

She thought of just hurrying past Addie, but she knew that wouldn't do any good. Someone else would tell her; people loved to spread bad news.

"Mrs. Pidbuhl died last night," Addie told her before she could ask.

Quinn dropped her books. They hit the concrete steps with a loud sound that echoed around in Quinn's head as though they'd slapped her instead of the steps. "What?" she breathed. This was so much worse than anything she could have imagined.

Addie nodded, then stooped to help Quinn pick up the books. "Last night in her home," she added, a little puzzled by Quinn's extreme reaction. "Some kind of accident, but I haven't really heard all the details. My mother heard it on the TV this morning, and everyone is talking about it."

"Are you sure?" was all Quinn could ask.

"Positive. Do you think they'll cancel school for the day? I wouldn't mind missing a day of school." As soon as she'd said these words, Addie, looked sorry. "Geez, that was really tacky of me, wasn't it? I didn't mean it that way. I'm not glad she's dead or anything. I wasn't crazy about the Pit—I mean Mrs. Pidbuhl, but she never did me any harm."

Once she had her books picked up, Quinn climbed up the steps slowly, leaving Addie behind. She had to find Lee and Mick.

Instead, Lee found her, almost as soon as she entered the school. Lee looked as though she'd seen a ghost, and as soon as she reached Quinn's side she knew that her friend had already heard.

"Where's Mick?" Lee asked.

Quinn walked to her locker and dumped her books inside. "I don't know. I haven't seen her yet."

"I hope she stays home today," Lee said.

Turning to look at her, Quinn asked, "Why?"

"I don't know. But I'm afraid."

"Why?" Quinn asked again.

Lee ran a hand through her hair. "I don't know," she repeated. Tears filled her eyes as they darted from one end of the hall to the other. "Mick had something to do with this."

"Oh, no. That's not possible. What have you heard?"

"Not much, just that Mrs. Pidbuhl had an accident last night and she's dead," said Lee.

"Then it was just that—an accident. Mick didn't do anything. She couldn't."

"Couldn't?" Lee asked. "Or wouldn't?"

"What's the difference? Both."

Lee leaned against the lockers, and the tears that had filled her eyes now overflowed and ran down her cheeks. "Four months ago I wouldn't have believed it, but something is going on with Mick. She's different. You know that, Quinn; we've talked about it."

"Yes, but she's not capable of violence."

"I'm not so sure. You remember what she said about your father."

"Lee, Mick was just talking crazy. Don't you start talking crazy on me now, too."

A boy they both knew stopped on his way past and said, "Hey, did you hear what happened to—"

"Yes, we heard," Quinn snapped, sending the boy on his way. She turned back to Lee. "Please, Lee. Whatever is going on with Mick right now, she needs us. If you start thinking like this, it'll only make things worse for her. Don't start thinking she's the bogeyman."

Lee frowned and wiped at her cheeks with the tail of her shirt. "Maybe you're right."

"Of course I am. I'm going to go find Mick right now. Are you coming with me?"

"Yeah," Lee sighed. "I'm sorry I went off the deep end for a minute there."

"That's okay," Quinn said. "Just don't let it happen again." To herself she kept the knowledge that outside, when Addie had first told her about Mrs. Pidbuhl, she had also experienced a brief certainty that somehow Mick was involved. She would have liked to have shared this with Lee, to unburden herself somewhat, but now she knew she had to be the strong one. If no one else was going to be the voice of sanity, then the job would fall on her shoulders.

As it turned out, they didn't get a chance to talk to Mick. Once outside the building's side door, they spotted Mick in the school's parking lot, standing beside her car. Addie had apparently beaten them to the punch and was talking to Mick.

Even from that distance they could see the look of horror that came over Mick's face as she listened to Addie. Then Mick turned and got back inside her car. She left Addie behind in a shower of small rocks and dust as her car raced out of the parking lot and into the street without stopping for on-coming traffic. A blue station wagon hit its brakes just in time, cursing Mick with a shrill blast of its horn.

Quinn and Lee looked at each other. "Now what?" Lee asked.

"Now we go to our classes," Quinn told her. "I don't see what else we can do. Maybe she'll come back in a little while. If not, I'll go to her house later and talk to her."

"She's not going to come back today. Did you see the look on her—"

"Yeah, I did," Quinn said. "Don't go making a big deal out of it. She was just as surprised by Mrs. Pidbuhl's death as we were, and it hit her wrong, that's all. I wish we'd had a chance to tell her about it ourselves, though."

The first bell rang inside the building, telling them that they had to get inside. Neither enjoyed the prospect of spending a full day listening to a rehashing of the latest tragedy, but they didn't see that they had any choice.

After barely missing a collision with the blue station wagon, Mick headed west, out of town. She drove without thought of what she was doing, driven only by a need to put some distance between herself and the nightmare that had become her life.

She didn't stop until almost an hour later, when the ocean, an insurmountable barrier, forced her to park her car and get out. She walked along a sandy beach that looked vaguely familiar, sand getting inside her shoes until she reached down and took them off.

Dressed in her school clothes of faded jeans and a sweatshirt, she collapsed on the continent's edge, ignoring the wet sand that soaked through the seat of her jeans. Mick sat there for a long time, looking out at the turbulent water, wishing she had the courage to walk in and keep going until the ocean covered her head and sucked her into itself, maybe never to be found.

But that was no way out. Her despair wasn't so deep yet that she could do such a thing, no matter how much she wished it.

There were a few strollers along the beach, but no one approached Mick. There was something forbidding about her, so deeply lonely that even those who preyed the beaches looking for such lost souls as herself stayed clear.

There was no doubt in her mind now that she had caused Mrs. Pidbuhl's death. The only question now was, could she live with it? Could she live with herself after what she'd done?

The sun was straight overhead when Mick got up and tried to brush off her jeans. She couldn't go home yet. It wasn't that she feared her mother would question her being home in the middle of the day. It was because she was no longer sure where her home was.

Getting back in her car, Mick drove slowly and carefully this time, back to Xavier, knowing that there was really only one place where she could go and not have to dodge the curious faces and questioning eyes that seemed to follow her everywhere.

The old Montagna house was her only place of peace.

When she parked her car in front of the house some time later and looked up at the decrepit building, some of her despair washed away. She went inside and immediately felt stronger and more capable of thinking through the events of the past twenty-four hours.

Mick went straight upstairs this time and got out Rosalie's diary. Reading it gave her a feeling of peace, as though she were having a conversation with an old friend. The words themselves weren't soothing. Rosalie had obviously been a woman of disturbed thoughts, but her thoughts seemed to reflect Mick's own and dissipate some of her loneliness.

She sat crossed-legged on the floor for a long time, letting the scrawled handwriting soothe her troubled conscience.

Lee opened the front door of her house and dropped her school books on the desk beside the door. Her mother's car had been parked in the driveway, so she called out, "I'm home."

She headed straight for the kitchen, starving after a day in which the cafeteria food had been almost inedible. She had just opened the refrigerator door when she heard her mother's voice coming from the other room.

"Lee, we have company. Come be sociable for a few minutes."

Great. That was just what she didn't need after today. Lee closed the refrigerator door and walked to the living room to see who it was she was going to have to put on a pleasant face for this time.

She stopped in the doorway, stunned. Bryan was sitting on the hard chair beside the couch. Kat was on the couch beside Joan Sternhagen, looking flushed and radiant as she held a small bundle in her arms.

Joan smiled at Lee. "Bryan and Kat were next door with the new baby while I was visiting with Gloria," Joan explained, "and I invited them over for a few minutes. Come see the baby, Lee." Bryan had the good grace to look embarrassed. Lee knew he had probably been against the idea of coming over here, but faced with Joan's determination he wouldn't have stood a chance.

Kat only smiled at Lee.

Lee barely had time to wonder why her mother was doing this to her when Joan gently lifted the bundle from Kat's arms and held it in her own.

"You have to see the baby, Lee," Joan gushed. "She's adorable. I'd forgotten how sweet they are." She stood and approached Lee.

Lee wanted to back away, but her legs wouldn't move. Her mother's voice and face were as smooth as glass as she carried the baby toward her, but something in Joan's eyes were hard with delight.

All the events of the day paled in comparison to

this. School had been a dismal affair, with a substitute teacher taking Mrs. Pidbuhl's place until a new teacher could be found to fill her spot, and all conversation had swirled around the sudden death. But for the first time all day Lee wasn't thinking about that as she tried to understand this torture her mother seemed determined to put her through.

She looked down and saw the red, tiny face of the infant barely peeking out of the blanket in her mother's arms. This was Bryan's baby, and although Lee no longer loved him, she had once, and the pain of loss was still too fresh for her to look upon this sign of his new life without feeling as though a knife had been thrust into her heart.

And her mother was knowingly twisting that knife.

"Isn't she precious?" Joan asked, her face arranged in a smile and her eyes watching Lee eagerly for her reaction.

"She's very small," Lee murmured.

"Do you want to hold her?"

Lee wanted to scream. "No, that's okay," she said instead. Her arms were at her sides, as frozen as her legs.

"Oh, go ahead, you can hold her for a minute" Joan held the baby out to Lee, and actually pressed the infant to her.

Given no choice, Lee lifted her arms. She held the baby and her mother stepped back, satisfied that she had done all she could to make Lee's life miserable.

The baby weighed nothing at all, and as Lee held it and looked down into the sleeping face, she felt nothing for it except a deep sadness that it had no idea what lay ahead for it. It might think it was safe and snug, but in a few years, maybe less, it would learn, as she had, that the world was a place of betrayal and pain.

Lee couldn't look at her mother. She didn't want to give her the satisfaction of seeing the anguish in her own eyes.

"What do you think of her?" Joan asked.

"She's very small."

"You said that already," Joan pointed out.

What did she want, blood? Was her mother hoping she would burst into tears in front of everyone? Lee was determined not to do that under any circumstances, and once she felt a decent interval had passed, she handed the bundle back to her mother.

"I have homework to do," Lee lied. She'd brought a couple of books home, but she didn't have anything to do that couldn't wait until later. That seemed the only way to make her escape, however, so she used the excuse and mumbled a few words to Kat and Bryan before turning away.

She didn't run out of the room, even though she wanted to. She walked out with as much dignity as she could muster, her back feeling as though three pairs of eyes were boring holes into it.

Only when she was safely out of sight did she let her shoulders sag and her head droop.

There was a knock on the front door as Lee passed it on her way to her bedroom. The sound was soft and tentative, as if whoever was there wasn't sure they really wanted anyone to answer. Lee opened the door automatically, her thoughts still on the people in the living room, and was surprised to see Mick standing there.

"Hi. Is this a bad time?" Mick asked in a small voice.

Lee had forgotten all about Mick. She didn't think about seeing Mick flee the parking lot this morning, or the endless conversations she and Quinn had had about their friend this past couple of months. All Lee thought of at that moment was that Mick would be a sympathetic ear, someone she could talk to about what had just happened inside her house. That was first and foremost in her mind, and she immediately began pouring out her heart to Mick.

"She tried to get me to go to the hospital with her to see the new baby after it was born," Lee explained after describing the incident to Mick. They were sitting side-by-side on the top step, their knees pulled up. "I think I spoiled a little of her fun then by just plain refusing to go. I don't know if this was her way of getting back at me, or if she just likes to see me suffer."

Mick, her face neutral when first listening to Lee's story, had grow stonily silent, and her eyes blazed with anger for her friend. "That was a rotten thing for her to do," she said when Lee had paused for a breath.

"I think it's a control thing with her," Lee said. "She scrubs this house like it was a hospital, instead of a place where people are supposed to live. And she treats me like one of her possessions. She has to always have the upper hand, or she's not happy. This is her way of keeping me in line."

"I don't know why you put up with her," Mick said.

Lee sighed deeply, feeling a little better for having gotten if off her chest. But then she looked—really looked—at the barely controlled fury in Mick's features, and she felt her blood turn to ice in her veins.

She jumped to her feet. "Mick, don't hurt my mother!"

Startled, Mick had also gotten to her feet, but Lee had backed up to the door.

"Lee, I only meant—"

But Lee was gone. She had gone back inside her house, slamming the door and leaving Mick alone on the porch.

Devastated, Mick ran a hand through her hair, wondering if she dared knock on the door again and try to explain to Lee that she had only been offering words of comfort. Instead, she turned and went to her car parked at the curb and got inside.

She had come to Lee's house after being at the Montagna house all afternoon because she had felt that need to touch base with reality. She'd wanted the normalcy of talking about everyday things, of being reminded that the world was not a place of creeping shadows and troubled thoughts.

But, instead of having the chance to share some of her feelings with Lee, she had again been reminded of the ever widening gap between them, and she knew now that there would be no more going back. It was time to sever all old ties, to admit to herself that she had lost something within herself that she had once treasured.

Mick started her car, and as she drove away from Lee's house, she had an odd feeling that she would never be back.

She didn't notice the rusted VW parked at the corner down the street from Lee's house, nor did she see the VW pull away from the curb and follow her.

"I probably overreacted," Lee said into the telephone a few minutes later, "but the look on her face absolutely spooked me. All I could think was that my mother would be the next person to meet with some weird accident."

Quinn, on the other end of the line, tried to reassure Lee, but she knew she wasn't doing a very good job of it. Mick hadn't been in school all day, and at first she had been relieved when Lee had called to tell her that Mick had just been at her house, but now that old gnawing worry was returning. She wasn't very good at soothing Lee's panic when she herself was afraid for Mick. "I bet I know where she was all day," she said.

"Where?" Lee asked.

"That old Montagna place she's been spending so much time at. I don't know what she sees in it, but she seems to like it there."

"Probably because it's spooky, just like her."

"Lee, don't say that."

"It's true, and you know it."

"No, I don't know it. Just because Mick is having problems, it doesn't mean you have to say things like that about her. I've been thinking of talking to her parents about it. Maybe the time has come. Will you do it with me?"

"What? Talk to Mick's parents? No way."

"Why not?" Quinn asked.

"Because I don't want to be any more involved in this than I already am. I don't think you should talk to them, either. You know how Mr. and Mrs. McGee are, Quinn. They've always thought Mick could do no wrong. You won't get anywhere with them."

Quinn chewed on her thumbnail as she thought about what Lee was saying. "I'm not so sure," she said after a minute. "As much as Mick has changed, I'm sure they've noticed something is wrong. They might even be grateful to have us bring the subject up. Please say you'll talk to them with me, Lee."

"No, Quinn, I can't. I'm afraid of Mick. I think she might really have it in her to do something to me—to us—if we interfere."

Quinn realized it was useless to try to change Lee's mind. She could hear the fear in the other girl's voice, so she knew that she had no choice but to try to handle this by herself. She wouldn't just walk away and abandon Mick, though. She had to at least try to get help for Mick, and if that meant going to Mick's parents, then she would do it.

After saying good-bye to Lee, Quinn went to her car as she tried to figure out her next move. Her first thought was that she should go to Mrs. McGee, but she quickly ruled that out. As nice as Mrs. McGee had always been to her, Quinn didn't know how useful she would be in a crisis situation.

That left Mr. McGee. Quinn didn't know him as well, but she knew she could go to him with any problem and he would at least listen. And he was a lawyer, so that meant he was probably used to sorting through problems and figuring out their solutions. Yes, she thought as she drove away from the house, Mr. McGee would be the person who would know what to do.

And if he told her that he thought she was exaggerating the problem, then Quinn would listen to him and try to believe him. But she had to talk to him about this. More than at any other time in her life, Quinn knew she needed the advice of an adult.

Brady was surprised when his secretary told him that Quinn Baker was waiting in the outer office to see him. He didn't know what Quinn could possibly want with him, and it seemed unlikely that she

231

wanted legal advice, but he told Mrs. Mitchell to give him a couple of minutes to finish looking at the papers he'd been going over, then send her in.

By the time Quinn was led into his office, Brady had convinced himself that Quinn probably did want legal advice. He knew he tended to think of Mick and her friends as children still, but the fact remained that they were almost out of high school, and they faced problems as adult as anyone else. And with the added burden of her father's recent death, Quinn probably didn't have anyone else to ask for a little friendly advice.

But the look on Quinn's face when she sat on the chair across from his desk quickly changed Brady's mind. This was no girl wanting to ask about colleges or job opportunities. He could see immediately that something serious was weighing on Quinn's mind, and that it was more than any girl her age should have to contend with.

"What can I do for you, Quinn?" he asked, deciding to let her begin in her own way.

Quinn took a moment to look around the big office, her eyes taking in the shelves of law books and expensive-looking paintings. She wasn't stalling, but only trying to calm the inner quaking that she feared would make her voice tremble when she spoke. She didn't want him to think she was just some nervous kid, so she waited until she was sure she would have her voice under control.

She squared her shoulders. "Mr. McGee, I'm very worried about Mick," she said.

Brady was taken aback, but an inner voice told him he should have seen this coming. "Why? What's wrong?"

"Everything," Quinn blurted. "Mick is in trouble,

and I don't know exactly what it's all about, but I think she needs help. I think she might even need a psychiatrist."

His eyes probing Quinn's for clues, Brady saw a young woman who had grown up since the last time he'd talked to her. Instead of brushing off her words, as he was ashamed to admit he wanted to do, Brady instead leaned forward in his seat and addressed her as an equal. "What is it, Quinn?" he asked. "What's wrong with Mick?"

"She's different. Since school started she's drifted farther and farther away from us — I mean from me and Lee — so that we hardly know her any more. Haven't you and Mrs. McGee noticed anything about her lately?"

Brady frowned, rubbing his hand along his jaw. "Yes, we have," he admitted. "But we'd pretty much decided that she was just going through the changes everyone goes through when they hit their teens. We haven't been thrilled by some of her behavior, but then I remember how difficult I was at that age, and how much I rebelled against my parents when I was in high school, so we've been trying not to make a big deal out of it. She'll outgrow it, probably soon."

Quinn was shaking her head even before he'd finished speaking. "No, Mr. McGee, it's a lot more than that. You see, Mick has these tarot cards —"

"Tarot what?" Brady interrupted. Then he said, "Sorry, Quinn, go ahead and tell me."

"Tarot cards. They're like for telling fortunes." Quinn flushed deeply, waiting for Brady to interrupt her again, but when he didn't, she continued. "She's had them since last summer, but just a couple of months ago she started really using them. It was all in fun at first, or so we thought, but the strange part is that Mick seems to think they really work, that they really can predict the future."

"You don't believe that, do you?" Brady asked.

"N-no," Quinn stammered, at the same time wondering why she was even hesitating. "No," she added, more firmly this time. "I don't believe it, but Mick does, and she's gotten so that she carries them around with her all the time, and is always bugging us to let her do readings with them—that's what she calls it, doing a reading. Weird things have happened, I have to admit, and the cards have actually seemed to be right a couple of times."

Brady watched Quinn, some distant memory of the mention of such cards trying to struggle to the surface.

"But I think Mick has become—unbalanced," Quinn continued. "She really believes in those cards, and what's more, she's even started saying that they can *make* things happen. Right after my father died, Mick came to me all upset and tried to tell me that she'd put the Death card down on top of my father's card, and maybe that was why he'd died. Of course I know that's not true, but I'm just trying to make you understand just how serious this whole thing is."

Brady found himself leaning forward in his seat, listening intently to everything Quinn was saying, and trying to believe her. He didn't want to. If she were telling him the truth, that Mick actually had a deck of cards that she'd come to associate with some sort of power, then he had to concede that Quinn was also right when she said Mick was in trouble.

He tried to picture his daughter as someone who was in danger of being emotionally unstable, and, to his dismay, he had to admit it was a possibility. If insanity could be transmitted genetically, then Mick

234

did, indeed, have a better than average chance of being affected. It was something he should have been considering years ago, but he hadn't wanted to think about it, so he'd created a mental block that was now crumbling around him.

That didn't mean Mick couldn't be helped, though, and Brady was already thinking of the best psychiatrists and treatment for his daughter. He would do everything he could for her, and would see her through this with the sheer force of his own will, if necessary.

But Quinn's next words so stunned Brady that he could only gape at her as she spoke.

"And it's not just those cards," Quinn was saying, wringing her hands on her lap. "It's that house, too. That deserted old Montagna house. She goes there all the time, and she's tried to get me to go with her a couple of times. She says she *likes* it there, but I don't see how she could possibly like it when it's just some crumbling old—"

"Quinn!" Brady barked, startling the girl into silence. "What about that house?"

"W-well, just like I said," Quinn said, staring at him. "She goes there, she says she feels at peace there, or something like that, and—"

"How *long* has she been going to that house?"

"Not long. A month or so, I guess."

"What does she do there?"

"I don't really know, Mr. McGee. Just hangs around. All the furniture is still there, she says, and she's even brought a few knickknacks home to put in her own room. I don't think that's stealing, exactly, because the house is empty, and it seems like if anyone wanted the things there, they would have taken them out already. She says they're Rosalie's things, and she likes having them around her."

"Yes," Brady said slowly. "I saw a mirror in her bedroom that must have come from that house, but I didn't recognize it at the time. Now I know why it looked familiar to me."

Quinn didn't know what she had expected from Brady McGee, but his reaction to her news far surpassed anything she could have imagined. His usually tanned features had paled, and she could see small beads of sweat on his forehead. She stared at him, wondering if he knew something he wasn't telling her. His eyes looked tortured. Quinn had seen a look like that once before. When she was about eight years old, she'd been walking on the outskirts of town when she'd come upon a young racoon with its foot caught in a metal trap. Quinn had run home and gotten her mother, but by the time they'd gotten back both racoon and trap were gone. Looking at Brady now, Quinn was reminded of that racoon, with its pain-filled eyes.

Brady asked, "Does she actually say that—'Rosalie's things'?"

Quinn nodded. "Yes. In fact, she talks about Rosalie as though she were a friend. It's always Rosalie this and Rosalie that. As if she *knows* her personally."

Brady leaned back in his seat, his hands gripping the armrests tightly. "That's not possible, Quinn," he said. "Rosalie Montagna has been dead for fifteen years."

236

Chapter Eighteen

Fran McGee picked up the phone on the third ring and propped it between her shoulder and her chin. "Hello?" she said. She kept her hands free as she tried to clip her hair back with a barrette.

But as Brady spoke to her, Fran felt the barrette fall from her fingers and land soundlessly on the carpet at her feet. She listened as Brady talked. "Yes, I think you're right," she said after a minute. "It must be the same cards . . . No, I haven't looked in ages . . . Yes, of course I'll be right there. As fast as I can."

After she'd hung up, she stood for a minute, unable to move. What he'd told her—about Rosalie Montagna's house, and about the tarot cards, had been like a cold hand squeezing her heart. How could this be happening, after all this time? She'd thought that episode in their lives had forever been put behind them, but now Fran realized she'd been deceiving herself when she'd believed that the past would not resurface to rip her life apart.

Instead of going to her car as she'd promised, Fran went instead to Mick's bedroom and looked at all the little clues she had been seeing but had refused to acknowledge. How could she have been so blind? Yes, that silver picture frame did look familiar to her, and she now knew why. She'd seen it once before, a long time ago, even though Mick had put a picture of her own in it. And although some of the other new pieces didn't strike a cord in her memory, she knew where they had come from, too.

She'd seen some of these things, or pieces like them, in Rosalie Montagna's living room so many years ago.

Next she went to her own bedroom and opened the closet door. Getting down on her knees, Fran pulled out the cardboard box that she kept there, and began to sift through it. The box contained all her treasures—the pictures, letters from long-forgotten friends, and other mementos she'd been accumulating since she was a little girl. She was a born pack rat so the box was almost full even though she hadn't thought about its contents in a long time.

It took Fran a few minutes to thoroughly check the box, but by the time she was finished, she knew the tarot cards she'd had all these years were gone.

They were gone, and Mick had them. Mick was always borrowing her clothes, and it wasn't so hard to believe that at some time she had noticed this box and gotten to snooping, but why had she taken the cards? They couldn't possibly mean anything to Mick.

All the old secrets Fran and Brady had tried so hard to keep were about to be exposed, dragged out into the daylight like a writing creature of the night.

Cursing herself for even keeping those damned cards, Fran felt herself suddenly filled with rage at Rosalie Montagna. She was reaching out from the grave to destroy them all for what they'd done to her, but that didn't mean Fran was going to give in without a fight.

Fran did go to her car then, but still she didn't drive straight to Brady's office. Instead, she drove to the department store where she knew Elaine Baker worked. Inside the store she scanned the aisles, hoping she would spot Elaine before she had to ask someone for help. She was just about to give up when she saw Elaine behind a counter of perfume displays, and she quickly approached.

"Hi, Fran, how are you?" Elaine asked, surprised to see her. She knew Fran did most of her shopping at the more expensive stores in San Diego, so she hadn't expected to see her here.

"Not good," Fran said in clipped tones. "Elaine, I have to talk to you."

"Well, sure. What's up?"

"Can you leave the store?"

Elaine's surprise gave way to apprehension. Something wasn't right here. "I'm not off for another couple of hours. Can't it wait until then?"

"No, it can't." Fran looked around and saw that the nearest person was several feet away. She lowered her voice so that only Elaine would hear her. Quickly she told Elaine that Quinn was at Brady's office, and that they were both waiting for her to get there. She wanted Elaine to go with her, for this involved Elaine as well, and the only way she could convince Elaine of the urgency of the situation was to bring up that shared incident from their past.

After hearing what Fran had to say, Elaine closed her eyes for a moment, not wanting to believe that Quinn was involved in any of this. But when she opened her eyes again, she only nodded at Fran. "Give me a minute," she said. "I'll have to tell my boss I'm leaving, then I'll meet you outside at your car. Where are you parked?"

"Right by the front doors," Fran told her.

A few minutes later they were both seated in the front seat of Fran's car, and Fran drove away from the department store toward Joan Sternhagen's office.

"I haven't talked to Joan in ages," Elaine said. "Do you think she'll come with us?"

"She has to," Fran said. "She's a part of this, and Lee as well. It's all come full circle, hasn't it, Elaine?"

"Maybe it's not as bad as it sounds," Elaine said hopefully.

"It's ten times worse than you can imagine," Fran could only tell her.

When they arrived at Joan's office, they learned that Joan had already gone home for the day, so Fran and Elaine then drove to the Sternhagen house, hoping to catch her there. Fran didn't want any more delays. Brady was probably already wondering what was keeping her, but this was something that had to be done. If Joan wasn't home, Fran didn't know what they would do.

But Joan was home, and when she answered the front door Fran quickly explained as much as she dared, then asked Joan to come with them.

Joan was not receptive to the idea as she stood in her doorway and frowned at them as though they'd never been close friends. "None of this makes any

240

sense, if you ask me, and I certainly don't see why you want to drag me into it."

"You're already in it, Joan," Fran struggled to explain. "You were there, remember?"

"That was a long time ago."

"Yes, but—"

"For your information, I'd forgotten all about that, and I don't see how it could possibly be important now. And Lee certainly is not involved."

"I think she might be," Fran said. "It seems our daughters are somehow—"

Joan cut her off. "No. I won't listen to any more of this nonsense."

"Mom? What's going on?" Lee appeared behind her mother and looked curiously at Fran and Elaine.

"Nothing," Joan said. "Go back inside."

Fran moved a little closer to the doorway, even though Joan was doing her best to block her way. "Lee," Fran said, "you know all about the problems Mick has been having lately, don't you? Quinn is at my husband's office right now and they're waiting for me. Quinn went to him because she was concerned."

"Yes," Lee nodded. "She told me she was going to talk to you about it, but I didn't want to go along because frankly, Mrs. McGee, Mick scares me. I've had a little time to calm down since I talked to Quinn, though. If you really think it would be best if I go with you, I will."

"No, you won't," Joan Sternhagen snapped. "Go back inside the house right now." She kept her shoulder between Lee and the doorway, and now she tried to close the door.

"Mom, maybe I should—"

"We don't need this kind of trouble. Don't I have enough problems around here?"

"Mom—"

Fran could see that Joan's mind was made up, and she didn't want to be the cause of trouble between Lee and her mother. "That's all right, Lee," she said, looking over Joan's shoulder. "We'll manage somehow."

She turned to go, but before she got down the first step Joan's voice stopped her. "By the way, Fran, your daughter has been dating that Santos boy, hasn't she?"

Fran turned and looked at her. "Yes, she did for awhile, but she isn't seeing him any more."

"I should think not," Joan said coolly, one eyebrow arched. "Only ten minutes ago I heard that his car was pulled out of the lake with his body inside. Apparently he and the car had been in the lake at least a couple of weeks, and from what I hear, Mick was one of the last people to be seen with him."

Before Fran could recover from her own shock, she saw Lee's eyes roll up in her head as the girl fell in a dead faint behind her mother.

Quinn had watched as Brady, moving slowly as though he needed to think through each step, had picked up the telephone on his desk and punched a series of numbers. She'd known then she'd done the right thing in coming to him, that he would do his best to handle the situation. It was all too much for her, and she'd felt a sense of relief in knowing that the burden had been removed from her shoulders and placed squarely on his.

Brady was just about to call his house again to try to find out what was keeping Fran when she and Elaine Baker walked into his office.

Surprised to see her mother arrive with Mrs. McGee, Quinn quickly jumped up from her seat. But before she could ask her mother what she was doing there, Elaine went to her and told her to sit down, that they all had something to talk about.

"I brought your mother here because I think this has something to do with her, too," Fran explained after they'd all taken seats around Brady's desk. Pushing her hair back from her face, Fran wondered where to start. There was so much to explain, but she didn't want to waste too much time talking about it. Turning to Quinn, Fran began: "A long time ago, Quinn, when your mother, Joan Sternhagen and I were only about sixteen, we went out one night on a scavenger hunt and ended up at Rosalie Montagna's house."

"The three of you?" Quinn asked, frowning in bewilderment.

"That's right. You see, Elaine, Joan and I were as close back then as you, Mick and Lee are now. The three of us were best friends all through high school, and it wasn't until after graduation that we drifted apart. That night of the scavenger hunt— God, it's been so long I can barely even remember it—we went to Rosalie's because the scavenger hunt list offered twenty-five points for something from her house. Rosalie was different from anyone else in town. She kept to herself, and the local kids used to dare each other to go out to her place as sort of a test of courage." Fran looked at Brady, and he nodded his encouragement. "Anyway," she continued, "we waited outside her house until we thought it was safe to go inside, then we went into her living room to look for some little thing that she might not miss and that we could use to win the game. She caught us, though, and chased us out of her house, but not before I picked up a little wooden box from the mantle that contained a deck of tarot cards.

Quinn gasped, and Elaine put a calming hand on her daughter's arm.

Fran nodded. "Yes, the very same deck of cards. I didn't know then why Rosalie didn't chase us until she caught us, but she stopped just outside her door and called to me to bring the cards back. I wanted to, but by then I was so scared that all I wanted to do was get as far away from there as I possibly could, so I kept running until I caught up with Elaine and Joan, and the three of us left."

"Why did you keep the cards all these years?" Quinn asked, her curiosity taking over.

"I don't really have an answer to that," Fran admitted. "I wanted to give them back to her, but I didn't know how. I sure wasn't going to go back to that house. I toyed with the idea of mailing them to her, but I never did get around to doing it, and eventually pretty much forgot I even had them. I stuck the cards in a box with a bunch of my other junk, and they stayed there." She looked at Quinn intently now, knowing that Quinn had the ability to provide some answers. "*When* did Mick find the cards?" she asked. "And why did she take them?"

Quinn squirmed uncomfortably, wishing her

mother didn't have to hear this next part. "Mick found them in the back of your closet about the middle of last summer," she told Fran. "I don't know what we were doing in your closet — just being nosy, I guess, and I'm really sorry for that. We were bored, and no one else was there at your house; so when we found that box in your closet, it just seemed like fun to look through all the stuff in it. We didn't mean any harm."

"I know you didn't," Fran said. The fact that the girls had invaded her privacy seemed a minor point now.

"I don't even know why Mick took the cards," Quinn admitted. "She just liked them from the first minute she saw them. Lee tried to get her to put them back, but Mick said you'd never even miss them, and it might be fun to figure out how they worked." Quinn looked guiltily at her mother, then leaned forward to speak directly to Fran. "The weird part is, she really did seem to figure them out. I mean, she went to the library to study up on the meaning of the deck, then she used them at a party right before school started. She spread the cards out for Jack — that was a boy I was going out with at the time — and then she looked at those cards and told Jack so much personal stuff about his family that he was mad at me because he thought I must have told Mick about it. But I hadn't. I hadn't told her a thing, yet she seemed to know, just by reading the cards." Quinn shook her head and looked at the adults in the room. "But it had to be just a coincidence. Those cards can't have any real power to tell fortunes — can they?"

No one spoke for the space of several heartbeats.

Brady broke the silence. "Quinn, I honestly don't know," he said.

Elaine spoke up. "Oh, now, Brady, you don't believe there's anything to this—magic, do you? That's too far-fetched even for me to believe."

Brady rubbed at his chin, and this time it was he who looked to Fran for a nod of encouragement. When he saw by her expression that she wanted him to tell the whole story, he squared his shoulders with an air of determination and decided that this was not the time to be keeping secrets. No matter how personal or painful, the truth had to finally come out.

"I don't know if the cards have any real power or not," he said. "But if they do, Mick would be the one person in the world they might actually work for." He stopped, finding the words too difficult to say.

"Tell them," Fran urged.

He nodded. Closing his eyes as though he couldn't bear to see the faces of the people in the room with him, Brady said, "Mick is Rosalie Montagna's daughter."

Chapter Nineteen

Brady McGee, as a young man, had been obsessed with Rosalie Montagna. She was a couple of years older than he, and was more often than not the subject of locker room talk and speculation, but he was drawn to her in a way that defied explanation. During the daylight hours, he told himself he wouldn't see her again — she was trouble, his reputation was at stake, and hers was in the gutter. He had a dozen reasons to stay as far away from her as humanly possible. At night, though, when rational thought hid for cover, and the reasons to stay away seemed less important, Brady was drawn to her again and again, always to her mocking delight.

He was ashamed of his need for her, and kept the relationship a secret, he thought, not realizing that this sort of thing was exactly what people loved to talk about, and it was no secret at all.

Rosalie was the wildest, most beautiful creature he'd ever known, but he wasn't blind to her emotional problems — problems that seemed to grow worse with the passing of time. He could almost see her mind crumbling, and he tried to help her. He told her she needed to see a doctor, even offered to take her to one himself, but his words always caused such an outburst from her that he eventually stopped trying.

Nothing could possibly have come of their affair. Brady knew this, but it wasn't enough to keep him away. Maybe it was what he liked about her—the fact that she just didn't give a damn what people thought. She ridiculed him for his conventional ways, and tormented him with her beauty.

And Rosalie liked men a little too much. She didn't care if they were married or single; all men were the same to her. She boasted that she was a witch, and if her hold on him was any indication, she might very well have been.

Only when he met and fell in love with Fran was Brady finally able to turn his back on Rosalie. He married Fran, who met his family's standards of acceptance, and for awhile they were as happy as two people could possibly be. They built a life together, along with all the pleasantly normal aspects of marriage—a mortgaged home, long nights cuddling in front of the fireplace and planning their future, meals together in their dining room as Fran learned, sometimes with comically disastrous results, to cook.

Then Fran had learned that she could never have the children they both wanted. The news had sent her into a tailspin. She withdrew, hating herself, taking her pain out on Brady. The marriage suffered as she underwent a partial hysterectomy, and they had to adjust to the knowledge that there would be no babies for them.

They began picking at each other, and fought until it seemed they wouldn't weather the crisis. Brady wanted to offer comfort but didn't know how.

Fran needed comforting but couldn't ask for it.

And, in his unhappiness, Brady began seeing Rosalie again. She became a lifeline for him, even though he knew that by seeing her he was only widening the rift between himself and Fran.

Then Rosalie became pregnant.

As the pregnancy progressed, Rosalie's mental condition grew worse. She was completely agoraphobic by then, but somehow she had the baby without aid of hospital or doctors. When Brady tried to question her about it, she only hinted at an aunt from Los Angeles who sometimes acted as a midwife.

Brady never doubted that the baby, named Michelle, was his daughter. She looked like baby pictures he'd seen of himself, and Rosalie had become so withdrawn in the past year or so that he was certain she hadn't been seeing anyone else when the baby would have been conceived. Besides, she'd never been one to keep secrets about the men in her life, and she hadn't recently tormented him with the names of her other lovers.

Brady had begged her to let him raise the baby. He'd wanted Michelle, and he knew he could give her a better home than Rosalie ever could, but she stubbornly refused to consider his suggestion.

Michelle was all she had—and probably the only thing keeping her from taking that last step over the edge into insanity.

Then Rosalie's behavior had grown increasingly bizarre, until Brady actually began to worry about Michelle's safety. Rosalie let her house fall apart around her, no longer making any attempt to clean it. Debris piled up in corners, soiled diapers rotted in the bathroom and made the entire downstairs stink.

When Brady stopped in to see her and the baby one evening, he was appalled at the conditions in which Michelle was being raised. As he cleaned up some of the worst of the mess, Rosalie ranted irrationally about the people she thought were after her.

"You're one of them, I know you are," Rosalie hissed at him as he carried a bag of garbage out the back door. "I see you looking in my windows at night, spying on me."

"Rosalie, I've never peeked in your windows," he tried to tell her. But by then she was beyond listening.

She picked up a heavy silver cigarette lighter and flung it at him, but Brady, accustomed to her outbursts, stepped easily out of the way.

"Where's Michelle?" he asked. "I brought some toys for her."

"She doesn't need them."

"She *does* need them. She's over a year old now, and she needs educational toys to stimulate her mind."

Rosalie wouldn't listen. Her once lovely hair was neglected and dirty, and she paced the room anxiously, never taking her eyes off him. "I give Michelle everything she could want," she said.

"I don't know how you manage that," he snapped, close to losing his temper. "You don't go out to shop for her. There's no baby food in the cupboards, no fresh milk."

"I order everything by telephone. They deliver it

250

right to the door. That way I know it isn't poisoned. Baby food is poisonous, and milk can be tampered with. Canned food is best; that way I know my enemies haven't touched it."

"Rosalie, what are you talking about? No one wants to hurt you."

"They all do. Even you. The things you bring here are all contaminated. That's why I always throw them away after you leave."

A gnawing fear began to grow in Brady's heart. "Where is Michelle?" he asked again.

Rosalie's eyes grew wary. "She's safe."

"Where is she?" Brady asked, going to her and grabbing her arms.

She struggled to pull away from him, but refused to answer any more questions. Brady wanted to shake her, though his anger and fear were overshadowed by a deep sympathy for the woman. Rosalie's beauty was fading along with her mind, but he couldn't forget what she'd once been, and he was saddened by the wreck before him.

Finally, when he could get no answer, he threw her aside and ran up the stairs to the room he knew the baby slept in.

To his relief he found Michelle in her bed, sleeping, but his relief soon gave way to a new anger as he saw that the child was filthy and dressed only in a wet cloth diaper on this chilly night. She didn't have a proper crib. Brady had brought one shortly after Michelle's birth, but Rosalie had thrown it out. The baby slept in a sagging twin bed, with a chair pushed up to the side to keep her from rolling out.

Picking her up, he took Michelle into the bathroom and cleaned her up, watching the recognition in her eyes as she awakened and looked up at him. She smiled at him with her delicately shaped mouth and put one tiny hand up to tug at his hair.

After he'd bathed the baby and found warm pajamas for her, Brady changed the sheets on her bed and put her down so she could go back to sleep. She immediately rolled over on her stomach and positioned herself with her butt in the air, one thumb in her mouth.

Brady knew then that he would have to get Michelle somehow, that Rosalie was no longer capable of taking care of her. If he didn't act quickly, Michelle might be permanently scarred by her unstable mother.

He began a campaign to get baby Michelle taken away from Rosalie. Even so, it took another year, but finally he managed to have Rosalie committed for a thirty-day mental evaluation. From that point the child welfare department stepped in and took Michelle to a foster home in San Diego.

Rosalie might have gotten through the observation period and been released, she might even have gotten Michelle back if she'd made an effort to prove she could be a responsible mother, but that was not to be. Rosalie refused to bend to convention, and grew increasingly violent in her confinement. She was like a wild animal suddenly thrust into a cage, and her behavior fluctuated between aggression and total withdrawal.

The moment Rosalie was confined, Brady began working to get Michelle. The first obstacle, of course, was Fran.

He was surprised to learn that she already knew about his affair with Rosalie. What he'd thought was a well-kept secret was, in fact, almost common knowledge. But Fran didn't know about Michelle simply because no one in town knew Rosalie had a baby, so complete was her isolation.

Telling Fran about his daughter almost destroyed her, and was nearly the last straw to break the back of their shaky marriage. But she came around eventually, guilt about her infertility stronger than her anger, and she'd agreed that Brady had the right to raise the child he'd fathered.

If she couldn't give him a child, she felt she had no right to refuse him the one he had, and she knew his chances of getting custody of Michelle would be almost zero if his marriage were to break up.

Also, he agreed that they would let no one know that Michelle was actually his, that it would be better if the town believed they'd adopted a stranger's baby, and this was what finally convinced Fran. She couldn't face having everyone know the painful details of Michelle's birth, but she didn't mind so much if people were to think they'd adopted a child through the usual channels.

It made so much more sense to let Michelle grow up without the stigma of her crazy mother hanging over her head.

They prepared themselves for the legal battle ahead.

Then, unexpectedly, Rosalie died in the mental institution. Trying to escape from her prison, she fell from a third story window she'd somehow managed to get open.

The way was clear for Brady and Fran to legally adopt Michelle.

"I'm not going to pretend it was easy," Fran said after Brady finished his story. She and her husband shared a look of pain and love. "Michelle was a little over two years old by then, and I was terrified of what I was getting myself in for. But she was so helpless, and the sweetest baby you'd ever want to know."

Mrs. Mitchell opened the door to Brady's office and peeked in, asking him if he needed anything else. He told her to go on home, that he would lock up when they were finished. The secretary closed the door softly.

"You never told Mick she was adopted?" Elaine asked.

"No," Fran said. "We always intended to, but after a few months she seemed to have no memory of her natural mother, and as time went on we didn't know how to bring it up. And we really couldn't think of any reason why we should. By then she *was* mine, and I loved her as much as any mother could love a child. Our families knew she was adopted, of course, and so did everyone in town. For awhile I worried that someone would mention it to her, and that the whole thing would come out, but that never happened, and we stopped thinking about it."

"I can't believe this," Quinn said. "Mick is adopted."

Elaine made a gesture with her hands. "Now that

254

I think about it, I do remember something about that. I mean, secrets are pretty hard to keep in this town, and I heard about it at the time, but then it just sort of faded into the background, and I never thought about it again, even later, when Mick and Quinn became such good friends."

"I think that's how it is with most people," Brady said. "And why hurt Mick? None of this was her fault."

But now it was all coming back to haunt them, Brady knew, and somehow they were going to have to deal with it. Probably Mick had run across Rosalie's deserted old house quite by accident, and it had triggered memories in her she didn't understand or even really know she had. Going there, then saying she liked it and felt comfortable there were merely the mental scraps from the first two years of her life when she'd lived with her natural mother.

"How do the cards enter into this?" Quinn asked. "If what you're saying is true, then the cards would have been gone long before Mick was born, so she couldn't possibly remember them."

"I don't know," Brady admitted. "But as far as Rosalie being a witch—I know she believed it, and at times she almost had me believing it. She told me once that she'd cast a spell over me and made me hers, and it did seem as though I was helpless to stay away from her." He shook his head. "But she was crazy."

"It's like she cast a spell on all of us," Fran said softly. She looked out the window behind Brady's desk and saw that it was dark outside, that they'd talked away the late afternoon hours, and it was

255

now evening. That seemed fitting, somehow, for this conversation was almost like the late-night talks she and her friends had had as children when, at slumber parties, they'd tried to scare each other with ghost stories.

But this was no ghost story. This was real.

Fran said, "I can believe Rosalie was a witch."

"I don't," Elaine spoke up. "She was eccentric, and she eventually did go insane, as Brady says, but I cannot believe in witchcraft and spells and—well, I just don't buy it."

"But think about it," Fran said to her. "The three of us—you, me and Joan—years ago stole something from Rosalie. Now, almost a quarter of a century later, *our* three daughters have been dragged into Rosalie's life all over again."

"She's dead," Elaine said sharply.

"Yes, but she's reached right out of the grave to teach us all a lesson, hasn't she?"

Before the women could continue their argument, Brady stepped in to redirect the conversation. "We could debate that point forever and never get anywhere," he said. "The important thing now is that we find Mick and help her."

"I know where she is."

The three adults turned to look at Quinn. She'd spoken softly, but with conviction.

"Where?" Brady asked.

"At that house, again," she told them. "I'm sure that's where she's at right now. I think we should go there and try to talk to her."

"Not all of us," Brady said. "If she sees all four of us coming in she'll think we're ganging up on her.

256

I'd better go alone. Maybe I can get her to come home."

"Can I go with you?" Quinn asked, getting up from her seat. She felt as stiff as if she'd been sitting there all day. "She's always listened to me—at least she used to. I think I could talk some sense into her."

Brady took a moment to think it over. "Okay, you come with me, Quinn," he said. "Fran, you and Elaine go to the house and wait there for us. We'll try to bring her back with us."

"What if she won't come willingly?" Fran asked.

"I don't know," Brady said. "I'll deal with that when and if it comes up. But Mick is going to have to listen to us. We're the only ones who can explain to her what's been happening to her lately, and why she feels the way she does."

Chapter Twenty

Mick had lit candles when the sun went down, and she sat on the floor of Rosalie's bedroom and read the diary.

> . . . *when i sit very quietly i can see my family around me. mother with her cut wrists father smelling of gin. never could understand how he could drink gin. i prefer . . .*

Mick was nearing the end of the book, and in the past hours a great deal had been revealed to her. Several times she'd had to get up and pace around, nearly overwhelmed by what she'd learned.

When she'd gotten, finally, to the part where Rosalie had described the birth of her baby, Mick's eyes had filled with tears of sympathy for the woman.

> . . . *thought i was going to die Tia Celestine thought so to but she wouldn't admit it. that would be a blemish on her record . . .*

When Mick read that the baby's birth date coincided with her own, and that Rosalie had named her daughter Michelle Rose, Mick's sympathy changed to shock and outrage, and she had to put the book down for almost an hour to go to the dust-covered little bed in the other room and run her hands along its worn wooden frame and faded pastel blankets.

There was an overturned chair in the middle of the room. Mick picked it up and placed it beside the bed. It made a neat little crib, if that's what one wanted to use it for. How had she known to put the chair there? The room was almost dark because she hadn't lit any candles here, but enough light came in from the other room for her to see as much as she needed to.

The room whispered a lullaby in Mick's ear, a half forgotten song that skittered at the edge of her memory.

Did the bed really look familiar to her now, or was that only her imagination?

Fists clenched, Mick beat them against her thighs, a growl of frustration in her throat. Her life had been a lie all along. Fran and Brady—the people she could no longer think of as Mom and Dad—hadn't trusted her with the truth, had elected, instead, to let her believe her last name was McGee, when in fact she was the bastard child of Rosalie Montagna.

. . .he came by again last night thinks he can take Michelle away from me. i'll kill him before i'll let that happen. could still do it i think. haven't tried in a long time not since that time it backfired on me. i've been afraid my memory is hazy and i dont have the concentration needed to . . .

Even Rosalie hadn't trusted her with the truth.

Mick had found no mention of her father's name in the diary, as though Rosalie had known her diary would be read someday and had taken steps to conceal important facts.

Mick was filled with a new hunger to learn who her family really was, and where her father now lived. Fran and Brady might know who he was. It might even be on the adoption records they had hidden somewhere. Too bad she no longer had the opportunity to search for those records.

Mick went back to the diary and was looking for clues when she heard sounds downstairs. She tiptoed from the bedroom to find out who was invading the privacy of her home.

"She's here, all right," Brady said. He'd rounded the corner in the driveway in front of Rosalie's house, and they saw Mick's car parked near the front door. "Now let's hope she'll talk to us."

"Maybe I should go in alone at first," Quinn said.

"That's not a good idea, Quinn."

"Mick trusts me."

"You're probably right."

"Just give me a few minutes with her. Then, if I can't get her to come out by myself, you can come in."

Brady sat behind the steering wheel of his car and looked at the house. His first instinct was to go inside and drag Mick out. If it was possible to hate a dead woman, he hated Rosalie for what she was doing to their daughter. Maybe it would be best after all if Quinn talked to Mick first. He needed a little more time to get his emotions under control.

He wouldn't be doing anyone any good if he went barging in.

"All right," he said. "I'm giving you ten minutes."

"Thirty minutes," Quinn countered. "She was pretty upset when she left Lee's house. She might still need some time to calm down. I really do think it will be better if I'm alone with her, Mr. McGee, even if it's just to tell her that Lee and I are sorry for the way we've been treating her."

Brady still wasn't comfortable with the idea, but he finally agreed that he would give Quinn thirty minutes and not one minute more, and then if they didn't come out he was going in.

Quinn got out of the car and walked toward the house. She tried knocking on the front door first, but when that brought no response, she tried the knob and was surprised to find it open. She didn't know if it had been unlocked all along, or if Mick had opened it some time during her visits here, but Quinn went inside and looked around at the half dozen candles that dimly illuminated the living room.

She shuddered as she walked through the room, the candles giving everything an eerie glow that she didn't like. It was beyond her understanding how Mick could possibly find anything of interest here, but she smothered her fearful thoughts and looked around, hoping she wouldn't have to stay here the required thirty minutes.

"Mick?" she called out softly, realizing this place reminded her of a spook house at a carnival she'd once gone to years ago. This one was even worse because she knew it was the real thing.

"What do you want?" a soft voice asked.

Quinn jumped and put one hand over her wildly thumping heart. Looking around, she finally located Mick only a few feet away, standing in the shadows beside the fireplace.

"Mick, you scared me," Quinn said.

"What are you doing here?"

"I need to talk to you."

"Why?"

"Come on, Mick—we're friends. Since when do we need an excuse to talk?"

"Since you and Lee started avoiding me."

Quinn winced. "Yeah, I guess we haven't been around much lately, and I'm sorry about that. But it hasn't been all our doing, you know. You haven't exactly been Miss Congeniality yourself, Mick. I'm here now. That's the important thing."

"It's too late now," Mick said sadly. Her voice was as mercurial as fog, swirling around Quinn and getting into her head.

Quinn smelled death here. It was dust, and melting candlewax, and the sweat coming from her own pores—but it was also much more than that.

She pushed her fear down, smothering it as best she could so that Mick wouldn't sense her weakness. Taking three careful steps, Quinn approached Mick as though she were a wild bird that might suddenly take flight. "Lee told me what happened today after school," she said. "She feels really bad about it. She says she went a little bonkers because of what has happened to Mrs. Pidbuhl. You heard about that, didn't you?"

"You know I did. Do you think I killed her?"

"No, of course not," Quinn said.

"Well, I did."

"You couldn't have, Mick. I've been hearing about it all day, and I know it was an accident."

Mick stepped back into the shadows so that her face was hidden. "It was the cards, but I'm still the one responsible," she said.

Quinn took another couple of steps forward. She was now in the middle of the room. This wasn't the direction in which she'd wanted the conversation to go. "Your mother and father are worried about you," she said.

Mick's reaction startled Quinn. "They're not my mother and father," she spat. "I'm adopted. Or maybe they just bought me on the black market. I've been hearing a lot about *that* on the news lately."

"They adopted you legally," Quinn said quickly, trying to keep a soothing tone to her voice while she hid her surprise. "But I didn't know you knew about it."

"Come upstairs with me," Mick said suddenly. "I'll show you."

Accepting the invitation reluctantly, Quinn stepped aside as Mick came out from the shadows and headed for the stairway.

"Come on," Mick said, climbing the stairs. She stopped and looked back over her shoulder. "Are you coming, or are you afraid?"

"I'm not afraid," Quinn lied.

"Sure you are; it's written all over your face. You always were a big chicken, scared of the dark."

Mick reached the top of the stairs, and Quinn took a deep breath and followed her. The steps creaked under her weight, and halfway up Quinn felt a closing in, as though dark arms were wrapping themselves around her. It's only the surrounding gloom, she told herself. She squared her shoulders and went the rest of the way up.

She found herself in a bedroom, or what had once been a bedroom. Now it was only the ruins of some long-ago life, and she didn't like the vibrations she felt here. She wasn't welcome. The house was rejecting her, despite Mick's invitation, but Quinn kept up a brave front, knowing it was the only chance she had of gaining Mick's trust.

"This isn't so bad," Quinn said, looking around at the candles placed on a dresser beside the window.

"But it's spooky, isn't it?" Mick teased.

"Yeah, little bit. What's that you're wearing?"

Mick fingered the gauze blouse she'd put on over her own shirt. "It was my mother's. I took it out of her closet because it makes me feel closer to her when I wear it. Rosalie Montagna was my mother."

Quinn couldn't stop the gasp of surprise that came out of her mouth, so she turned away from Mick and touched the quilted bedspread that felt like it might fall apart if she pressed too hard. The shadows in the room had taken on a life of their own. They seemed to creep toward her until she looked directly at them, then they slunk back into the corners like animals of the night. She could almost imagine that she was an object of ridicule with her quaking limbs and false bravado.

"How could you know something like that?" she asked Mick as soon as she trusted her voice.

Her anger fading with the desire to share with Quinn all she'd learned, Mick spoke eagerly. "I've been reading her diary. It's all in there, all except who my real father is. I'm not quite finished, though. I'm still hoping maybe she'll name him. I have the right to know that much."

Sitting down on the floor beside her purse, Mick picked up the diary again and opened it. "I think my mother might have been a few bricks short of a full load," she explained as Quinn sat down a few feet away. "She sure sounds nuts in the diary, especially as I get closer to the end. But I don't think it was all her fault. This town treated her badly, and that probably helped send her over the edge. No one tried to help her. They all treated her like dirt."

"I've been talking to your dad about this, Mick, and he—"

"He's not my father!" Mick shouted, letting the diary fall to the floor.

Newly frightened at this outburst, Quinn fought the urge to run. Instead, she got slowly to her feet. She felt she was in over her head, especially when she saw the wild look that had come into Mick's eyes. The possibility that Mick had inherited some of her mother's insanity seemed all too real.

"Yes, he is," Quinn said.

Mick's hands were knotted into fists as she stood. She took a menacing step forward, but stopped when Quinn didn't back away. "He adopted me," she said. "And instead of telling me, like you're supposed to, he lied to me all these years. I'll never forgive him for that. I'll never forgive either of them."

"Mick, Brady McGee *is* your father," Quinn said. She didn't know how Mr. McGee was going to feel about her telling Mick this. She hoped he wouldn't be too mad at her. "He told me all about it just a little while ago," she continued. "When I went to his office because I was worried about you. He had an affair with Rosalie Montagna a long time ago, and after you were born he arranged to adopt you and raise you because he wanted what was best for you. He loves you, Mick. They both do, no matter what you might think."

The fury that had twisted Mick's features faded somewhat, but she still looked at Quinn with suspicion. She seemed to be struggling to accept this newest development on top of everything else she'd learned.

Seeing her advantage, Quinn explained to Mick as quickly as possible about Brady's relationship with Rosalie, leaving out some of the more painful details of Rosalie's last days. She would leave that much up to Brady, and let him decide how much Mick really needed to know. "But it is true that he's your real father, and he wants you to go home now so he can try to explain it to you himself."

Mick walked toward the window, her back to Quinn. When she turned to face Quinn again, she looked hard, harder than anyone Quinn had ever seen.

"It doesn't really change anything," Mick whispered.

"How can you say that? He's your father—I thought that was what you wanted to know."

"But I'm more Rosalie than I am him."

"You're part of both of them, you—"

"My father could have been anyone. That doesn't matter. I'm a Montagna. Rosalie's diary has told me that much. She could do things, special things, despite her problems. And I have her powers. I know it because of what I've been able to make the tarot

266

cards do, how they've worked for me. I'm not sure I like it, but I can't deny what I am."

Mick bent down and picked up her purse from the floor. She took out the box and opened it.

"This is my life now," Mick said. She held her left hand flat, the cards resting on her palm. The box had fallen to the floor, but she ignored it. "See this—" She flipped the top card. "The Lovers. That can mean romance, of course, but it also means making a choice. Choosing between two things."

Quinn stared at her.

Mick turned up another card. "Ah—the Ten of Swords. Treachery. A stab in the back. Appropriate, don't you think?"

"Mick—"

"Don't interrupt." Another card. "The Fool. Is that you—or me?"

"Mick, stop it."

"Can't you see?" Mick was smiling, but it was like a facial tick, totally without humor. "This is all I have. My parents—the people I thought were my parents—are really strangers. Brady might be my biological father, but that doesn't really matter any more."

"Throw the cards away," Quinn said.

Mick shook her head. "Are you crazy? I was *meant* to have them. They waited, through Fran, all those years for me to find them. I used to wonder why Fran had the cards all that time without using them, but now I know it's because only a Montagna can really benefit from them."

"I don't see that they've done you any good," Quinn said.

"That's because you're one of *them*."

Quinn held her hands out. "I'm just your friend, Mick, and I wish you'd leave here with me. You need time to absorb everything that's happened to you."

"Oh, you don't know the half of it," Mick said. "I can't ever go back home, Quinn. Too much has happened, and it's all going to come out soon. I took all my money out of my savings account this afternoon, and it's a good thing I did because I've got to leave this town and never come back. I've gotten myself in deep trouble this time."

"Nothing has happened that can't be worked out," Quinn said. "Please, just—"

"Go away, Quinn. You can't help me, and I don't want you to get hurt, too."

"I'm not leaving without you."

Mick made an exasperated sound. "Boy, you sure are stubborn. Don't you understand that I don't want you here? If you really are my friend, then give me a head start before you call out the troops."

Quinn had no idea how much time had passed, but she knew Brady would be coming in soon, and she also knew that Mick's state of mind was such that she wouldn't be happy to see her father. In growing desperation, she approached Mick and put her hand on the other girl's arm, surprised when it wasn't immediately thrown off. She took that as an encouraging sign. "Mick, whatever it is you think you've done, we all only want to help you."

"You don't know anything about it!" Mick cried suddenly, pushing Quinn aside. The rest of the cards fluttered to the floor.

Startled by the sudden movement, Quinn was thrown off balance and her hip hit the chest of drawers heavily, sending a bolt of pain shooting down her leg. She reached out to catch herself, and her arm knocked over one of the candles.

As the candle tipped, the flame caught in the aged curtains and quickly spread upward, toward the ceiling, eating at the rotted fabric.

Mick and Quinn stared at it for a moment, caught by the spectacular sight as the wallpaper around the curtains began to blacken and peel.

"Oh, shit!" Mick shouted. She pushed Quinn again, out of the way this time, and tried to pull the flaming curtains from the window before the fire could spread.

She was too late. Even as she beat at the flames, they spread throughout the room, devouring furniture, leaping to the nearby bedspread and filling the room with smoke.

Quinn began to choke and gasp. Her eyes filled with tears, and she covered her head instinctively with her arms. By the time her numb brain began to function enough to tell her that they had to get out of the house, she could no longer tell where the door was.

Brady stood beside his car with his back to the house, looking at his watch. Quinn's time was up. He'd just decided to go in and get the girls when he saw a set of headlights coming around the bend in the driveway.

He walked a few feet toward it and didn't recognize Fran's car until it stopped in front of him. "What are you doing here?" he asked, leaning down to the open driver's side window.

Fran and Elaine looked at him. "We couldn't stand just waiting and not knowing what was going on," Fran explained. "Why are you outside?"

"Quinn wanted to go in and talk to Mick alone for a bit."

"And you just let her?" Elaine asked incredulously.

"I hate to admit it, Elaine," he said, "but Quinn probably knows Mick better than any of us. I told her I'd gave her thirty minutes, and her time is up. I'm going in now, but I want you both to wait out here."

Elaine had opened her door and gotten out of the car. "I'm going with you," she said.

Almost blinded by the heavy black smoke, Quinn felt a pair of hands on her shoulders.

"Come on," Mick said, coughing. "The door is this way."

She led Quinn out of the room. The fire had somehow already spread from the bedroom to the rug in the hallway, and the girls dodged the flames and felt their way along the wall to where they knew the stairs were.

Quinn thought she was following Mick until she smacked nose-first into a wall. "Mick?" she called, trying to tell by touch where she was. The hallway was gone, and she could tell she had turned somewhere along the way and gone into another bedroom. She didn't know the layout of the house as Mick did. With her hands flat against the wall she moved slowly, trying to find a doorway but meeting only solid resistance. The hostility she'd felt earlier in the house now manifested itself in the smothering smoke, and she had the sense that something was trying to pull her down into itself. She fought the feeling, not wanting to become a part of this house. It already held years of barely-contained rage and vengeance; if she died here, her soul would be trapped forever with four generations of bitter Montagnas.

She stopped when she bumped into a piece of furniture, and her hands told her it was a low bed. She called out again, but could hear nothing but the roar of the flames all around her and, she imagined, distant laughter.

"I'll get the girls and bring them out," Brady told Elaine, blocking her path.

"You shouldn't have let her go in there alone," Elaine said.

"I'm sure she's fine, she—"

But Elaine was looking past him, and her eyes widened as she pointed. "Oh, my God. Look!"

Brady turned and felt as though someone had punched him in the stomach. The upper half of the house was aglow with an orange light, and even as they watched the flames burst through a window, sending sharp pieces of glass to fall to the ground below.

Quinn felt her strength leaving her, and no matter how many times she turned, she couldn't find the door of the bedroom. She fell to her knees, her lungs tightening as they refused to take in any more

271

smoke.

It was over. She knew she wasn't going to get out. As she felt herself slipping away, she wondered what her mother would do now.

Then she was pulled roughly to her feet, and she heard Mick shouting at her as though from a great distance.

Mick had been halfway down the stairs when she realized Quinn was no longer behind her. At first she wanted to keep going, but she was unable to make herself leave her friend. Doubling back, she went back up the stairs, knowing that if she didn't find Quinn soon, they would both perish.

At the top of the stairs Mick realized the hem of her gauze blouse was burning. She shrugged it off, and let it drop to the floor.

She heard Quinn coughing, and went into the bedroom that had been hers as a baby. She almost tripped over Quinn, then reached down and began to pull the other girl bodily from the room.

Clinging to each other, they descended the stairway. The entire house seemed to be in flames around them, but when Mick and Quinn reached the bottom step they could at least now see where they were going.

"Get out," Mick ordered, pushing Quinn roughly. She turned as though to go back up the stairs.

Quinn held onto her. "You're coming with me!"

There was an inferno around them. They might have been in hell.

"My cards are upstairs," Mick shouted.

"Forget the cards, Mick. Everything is burning up there."

The flames crackled and roared, so that their

voices were almost drowned out.

"I have to get them," Mick shouted again.

"It's too late. Give it up." Quinn tried to pull Mick out with her, but Mick was stronger, and she managed to jerk out of Quinn's grasp.

"Those cards are all I have of my mother. I need them."

A crystal bowl to their left shattered with the heat. The skin on Quinn's face felt too tight, and somewhere a window exploded. Again, Quinn thought she heard the laughter of a demented soul.

Before Quinn could protest further, Mick turned and ran back up the stairs, into the heart of the fire. Quinn started to follow, but then she remembered that Brady was still outside. He could get Mick and bring her out. She had no more strength left.

She stumbled out the front door of the house, calling for help, just as Brady reached her. Through her tears she could see the question in his eyes. She fell into his arms, her hair singed, and her face blackened with soot.

"She went back upstairs," Quinn gasped. "Get her out, Mr. McGee. She's going to burn to death!"

Brady threw Quinn out of the house into her mother's waiting arms and went back for Mick. The house was crumbling around him, but he put one arm over his head and grabbed the banister.

He'd taken only two steps up when the stairway, nearly completely in flames by now, crashed down around him.

Chapter Twenty-one

Lee stood looking down at the pink marble head-stone that read MICHELLE ROSE MCGEE. There was nothing else on it. No dates, no poetic sayings, just her name.

"I still sometimes wake up in the morning and for-get—just for a few seconds—that any of it happened," she said softly.

"Yeah. Me, too," Quinn said. She stood a little be-hind Lee, and to her left. "Then it hits me all of a sudden. It's been almost two months. Do you think we'll ever get used to the idea that she's really gone?"

"Eventually. Maybe it'll be better next year, when we're no longer in high school." Lee brushed at a dead leaf that had blown onto her sweater by the crisp January breeze. "I've been accepted at Regis College in Colorado. I don't know yet if the scholar-ship will go through, but I've decided that's where I'm going to go."

"That's so far away," Quinn said. "Why don't you go to UCLA with me?" Quinn's hair had been cut short, so that it barely covered her ears, a necessity after so much had been singed off. She looked over at Lee. They'd both changed so much in the past months, in ways that had nothing to do with physical appearance.

Lee shook her head in response to Quinn's question. "No offense," she said, "but I think our being together is what keeps us thinking about Mick. I want to be off on my own for awhile, where I won't run into anyone from Xavier." She sniffled a little and pulled a tissue from her purse.

"It'll seem strange, us going off in different directions," Quinn said. "But I guess I can see your point. This has been some half a year, hasn't it? My father, Danny Santos, Mrs. Pidbuhl—all dead. And Emma gone off somewhere with no word to anyone. It was funny, her running away like that just about the time everything was coming down."

Lee shrugged and put the damp tissue back in her purse. "Well, Emma's run away before. Maybe she's happy wherever she is. I know I'll be glad to leave town." She looked up at the cobalt sky. "I'm going now. I have to be at work in an hour."

"I'll give you a ride," Quinn said.

"No, I'll walk," Lee said. "It's not far, and I feel like the exercise. I'll see you in school Monday."

Quinn only nodded.

She watched Lee walk until she was out of sight, then Quinn turned back to Mick's grave. Mick wasn't the only one who was lost to Quinn. Though she saw Lee in school every day, and they occasionally talked on the phone, the closeness that had once been the core of their relationship was gone. Mick had taken it with her.

But Quinn couldn't mourn the loss. Lee was doing okay. She was getting along better with her mother, probably because they both realized how close they'd come to destruction, and her life was heading in a direction that, though away from Xavier—and away from Quinn—was positive.

Quinn didn't know why she spent so much time here, at Mick's grave, except that next year she, too, would be gone, and she wouldn't have many chances to do this. She liked to bring flowers when she could spare a couple of dollars to buy a small bouquet from the floral shop. She didn't know if it really made any difference, but she liked to think that Mick knew what she was doing and appreciated the gesture.

She turned when she heard the sound of tires crunching on gravel, and saw Brady McGee get out of his car and walk toward her.

"Hello, Quinn," he said as soon as he was close enough.

"Hi," she said, looking down at his hands.

Brady had been burned in the fire that had killed Mick, and had spent some time in the hospital. His hands were still scarred with new pink skin, but the last she'd heard, he wasn't going to need grafts. She turned away, hoping he hadn't noticed her staring.

"Looks like you've been thinking about her, too," he said.

"Every day. Lee was here with me, but she left a little while ago."

"How is Lee doing?" he asked.

Quinn brushed her hair back from her face. "She still feels bad that she didn't go to the house with us that night."

"There's no reason why she should feel bad. She couldn't have done anything." Brady put his hands in his pockets. "I've been meaning to talk to you, Quinn. Mrs. McGee and I have been discussing this a lot lately, and we've decided that we want to take the money we'd set aside for Mick's college education and give it to you and Lee. Think of it as a gift from Mick."

"You don't need to do that," Quinn said after she'd absorbed this news.

"We want to. We couldn't in good conscience use the money ourselves, and if you girls don't take it, we'll just give it to charity. Please let us do this."

Quinn thought about it, and she realized that she understood what Lee had said about wanting to get away from Xavier. There were so many unhappy memories that Quinn wanted to put far behind her, but if she used Mick's money for college it would be a daily reminder that Mick had died after saving her. Still, she couldn't refuse Mr. McGee's offer. His pain had to be even greater than her own, and she knew this was something he needed to do.

"Thank you," she murmured, looking down at the ground. "I have some insurance money from my father, but it won't be enough to see me through four years. This will help a lot."

"Good," he said simply.

They stood in silence for awhile. Quinn thought about the two deaths that had brought her and her mother out of the financial hole. First her father, and now Mick, in their passing, had made it possible for Quinn to have a future other than waiting on tables or standing behind some counter. Death wasn't supposed to result in good things happening to people, yet that was how it had turned out.

She could find no happiness in her windfall. If she could go back in time, Quinn knew she would wish none of it had ever happened. Even her father. He might have been a beast, but she would have gotten out from under his thumb eventually. No one deserved to die like that.

"I keep wondering if things could have turned out differently," Quinn said when the silence had

277

stretched on too long. "Mick had so much potential— I can't help but feel that if I'd come to you sooner, we might have been able to help her."

"Mick was doomed from the beginning," Brady said abruptly, his eyes on the marble headstone. "Don't get me wrong—I loved her more than life itself, and I would have died for her that night if it would have made any difference. But now that enough time has passed so that I can think about it clearly, I believe she had too much of Rosalie in her for her to overcome."

"Mick said something almost exactly like that to me the night of"—Quinn almost choked but made herself go on—"the night of the fire. She said she had more of Rosalie in her than of you."

"She was right." He shook his head sorrowfully. "Rosalie got her revenge, even after all these years, but she had to destroy her own daughter in the process. It might be for the best that the Montagna line died with Mick. There was something truly evil there."

"Mick wasn't evil," Quinn said sharply, temporarily forgetting that her mother had raised her to never argue with her elders. She had also, with the passage of time, forgotten what it had been like in that house— the feeling of being sucked down by something beyond her comprehension. It all had the feeling now of a bad dream, too vague to get a firm hold on and fading a little more every time she tried. "Mick took a wrong turn somewhere along the line," she continued, "but she wasn't a bad person. She pulled me out of that fire."

Brady looked at her, and Quinn noticed that the lines around his eyes seemed much deeper than they had a few months ago, and his hair, which had previously been lightly peppered with gray, was now more than half so. But his expression brightened slightly at her words. "That's right, she did," he said. "That's something to remember. You'll have to forgive me, Quinn. Sometimes my thoughts do take a morbid turn, but it isn't always like that. I do remember the good times, as well. Most of the time we had her, Mick was a joy to be around. She had so much spirit. And she found fun in every situation. Remember that slumber party Mick had when she was fifteen, and the dozen or so giggling, whispering girls she had over that night?"

"I remember it well," Quinn said. "We had a great time.

"I'll bet you girls never realized Fran and I knew all along about the five boys you and Mick smuggled in through the family room window that night."

Quinn put one hand up to her mouth, her eyes dancing at the memory. "How come you didn't barge in and kick them all out?" she asked.

"And spoil your fun? Never. Besides, we were right outside the door the whole time, listening and making sure things didn't get out of hand."

Quinn burst out laughing, and Brady joined her. After a moment, he put one arm around her shoulder and gave her a brief hug. "You kids kept us on our toes, all right, but we had a few tricks of our own. I used to do a lot of the same stuff when I was kid, so I managed to anticipate Mick's moves before she even made them, even though she thought Fran and I were a couple of the squarest people in the world."

"I never thought that."

"You didn't?"

"No. I used to love to spend time at your house,

because I thought you were both so nice. I think Mick used to invite me to spend the night so much because she knew I needed it, considering how my own father was." She looked sideways at him. "Did you know Mick taught me how to drive?"

Brady laughed again, shaking his head. "No, that's a new one on me."

"So we did manage to fool you once in a while."

"I guess you did." Brady buttoned his coat and looked back at his car. "Thank you, Quinn," he said.

"For what?"

He lifted one shoulder and let it drop again. "For talking to me, and reminding me that life goes on. For making me laugh again. It's been a long time since I laughed. I have to go now. I know you'll be taking off in a few months, but will you keep in touch?"

"Of course I will," Quinn said.

"Good." He turned up the collar of his coat and walked away from her toward his car.

Quinn waved to him as he drove away, but she was never sure if he saw her.

Epilogue

"Hi, Michelle. Meet me for a cup of coffee later?"

Mick turned from locking the door of her trailer and waved at the skinny girl who had called to her from the next unit. "Sure," she said. "I have to get Gary to fix that latch on my booth first, then I'll be going to the tent."

The girl nodded and hurried off in another direction to tend to her own business.

Moving slowly through the trailers, Mick looked up at the morning sky and enjoyed the few moments of peace she would have before the carnival opened for the day and she would be too busy to even think, much less enjoy a cup of coffee with a friend. She liked it that way, liked being so busy that the hours flew by, just as she liked the fact that all her new friends called her Michelle.

Where were they, anyway? She had to think for a minute before it came to her that they were in east Texas, where they would stay for two weeks before moving on to the next small town. When the weather started to warm up, the carnival would then go north, through Missouri, Iowa, and on to Minnesota, a caravan of nameless carnival workers to the people who came to spend their money throwing darts at balloons and riding the Ferris wheel.

She enjoyed the small pleasures of life—like how good her Reeboks felt on her feet. She was glad she'd spent the extra money on good shoes because she spent so touch time on her feet that it really made a difference. And she was glad for the fact that no one here questioned her too closely. That was a hard rule among the carnival workers; many of them just preferred the anonymity of such a job, but some were running from something, as she was, and they all respected each others' privacy.

"Michelle, have you seen Gary?" a dark-skinned man asked as she walked past the truck he'd been working on.

"I was just going to find him, Tim," she said.

"Well, will you tell him this old clunker is going to need some major parts? If he's going into town later maybe he can pick me up what I'll need."

"I'll tell him," Mick promised. She rounded a corner and pulled the strap of her purse up onto her shoulder. Almost unconsciously, she ran her hand along the outside of the purse, feeling for the cards before she remembered that she no longer carried them with her. They were back in her trailer, locked in her trunk along with her mother's diary and the few clothes she owned, and there they would stay.

She'd lived a lifetime in the past few months, and she regretted much that had happened, but Mick knew there would be no going back. She hadn't meant to kill Quinn's father. That had been an accident, brought about by her own ignorance.

Even that night with Danny Santos she hadn't really known what she was doing. She'd had her suspicions by then, but that's all they'd really been, compounded by confusion and the increased alienation she'd felt.

Danny hadn't been much interested in her cards, but she'd spread them out on the front seat of his car as they'd parked by the lake that night of the Halloween dance. She'd even brought out the Death card again, but it had only been a careless game at the time.

She'd taken the cards with her when she'd told Danny she didn't feel well and needed some air, leaving him in the car to wait for her. She really had felt sick, or maybe she'd just known she had to get out of that car. But when the car had started slipping into the lake, and Danny hadn't been able to get out, she *had* tried to get to him, had actually gone into the water and tried to open the door until it had gone under and there was nothing more she could do.

Sometimes she really believed this.

She *wanted* to believe it. But sometimes—usually late at night, after she'd had a couple of drinks—the uncomfortable thought came to her that she was making excuses for herself. That maybe, just maybe, she hadn't been as innocent a bystander to Danny's last night of life as she would like to think she'd been.

But she couldn't claim ignorance when it came to Mrs. Pidbuhl. She'd known exactly what she was doing that time. She'd only wanted to help Lee, but that didn't justify what she'd done.

And there was more. No one else really knew the extent to which she'd manipulated lives with her cards. Some of the incidents had been small, and even she wasn't entirely sure she'd brought them about. Hilary Thomsen, next door to the McGee house, had fallen and broken her arm a half hour after opening her big mouth to Mick. Had she done that? She'd spread the cards after going back in the house, and had arranged them in such a way that illness or injury would befall someone around her, but that might not have had anything to do with Hilary's accident.

There was still so much she didn't know, but Mick

had decided to put the cards away for awhile nonetheless. She was trying to build a new life for herself, without controversy, and to do so she must blend in with her surroundings. She didn't want to attract attention to herself, or tempt the fates.

This was a lesson learned the hard way. Sometimes fate had a way of stepping in and taking over.

Like it had with Emma Mejia.

Her last night in Xavier, Mick had been in her mother's house, reading the diary, when Emma had arrived. Emma had been crying, and had told Mick that Danny's body had finally been found. She'd blamed Mick, and told her that she was going to tell everyone that Mick had killed Danny. She didn't know how, but she would make people listen.

When Emma had attacked her, Mick had had no choice but to defend herself. In the ensuing struggle she'd thrown Emma back, and Emma had hit her head on the fireplace. She'd been lying on the floor unconscious when Quinn arrived, and Mick barely had time to cover Emma with some draperies she pulled from a window when Quinn walked in the front door.

She'd honestly forgotten about Emma when the house began burning. All she'd wanted at the time was to get Quinn out safely, then to get her cards and her mother's diary. She'd almost left the cards behind, a fact that seemed incomprehensible to her now. It must have been the excitement of the fire that had caused her to abandon her precious tarot cards to the flames.

But she had gone back, into that burning hallway, and at the sight of the ceiling-high flames she'd felt a moment of total despair. There was no way for her to reach the cards. She knew they were in the bedroom, but the heat was too intense, the flames too all-consuming for Mick to dare enter.

Then something had happened. Mick still didn't completely understand it, and she'd spent countless hours trying to analyze what she'd seen.

The fire, so hot that she'd felt her eyebrows singing, had seemed to back off. Just when Mick had been about to give up, an opening had appeared before her, a pathway to her cards with a wall of flames on either side of it.

Still she'd hesitated, frightened by the sight of what was happening. She had no desire to die, and going into that room—even with the opening provided—had seemed a death sentence.

Then cool hands had touched her cheeks. To this day Mick could remember the feeling of protection that had come over her at the touch of those invisible and loving hands. She knew she would be safe, that her mother wanted her to have the cards and would see to it that she retrieved them without being hurt by the fire.

She'd thrown herself into the room, the flames at a safe, respectful distance, and had picked up the cards, the box and the diary from the floor. It had been close, and a couple of the cards did have scorched edges.

But, with her belonging safely in her purse, she'd realized she couldn't get out the same way. She could hear the hallway outside the bedroom crumbling as it was eaten by flames, and she'd had to climb out and down through a back window, again guided by the encouraging touch of Rosalie Montagna.

Once safely out she'd known that she would never again feel Rosalie's presense so clearly. That was gone, doomed to stay with the rapidly disintegrating house, and Mick had allowed herself a moment of sadness at the loss. She'd had Rosalie so briefly. All she had now of her mother were the cards and the diary.

Behind the house she'd found Emma's car with the keys in it. The house had been fully in flames by then, and Mick had used Emma's car to make her getaway.

She'd driven around the state for days before the shock had begun to wear off. By the time she hunted up some Xavier newspapers to find out what had happened, she realized that everyone thought it was her body found in the rubble of the house later. It hadn't taken her long to figure out that this might be for the best. At least now no one would come looking for her. She really could fade away, take a new name, and start over fresh.

If a part of her missed Xavier at times, she didn't dwell on that. Likewise, she tried not to think of Brady and Fran too often. They were better off without her, and the most merciful thing she could do for them was to let them believe she was dead.

Mick reached the little booth that she ran during the days, the one with fifty stuffed toys people could win by throwing a basketball through a hoop. It wasn't a completely fair game because the hoop was slightly smaller than regulation size, and the balls didn't go through easily, but enough people won the inexpensive toys to keep them satisfied and coming back for more.

She was examining the latch on the door, the one Gary was going to have to fix because it didn't close properly, when she felt a pair of arms slip around her waist.

Gary, tall and blond, and with eyes that held as many secrets as her own, pulled her to him. "I was beginning to think you were going to sleep all morning," he said, his voice low and seductive.

"It's only nine o'clock," she pointed out.

"Yeah, but the gates open in an hour. Are you going to have everything ready?"

"Don't I always?" She pulled away from him, looking around to see if anyone had witnessed their brief contact.

He caught the look and frowned. "Why do you always act like that?" he asked. "Nobody here cares what we're up to. And if you'd just stay in my trailer all night, instead of getting up at some god-awful hour to sneak back to your own place, you wouldn't have to worry so much about oversleeping."

"We've discussed this before," Mick said. "I can't sleep with another person in the same bed with me."

"We sleep together just fine."

"You know what I mean. Are you going to fix this latch or not? I've been asking you all week."

"Yeah, I'll get to it," he mumbled, reaching for the mini tool pouch he kept clipped to his belt.

"And Tim wants to see you," Mick told him. "Something about his truck needing parts."

Gary was bent over looking at the latch, but now he straightened up to glare at her. "How long did you talk to Tim?"

"Just long enough for him to tell me what he needed." Mick crossed her arms and looked down at her shoes. Gary was getting to be a bore.

"He could have told me that himself," Gary said. "I don't like the way he's always hanging around you."

"He was hanging around his truck, and I just happened to be walking by. What's the big deal?"

Gary reached over and grabbed her arm hard. "The big deal is I don't want you talking to him anymore."

Mick pulled her arm away. "I'll talk to anyone I like."

"Not if I say you can't."

She turned away from him, angry that he'd ruined her day already. Gary was getting to be a problem. At first he'd been a lot of fun, and he followed the rules of not asking questions about her past, but he seemed to be getting the idea that he'd staked out some claim on her future.

He was too much like Danny. Was there something about her that attracted this kind of man? Like Danny, Gary was territorial.

And she was very tired of it.

"I'm going now," she said. "I'll be back before it's time to open up."

Gary started to put the tool pouch back on his belt. "I'll go with you."

"No, you won't," she said firmly. "The latch has to be fixed, and I'm tired of waiting."

He looked at her suspiciously. "You seem awfully eager to get rid of me. Who are you meeting?"

God, it was Danny all over again.

Walking away from him, Mick headed for the tent where all the workers had their meals, determined to have that cup of coffee and maybe some breakfast. The company there would surely be more agreeable.

As she walked, Mick thought about the cards again. Maybe she would get them out, and see if she couldn't do something about Gary. Nothing serious, but she might be able to get rid of him, or at least direct his attentions on someone else. Just because she'd used the cards badly before didn't mean she couldn't learn to control them.

If she learned from her mother's mistakes and didn't let things get out of hand, there was no telling what she could do.

She was, after all, a Montagna.